Praise for *Glorie* by Caryn James

"An impressive first novel . . . Until the last page there is virtually nothing sentimental, and much that is wryly comic, in Caryn James's depiction of this elderly widow. It is an unflinching portrait, merciless as certain Rembrandts, of a shrewd, sly, vain, tough old lady. . . . She is a splendid character."

—*The Washington Post*

"Glorie emerges in all her vanity, irascibility, fearfulness and tenderness. . . . She is startlingly alive—full of doubt and conviction, regret and good intentions. One cannot help being moved by her plight, and by the unanswerable questions she asks."

—*The New York Times Book Review*

"Invites comparisons to Anita Brookner's best work."

—*The Baltimore Sun*

"*Glorie* is that rare gift, a treasure of wisdom and humor, all the pain and joy that come in a lifetime of love. Caryn James has written a beautiful story, as stunning in its pitch-perfect clarity as its resonant depth. Glorie's voice is unforgettable."

—Mary McGarry Morris, author of *Songs in Ordinary Time*

"The story of *Glorie* beautifully chronicles the steadying effect of a woman's imagination on her passage through life. It shows, in detail, that no matter how much life takes away from us, as long as we keep our inner vitality intact, we can count ourselves still rich."

—Gail Godwin, author of *The Good Husband*

"A dazzling accomplishment: Caryn James has managed to infiltrate the soul of a most ordinary woman, and what a soul it turns out to be! *Glorie* is a moving and satisfying novel."

—Susan Isaacs, author of *Compromising Positions*

PENGUIN BOOKS

GLORIE

Caryn James is the chief television critic for *The New York Times.* For six years she was a *Times* film reviewer, and remains a frequent film and book critic. *Glorie* is her first novel.

Glorie

A NOVEL BY Caryn James

PENGUIN BOOKS

PENGUIN BOOKS
Published by the Penguin Group
Penguin Putnam Inc., 375 Hudson Street,
New York, New York 10014, U.S.A.
Penguin Books Ltd, 27 Wrights Lane,
London W8 5TZ, England
Penguin Books Australia Ltd, Ringwood,
Victoria, Australia
Penguin Books Canada Ltd, 10 Alcorn Avenue,
Toronto, Ontario, Canada M4V 3B2
Penguin Books (N.Z.) Ltd, 182–190 Wairau Road,
Auckland 10, New Zealand

Penguin Books Ltd, Registered Offices:
Harmondsworth, Middlesex, England

First published in the United States of America by Zoland Books, Inc. 1998
Published in Penguin Books 1999

1 3 5 7 9 10 8 6 4 2

PUBLISHER'S NOTE
This is a work of fiction. Names, characters, places, and incidents either are the product of the author's imagination or are used fictitiously, and any resemblance to actual persons, living or dead, events, or locales is entirely coincidental.

THE LIBRARY OF CONGRESS HAS CATALOGED THE HARDCOVER AS FOLLOWS:
James, Caryn.
Glorie: a novel / by Caryn James—1st edition.
p. cm.
ISBN 0-944072-87-9 (hc.)
ISBN 0 14 02.8154 1 (pbk.)
I. Title.
PS3560.A37845G58 1998
813'.54–dc21 97–50386

Printed in the United States of America
Set in Minion
Designed by Boskydell Studio

IN MEMORY

OF MY GRANDMOTHER

May Gloria Fuoroli

Acknowledgments

When I was a child, my grandfather told me stories he called make-a-believe. Deep thanks to my parents, James and Joan Fuoroli, and to my aunt and uncle, Mary and Salvatore Compagnone, for allowing me to take the seed of a family story and turn it into make-a-believe.

For their never-failing encouragement and friendship, many thanks to Ellen Pall, Angeline Goreau, Vincent Canby, Charles Salzberg, and my agent, Gloria Loomis.

And deepest thanks to my sister, Kim Smeltzer, for always being there with endless encouragement, complete understanding, sharp wit and smart advice. Like so much in my life, this could not have been done without her.

Glorie

Chapter 1

"WHERE DID YOU GET that little red-haired girl?" The man's voice came from close behind her mother and sounded scarier than the dark. One of Glorie's hands was in her mother's as they stood side by side on the ship's deck. With the other she reached up to grab the railing, standing on her toes to try to see what her mother was staring at far away. She saw only fog and darkness, but felt her mother's hand holding tighter as the ship rocked and Glorie slid toward the edge. The kerchief on her mother's head made a loud flapping sound, like birds' wings. From the blackness behind her had come slow, heavy footsteps and the deep voice that said, "Where did you get that little red-haired girl?"

Then her mother calmly let go of her hand. There were stars in the sky Glorie hadn't noticed before and in their faint sparkle she saw the wind lift her mother over the railing and carry her over the sea. Her mother was flying away fast, her arms stretched out as if she were swimming, and as she sped across the ocean she turned her head back toward the ship. Her voice was fading in the wind but the flapping sound of her kerchief grew louder in Glorie's ears. As the black wind took her mother away, Glorie heard her yell, "I'll wait for you. I'll see you in America. I'll see you again."

Then Glorie was lying on the deck, wrapped in red plaid blankets up to her neck, her arms trapped like a mummy's. She rolled helplessly back and forth, to the edge of the deck then back again. "Jack!" she screamed, "Jack!" and her whole life must have passed by because now she was an old lady alone on the deck, sweating in her curled-up blankets.

I *am* an old lady, she thought as she sat up in the dark and tossed off the extra blanket. I'm sweating, the blankets are tangled and the heat is up too high. I'm a goddamn fool.

She lay on her side in the tiny twin bed, squinting at the red numbers on the bedside clock: 5:45. What day was this?

She closed her eyes again. "Where did you get that little red-haired girl?" She would never know what that man's voice had sounded like in real life or what he meant, but she knew the story. She knew it as her mother had told it, more than seventy years ago, and that was what the man said.

He had appeared on a calm bright day while Glorie and her mother were walking on the crowded deck. Her mother never liked to talk about the trip to America. "It was awful, Gloria, very bad. Better you don't remember," she would say, frowning and shaking her head. Glorie wished she could remember something about the old country. "The Azores. Pftt!" her brother Manny would spit whenever she mentioned it. She pictured São Miguel as a long grove of tall leafy trees, oranges and lemons mixed together on the very same tree, but she could never see herself there.

Her only memory of the long trip in the dirty, smelly steerage — she wasn't sure, maybe her first memory ever — was terror that she would lose her parents, and Manny and Frank and Josie, among all these mean-looking strangers.

From the time she was a small girl, she had tried asking the family about the boat, sneakily, one by one. Frank shrugged his shoulders. "If you were four I was what? Seven?"

"Seven," Glorie said.

"So what do *I* remember? I was seven."

Josie said, "Don't ask me, ask Mama."

Manny held his nose and made a face. "Pftt!"

Her father grumbled, "I got you over here. That's what counts," as if she had accused him of leaving her behind.

And no matter what questions Glorie asked, her mother would tell the story about the strange man.

"I went up to the deck as much as I could, no matter how cold," her mother began. "One day you was with me, and a man came up to us and asked in Portuguese, 'Where did you get that little red-haired girl?' I turned around and started to walk away.

"He said, 'No, don't be afraid. I'm from São Miguel too.' He spoke our language the way we did in Povoacao, he even knew the street where my cousin Roberto lived, with the horse barn at the end. He meant no harm.

"He told me, 'We're probably cousins ourselves,' and to say the truth he looked like Roberto. He had that same thick black hair and olive skin. Maybe everybody looked alike there," her mother said.

"But not you, Gloria. The man noticed that you stood out. 'Look at that light skin and those pretty blue eyes,' he said. 'She's lucky. They'll love her in America. She looks like she belongs there.' "

Glorie's mother thought the man must be lonely and asked him to meet the rest of her family. He said he would find them later on the trip, but he never did. "He was like a good angel," her mother always said. "He came to give us a message. You'll be the best of us all." From as early as she could remember until she was twelve and her mother died, Glorie heard this story. She had repeated it to herself all her life, had told it to Jack so often that it had become as real as that little girl's feeling of panic at the thought of being lost on the ship. It always ended with the same words. "You'll rise over everybody, Gloria," her mother would say. "You'll better us all." Her mother promised this, smiling and nodding, as if it had already come true.

Glorie sat on the edge of the narrow bed, slid her feet into her pink velvet slippers and snuck halfway down the hall to the bathroom. If she could have held off she wouldn't even have made this much noise, this one slow flush. It didn't seem to wake Louisa and Patrick down the hall, but you never knew. She washed her hands in a trickle of water and didn't bother to splash any on her face or rinse her mouth. She'd be home soon enough.

As she crept past Louisa and Patrick's door and back to her room the boat dream seemed to trail behind her like a bad smell. She pulled on yesterday's clothes as fast as she could: the black pants, the satiny green overblouse, even the crumpled knee-highs. Her back twinged when she bent over in the chair to tie the blue rubber-soled shoes. She peeked out from the drapes and saw the tree branches moving in the wind, so she pulled the first scarf she could grab from a drawer — an orange chiffon thing some no-taste in-law had given her and she had forgotten to throw away. She tied the ugly scarf under her chin; the green blouse hung under her car coat; she didn't dare look in the mirror.

It doesn't matter, she thought, and closed the door behind her on the unmade bed.

She didn't care how she dressed to cross the street before dawn. No one would see her make the short daily walk straight across from her daughter's house to her own. Thank God there were no more milkmen.

On most days Glorie saw the two white ranch houses as giant faces, their picture windows staring at each other cross-eyed from opposite sides of Jasmine Street. The granite-and-marble stones beneath the windows were like clamped mouths that didn't tell anybody's business. Today as the wind came up she saw Louisa's house as a puffy cloud with puckered lips that gently blew her toward her home.

She would definitely be crossing back in the dark that night.

Maybe I should get one of those miner's hats, the kind with the flashlight built in, she thought.

She smiled at the picture of herself, wearing gas station coveralls with "Glorie" embroidered over the pocket, a couple of red spit curls peeking out from beneath the hat that guided her across. It wasn't her usual style, of course, but she could start a trend, maybe turn up in *Vogue.* "The jumpsuit and the hat with a lamp. Elegant and practical for those crisp New England autumns," it would say. "Worn by its brilliant designer, Mrs. Gloria Carcieri."

The wind must have snapped her to her senses, because when she reached her front steps she remembered the alarm clock back in her bedroom, set to go off at 7:00. It would buzz while Louisa was right across the hall from Glorie's door, making coffee. Louisa would worry when the alarm kept going. She would pound on her mother's door, then barge in, terrified, hoping Glorie was still alive.

Oh, well, she'll get over it, Glorie thought. I'm not going back now.

She punched in the alarm code, unlocked her front door and stepped in.

"I'm here, Jack," she said. She thought this every morning

when she entered the house. Sometimes, when she felt so tough that she wasn't afraid of turning into a crazy old lady, or so annoyed she didn't care anymore, she said it out loud. Today she wanted to hear herself talk, to banish the creepy, lingering voice of the dream.

As long as it doesn't become a habit, she told herself.

There had been bad days when she'd stood still just inside the doorway, wondering whether she had said Jack's name out loud or not. Those days were the worst; she spent them checking for telltale signs of senility. She would sit down with a cup of tea in the television room and go back to make sure she had turned off the stove. Then she worried she was checking the stove too much, as if somebody might see her and think she had lost her marbles. So she would make herself sit in front of *Oprah* and sip her tea, getting anxious because the empty kettle could be melting in the kitchen as she sat there, getting more anxious because she knew this stove-checking routine was no use. She would never find signs of old-lady craziness while she was still sane enough to look for them. That was part of the disease, wasn't it?

"Calm down, Glorie," Jack would say. "You're fine, you're worrying for nothing."

"I know I am."

She wasn't too old to learn from her mistakes. Already she was smarter than she'd been a month ago, when she had climbed on the stepladder and held a match to the smoke alarm just to see if it was working. Was it her fault it worked fine coming on but didn't turn off? On the ladder, she fanned the alarm with a dishrag; she glared at it; she blew on it. In a fit of inspiration she got out the old canister vacuum cleaner and aimed the air hose at it. Finally she gave up and called Louisa.

"I was testing it," she yelled over the blare as Louisa climbed up the stepladder to unhook the battery. "I wasn't even cooking."

"I don't care if you were smoking cigars, Ma," Louisa yelled back from the ladder. "Let me get this thing undone."

"It's defective," Glorie said smugly once the noise had stopped and Louisa was back on solid ground. "Good thing we checked."

"Yeah, Ma, good thing. Do me a favor. Next time you get that urge to test, call me up, I'll talk you out of it."

Glorie shrugged. Nobody understood all the things that could go wrong when you were by yourself.

Nobody understands, she thought now, as she hung up her coat in the front hall — no one in there — turned up the heat and went from room to room doing her morning check for burglars who had crept in during the night.

She walked from one end of the house to the other, first from the TV room into the kitchen, where she opened the big cupboards under the counters. They were full of pans, but a man could hide the pans in another room and crouch in there. A short man could. She checked all three locks on the door that led from the kitchen to Jack's old shop and office in the basement.

I'm not going down there today, she told herself.

Sometimes she did, just to sit at his wooden desk and get weepy, though she knew this couldn't be healthy. And every time she went into the office she was taking a chance that somebody might be hiding in the next room, among the uncut slabs of marble in the shop. Today she wasn't tempted.

She moved to the rooms beyond the kitchen, into the sewing room and the small bathroom, checking the shower stall — a clear glass door, burglarproof — and the walk-in linen closet.

She used to wonder, What will I do if I find someone? What crook would be afraid of an old woman armed with pinking shears?

She was afraid of guns and never liked dogs.

What could I do, yell "You're it" and run?

She decided she could use a broom to trip him. Odds were he'd hit his head on one of the marble thresholds that were everywhere in the house. She kept mops and brooms hidden for these emergencies, the way some people kept heavier weapons.

In a pinch, she decided, shock value might be the best strategy after all. She could widen her eyes, make whooping sounds, then reach out a hand — without actually touching the burglar, of course, because he'd be filthy — yell "You're it!" and run like hell to the door. She couldn't run fast, but with luck he'd be too stunned to chase someone who was acting so loony. As a backup, she'd had alarms installed everywhere.

She walked through the large formal living room to the other end of the house and started filling the tub in the purple-tiled master bathroom next to their bedroom. She had given up getting down on her knees to look under the bed. Instead she got her clean mop from the clothes closet, leaned over and made one large swoop under the bed; if someone were there she'd know it. If she'd had hardwood floors instead of carpeting she could have cleaned and done a security check all at once, but no system was perfect. She put the mop back fast, before she had time to start wondering if she had swooped wide and carefully enough.

When she climbed into the tub she noticed that the towel bar felt a little wobbly. Already? It was only fifteen years old.

Jack had put it in not long after her seventieth birthday. "What? Do you think I'm old?" she had asked.

"No, Glorie, come on, I'm older than you, it's for me."

For him. He showered. In the other bathroom.

"For you?" she asked. "Do you think I'm feebleminded now, to believe that?"

"I think I don't want you to crack your skull. It's a thick skull but I don't want to take any chances."

"All right."

"It's a pretty skull, by the way." He always knew how to save himself at the last minute. He didn't fool her, but she appreciated the thought.

Maybe that bar should be shaky after fifteen years, she didn't know, but it reassured her as she held it and climbed carefully into the water. She sat very straight these days; if she leaned back and rested her weak neck against the edge of the tub, she might never be able to get up again.

"Tell Patrick to fix that bar," Jack said, annoyed. "It'll take him five minutes."

"I will, I will," she said, to satisfy him. Invite Patrick into this house when it wasn't an emergency? Change something Jack had done for her?

"You're not going to do it, are you? Then give a few bucks to one of those midget burglars you're so afraid of, have *him* fix the damn towel bar. Just get it done before you get hurt, Glorie."

"OK, OK."

"I mean it. You have to take care of yourself."

"I will, I promise."

She splashed warm water on her shoulders and chuckled. "Want to scrub my back?"

How was I so stupid, to waste all those years? she asked herself.

She had always bathed at night, washing away perfume and cooking smells, then sinking calm and refreshed into bed. One night, long after Louisa had married and left this house, the bathroom radiator was acting up and she left the door open while she bathed. Jack came in and sat on the small white chair next to the dressing table while she soaked; he never really left. Her bath became the romantic ritual of their last years, though she never thought of it that way until he was gone. At the time, she was too stunned and pleased with herself, too dazzled by this exotic side of Jack, too fearful that one day he would simply forget to join her.

Almost every night he sat in the chair talking about who had been by the office that day. She soaked while he read the evening paper, shook his head and grumbled, "That goddamn mayor is as crooked as they come, just like old man Molloy. Politicians. They were always corrupt but they never used to be this stupid. Roosevelt was a sonofabitch but he was a smart sonofabitch."

She looked up and saw this man she adored: in his gray plaid flannel shirt, suspenders loose around his waist, a fringe of white hair around his head. As he sat reading the paper she swirled the water around, tingling in parts of her body she never quite knew how to name, feeling as luxurious as if the two of them were locked together in bed. She lay back in the water, smiling.

Sometimes he would put his hand in the water, then silently turn on the hot water tap and swish the fresh warm water around in the tub. Once or twice he had climbed in, but this tub wasn't meant for two people, especially two people with stiffening bones.

Why didn't we do this when we were young? she had wondered often, but never asked. She didn't want him to feel bad or old.

So he talked and she closed her eyes and soaked. Glorie wished her body were young again and at the same time knew it didn't matter. Even with her eyes shut she could feel the twenty extra pounds that seemed to hang in her lap and spill over her thighs in the bath, as if someone else's larger body had been slipped on top of her own. Her granddaughter complained about thunder thighs, but what did she know? In a pinch Blanche would leave her two little boys with Louisa and go to exercise class. That girl didn't know what thunder thighs were. She didn't know about wearing scarves to cover a jowly neck and short sleeves in summer to cover flabby arms. She didn't know about eating whole-wheat toast with margarine instead of muffins with jam, just to keep the damage from getting out of control. She didn't know how slowly this fat and flab crept up on you, until one day you sat on the side of the bed in your underwear and cried because you'd never be able to go without a girdle again.

Glorie kept her eyes closed and inhaled the slightly musty smell that Jack's body had taken on in old age. She loved putting her nose against his neck and kissing it, she loved that smell, but she never knew how to tell him without insulting him. She would put her head on his chest and he would wrap her in his arms, and a faint, unmistakable scent would creep out toward her. "It *is* musty, but I *like* this," she thought, always. She liked the way a trace of that smell stayed on his shirts and pillows and sheets.

She almost told him once. They were sitting on the couch in the TV room watching some National Geographic special about an odd wild animal that left a strong sexual scent wherever it walked. She wanted to tell Jack he was like that, but the animal was ratty looking and vicious and she let the moment pass. But she imagined over and over saying to him, "I love the way you smell," mumbling it against his chest or raising her head and looking up into his eyes so sincerely he would have to understand what a compliment it was. He would smile, then kiss her, his arms around her. She opened her eyes to look at him, and shuddered. She was alone in the icy bathwater.

She did not believe that Jack was a ghost walking this earth, looking over her shoulder. When she talked to him in her head, when she said, "I love you," or asked, "Do we need bread?" she did not think he was some spirit at her side. But in the seven years she had been alone, she had never been able to let him go.

She missed being called Glorie, though even while he was alive she had looked with murderous eyes at anyone else who dared to call her that. She could not lose the feeling that somehow he had kept up with her. She would not think time had ended for him. There was a version of her husband that could follow her anywhere.

She sat on the edge of the wide bed in her robe and looked into the closet. There were rows of black pull-on pants and tunic tops she had made — in rose and royal blue satin, prettier and roomier than anything she could have bought. She had never walked around in threadbare sweaters or cheap housedresses, figuring she was just at home. What could she possibly be saving her good clothes for now? Maybe she had one foot in the grave but she wasn't about to put the other one in with a hole in the toe of her stocking.

She picked out a blue blouse and pearl button earrings, though she guessed she would see no one except the mailman all day. Then she sat at the dresser to comb her hair. It was one of her favorite spots. In the mirror she could see Jack's brown armchair in the corner, and the big bed with the ivory satin comforter. For a few years after Jack died there had been a bright patch of wallpaper in the shape of a cross right over the bed, where the crucifix had hung forever and the paper had faded around it. On her first day back home after the funeral she had taken the cross down and tossed it in the trash without hesitating or telling a soul. What good had it done her, all those prayers, all those desperate Hail Marys for Jack? Except for a few guilt-stricken moments — she imagined lightning striking some garbage dump where the crucifix had landed — her only regret was that she still had a flowered-wallpaper cross staring at her in the mirror.

Now and then she had amused herself by sitting at the dressing table and wondering what she might hang on that spot. On the dresser was a good picture of Louisa and Patrick with the kids and grandkids, but it didn't seem right to have them standing over the bed looking down like spies. Jack had never sat still for a good picture. Sometimes at the mall she wandered into art shops, looking at paintings of awful brown mountains or giant flowers that were overpriced — hundreds of dollars — and that Jack would have hated. One day, she knew, she would come across just the right thing. But now the paper where the cross had been was faded too. It looked less like a cross than a birthmark, familiar and comforting and imperfect, like the worn-out fabric on Jack's brown chair.

"I guess you like old things," Jack said.

"Like you!" she teased, combing her hair into tasteful curls around her cheeks. She still wore what her old hairdresser, Gilda, called the *Here's Lucy,* the hairdo Lucy Ball wore in the seventies when she had that show with her grown-up kids. Anyone could see the kids couldn't act, and by then Lucy sounded like a foghorn, but Glorie and Jack watched anyway. "The show was a dog, but the hair was a classic," Gilda always said. "You can live with this 'do forever." By the time Lucy died Gilda had retired, but she made a point of calling Glorie. "What did I tell you? She lived with that 'do to the end," Gilda said. Glorie's hair was darker than Lucy's, and she didn't really look like her, but she accepted the compliment when people said she did.

No one could believe her hair was naturally red anymore, but that didn't bother her. White roots poking out bothered her. Trashy color bothered her. She was upset for months after Gilda left and turned her over to some boy who looked like he wore rouge and made her hair bright red. Jack was gone by then, but she was embarrassed anyway. She had come home, looked in the mirror, and walked around with a kerchief on her head for two hours.

"Let me see the whole thing, Glorie," she heard Jack say.

"You'll hate it, I'm warning you. It looks cheap, it looks trampy and all I can do is wait for it to fade. You'll be ashamed of me."

"You always exaggerate," he said. "It can't look as bad as you think."

"It does."

"Stop being silly and let me *see.*"

She pulled off the kerchief slowly and stood there.

"It won't take long to fade," he said. "Don't worry."

Her eyes filled but she stopped herself from crying. She wouldn't worry; it would fade.

But what would she do in the meantime? Everyone would be sure to stare at fire-engine hair. She could see herself walking with Jack, maybe into the Towne Diner for lunch. A man's voice came from behind them. "Where did you get that pretty red-haired woman?" he asked, tapping Jack on the shoulder but keeping his eyes on Glorie. Jack glared, put his arm around Glorie and led her to their booth.

Glorie stared at herself in the mirror, snuck a scared look at her watch and sighed. Thank God, it was still early. Her stomach turned over with relief. Actually, it growled, so maybe she was only hungry and not upset with herself. But she worried. There were days when she moved so slowly or daydreamed so long, it seemed she was dressed just in time to take her afternoon nap. Today she was too tired to have much sense of time. She put on lipstick. She stood up from the dressing table and tried to concentrate on keeping her shoulders from curving forward.

She smoothed out the bedspread where she had sat.

One day, I'll sleep here with you again, she thought. As if she didn't doze off in her single bed across the street with Jack's arm around her and her head on his shoulder. But it wasn't the same. It would be sweetness itself to spend a night here again.

"What can I do? It's Louisa," she told him, shaking her head.

It was burglars, too. There were house creaks in the night that she would never be able to tell apart from a midget robber in the pan cupboard. But mostly it was Louisa, who had done a good thing seven years ago without knowing it would become a way of life.

Glorie walked from the bedroom back through the living room. Some days she could walk straight through without thinking at all. On cheery days, that vague hum of memories always in the back of her mind let her laugh at herself, at the waste this room had turned out to be. It had always been her house to design, and Jack didn't blink when she wanted a formal living room, this room that had scarcely changed since the day the three of them had moved in. There was the fireplace with the black marble mantel; the hearth that was remarkably clean because they had only lit a few fires, when the heat went off during blizzards; the picture window that had stared across at an empty lot until it became Louisa's new house; the green-and-ivory brocade couch and chairs that looked in perfect condition if you didn't know they had started out as emerald and turned pale over the years. Glorie declared the room off limits to children, pets, food and most adults, except on holidays, and for the first few years she referred to it as the Christmas Room.

One Easter, while Louisa's younger cousins scrambled around looking for colored eggs, Glorie heard Margaret, the nastiest of all the Carcieri sister-in-laws, mumble to Angelo, "Oh, we're allowed in the *Christmas* Room today, aren't we lucky? Out of season, too." Glorie didn't make a remark. She didn't have to. Jack's brother Angelo elbowed his wife in the side, and her glass of Chianti spilled down the skirt of her pink Easter dress.

Glorie tried not to smile as she handed Margaret a damp dishcloth. She had taken her time getting it ("I'm letting the water get nice and cold," she yelled from the kitchen) so the stain would set. "I hope it doesn't stain," Glorie said, handing Margaret the rag. She stopped calling it the Christmas Room anyway.

When Pat Jr. was about five he had raced one day from the TV room through the living room with his tiny untrained puppy running behind him. He knew better than to stop in the special green room as he ran past the fireplace, circled around the armchairs, sprinted to the bedroom and slid under his grandparents' bed, pulling the puppy behind him. By the time Glorie got there, yelling after her grandson, he was giggling under the bed, the dog skittering to get free, a paw poking out from under the spread. Jack had gotten there first, and he was sitting on the bed winking at her as he pretended to hide Pat Jr. by moving his legs back and forth. "I don't know where they could be, I looked everywhere," Jack said in an exaggerated voice as another giggle came from beneath the bed.

Why can't I be like that? she thought, and even as she thought it she heard herself scolding, "Patrick Mariano, Jr., get out from under that bed right now!" He poked his head out and looked up at her with wide brown eyes. "I think I found some dust under here, Grandma," he said, trying not to laugh.

"And you," she said to Jack, exaggerating her voice, waving a finger sternly, trying to joke now that it was far too late. "No more," she warned.

The three of them walked out of the room, with Pat Jr. holding the dog and swirling around in circles as they passed through

remembered from that one time she saw it in the substitute teacher's book.

"Ma."

"I'll be right there, I'm buying this picture," she said, pointing to the poster. Reckless and extravagant, she pulled out her wallet. Then it occurred to her that the real painting must be here, in this very building, that she could actually walk in and see it. Louisa would have to stay with her and they would make their own way home. It was only an hour away; she'd figure out how.

"I didn't see this picture inside," she said to the young man as she handed him the twenty dollars — enough for a coat, but this would last much longer. "Where would I find it?" she asked, as easy as that.

He stared at her coldly for a few seconds, then turned over the picture and pointed to the words on the other side:

Leonardo da Vinci (1452–1519)
The Virgin of the Rocks

"The original," he said slowly, "is in the National Gallery in London. There is another version in the Louvre. You might try Paris."

She knew he was making fun of her, but she didn't care. He rolled up the picture and handed it to her. It was hers.

Louisa looked as if her mother had lost her mind. "The whole bus is *waiting,*" she said. "They're *staring.*"

When they got home Glorie showed the picture to Jack, who said, "Why do we need a religious picture in the house? Put it in your sewing room, if you like it so much."

"You don't understand, I saw this when I was a girl. I looked everywhere for a book that had it."

"OK, Glorie, put it wherever you want," he said.

It belonged in the Christmas Room, the special room, but she knew Jack wouldn't want to see it every time he passed through. So she bought the golden frame and had him hang it in the corner, on that little inset part of the wall on the far side of the fireplace. She wished it didn't look so much like a shrine, but Jack agreed that was where the picture belonged.

"That's good, you can hardly see it unless you walk over there on purpose," he said, and when he saw her face take on that fierce, hurt look, he went on, "I'm joking, I'm joking, it's fine."

She relaxed.

"I like it," he said. "Behind that glass it looks like one of those advertisements for coming attractions outside the moving pictures. It looks like we're playing a holy movie next."

Louisa never took another class trip to the museum, and Glorie could never find another reason to go. On her own, it would have seemed like traveling to the moon. What else did she need there, anyway?

That Christmas, Margaret asked if they were supposed to pray in front of the new picture (gripping her glass of wine tight because she was within elbow range of Angelo). "It's not a holy picture, it's a painting by one of the most famous artists who ever lived," Glorie said, then left the room fast to check on dinner before anyone could ask her things she didn't know. Even now she couldn't tell if that angel was a boy or a girl.

On her best days, as she walked through the living room she could see her grandson swirling around in here. She imagined she had let him run free in it all he wanted, with puppies, friends, hamsters, anything. Sometimes she walked to the other side of the fireplace, to the priceless angel picture, still the most beautiful face she had ever seen. Months at a time could go by without her noticing it, then she would see it again. It could almost always make her feel better, even though it made her sad.

But on bad days like this, especially when she was trailed by difficult dreams, nothing could keep away the memory of how Jack had died in this room they had never used. It was as if he sat down to rest on the long green sofa and never got up. Glorie had been in the kitchen making supper, and when she called and got no answer she walked to the doorway, thinking he was in their bedroom. She didn't have to see the way his head was slumped over on his shoulder, his mouth hanging open, to know something was wrong. She knew the second she saw him sitting down in this room they always passed through.

She could see the three men from the rescue squad crowding over him as he slumped on the couch. She had a picture in her mind that would never leave of one man shaking his head at the other, and she thought she remembered screaming at the way that man's head moved. For some reason, and it upset her even now, she could remember hearing Julia Child in the TV room, telling her how much brandy to use on cherries jubilee, sounding cheerful while her husband was dead. How could she have noticed such a thing? How could she have such a clear memory of that chipper voice and such a dim sense of what happened next? She thought she remembered, but maybe it was only what Louisa had told her.

Did my memory start to slip as soon as you died? she asked. Did I go back to being four years old on the boat right then, too young and stupid to notice what was going on?

She took her delicate china teacup, the one with deep pink orchids on the outside and gold around the rim, and sat on the brocade couch, sipping coffee and looking out the big picture window across at the drawn curtains of her tiny room. This was one of those times when she had to try hard not to be angry at Jack. "Why did you slip away like that? So fast? Without even thinking of me?"

"It was for the best," he said as she sat on the very spot where he died. "I knew you always hated good-byes. And I knew Louisa would take care of you." No, that wasn't his voice, he would never have said that, it was too pat, all wrong. She stood up quickly and walked into the kitchen.

I know the difference, she reminded herself.

She knew the difference between what Jack would have said and what she wanted to hear. It was worth the struggle to keep things straight.

She definitely remembered that Louisa had been there before the rescue squad. When Patrick followed the men away Louisa said, "You'll come home with us, Ma. We'll come back and get some things tomorrow." Glorie crossed the street, and never slept in her own bed again.

Glorie stood at the kitchen sink looking out the picture window as she ate a half slice of toast and finished her coffee. When she saw Patrick drive away at 8:48, she knew the coast was clear, that Ada's house must be empty by now too. She was feeling down, but that was no reason to waste an opportunity like this.

She carried her cup into the TV room and sat down by the phone. I can't believe I'm doing this, she thought as she hit the buttons. Getting buddy-buddy with a person I don't even like.

That feeling went way back. Of all the Carcieri sister-in-laws, Ada was always the loudest. She wasn't as mean as Margaret, but she was boring enough. Through more than fifty years of family dinners, Jack and his brothers left the table and put their feet up. Glorie made coffee, Ada scrubbed pans, and during all that time Ada never said anything more memorable than "We think Big Anthony has an ingrown toenail. Anybody know what that looks like for sure?"

But now they had husbands in the same cemetery. And Ada had something Glorie didn't: a license and a car.

"Ada, it's Gloria," she said.

"Gloria, hi, honey," Ada said. "I been thinking about you. How you been?"

"I can't complain," Glorie said.

"Oh, sure you can," said Ada, cheerful and goofy first thing in the morning. "Just because we don't have big problems doesn't mean we can't complain about our little ones, right? Like now, I'm wondering why Barbara couldn't put the dishes in the dishwasher before she left for work. What am I, the maid? But never mind. What you been up to?"

"Oh, the usual, sewing, shopping. How is Anthony?"

"Like his father was, a grump. And Louisa?"

Why waste time, Glorie thought. I've led her to the perfect opening. "She's going to get her roots done tomorrow," she said, her tone loaded with meaning. Ada could take it from there.

"Oh, no, that's so painful," said Ada. "Anthony Jr. had that done and he was in such agony, you wouldn't believe."

"Anthony dyes his hair?"

"No, of course not. What are you talking about? He had that root canal done."

"No, no," said Glorie. "Louisa is having the roots of her hair dyed. To cover the gray. At the hairdresser's. She has an extra long hairdresser's appointment at ten o'clock tomorrow morning."

"Oh, I get it," Ada whispered. "I'll pick you up at ten-thirty, honey. We can go to Papa Gino's for lunch after."

That's Ada all over, whispering when she's alone in her house, Glorie thought. Goddamn fool.

After she hung up she thought, "I'll see you tomorrow, Jack," but it felt forced talking to him that way, as if he were in prison and tomorrow were visiting day. She wouldn't worry about where he was. Tomorrow was set; she felt better already.

At noon she ate cottage cheese and watched the news, then lay on top of the satin bedspread for her nap. As she closed her eyes she saw Jack turn into the driveway in the big green Ford she had sold right after he died.

"I had to sell it. I couldn't stand to look at it sitting in the driveway. I couldn't stand to have it rot away in the garage."

Jack's car stopped at the end of the driveway. It was empty. "Oh no," she mumbled, "no, I don't want to dream anymore today." But she was too tired to get up or to keep her eyes open. All morning she had puttered around, full of energy, putting a little Pledge on the sewing machine cabinet, passing a dry mop over the floor. She had been acting as if Jack were just at work, in the old days when he rented a shop, before the men who worked for him started calling him "the old man," before he cut back and moved the shop to the basement. She had gotten through the morning without even realizing how much she had put him out of her mind. It had almost been pleasant not to worry about him.

"Almost," she said out loud. "Almost. Almost."

Sometimes she wondered why she was so tired when all she did was spend an hour or two cleaning. But her brain got tired. Sometimes paying so much attention to Jack exhausted her. Sometimes she just couldn't think anymore.

When she opened her eyes, still facing the window, a streetlight was gleaming into the dark room. She sat up fast and a couple of tears ran down her face before she forced herself to stop, then put her head in her hands to steady the dizziness.

"You idiot!" she screamed. You goddamn fool, she thought, sleeping away the day. Her fists were clenched over her eyes in anger. Then she began to tremble, terrified, as if some evil power had willed her to sleep for a long, long time. Whenever she slept, she never knew if that evil spirit would knock her out, as quickly and surely as if someone had slipped a Mickey in her tea.

I'm OK, she kept thinking, as she got up, splashed cool water on her face and turned on the last minutes of *Oprah*, trying to catch up as if the day hadn't slipped away from her.

It's OK. Calm down. There's no reason to be upset, she thought, pacing around the room. I can do whatever I want. I must have needed the sleep. It's only 5:00. No one will know.

She took deep breaths and pretended she'd had an ordinary day. She didn't have to cross the street for another twenty minutes or so, but she decided to go back early and see if Louisa wanted help with dinner. Fat chance. Louisa would say, "Relax, Ma, sit down and watch television." Or she might say, "Yes, why don't you make the salad? As long as you don't add any of those secret ingredients." All right, once she made a mistake by crumbling in that leftover meatball so it wouldn't go to waste. Who would notice with all the carrots and olives, but Patrick had gagged and yelled, "What the hell is this?" and now Glorie could only make the salad as long as it was as boring as Patrick. When Louisa had first brought him home Glorie had nicknamed him Ivory Soap, he was so dull. "Ivory Soap is coming for supper, I better not cook anything too spicy," she would say, until Jack warned her that Louisa was bound to overhear if she kept it up.

What a match, when Louisa was so daring, even now. Louisa drank milk past the expiration date if it still smelled good. Louisa could do anything. She invented long thrilling stories for her grandchildren, she sewed beautiful ball gowns that she wore out dancing with her husband, she gave dinner parties for Patrick's business clients. Louisa kept so busy it was a wonder she had time to hover over her own mother and tell her what to do.

Everyone said Louisa looked like a black-haired version of Glorie, with the same thin nose and blue eyes. But what did they know? Wonderful Louisa had turned out just like her father. She was smart, she was funny, she could blow up at someone who treated her wrong and be their best friend the next day, and she could hold a grudge when she had to.

Glorie worried about her anyway. Louisa was going to poison the family with her microwave, for one thing. Glorie zapped lunch for herself every day, but she'd be long gone before any bad effects turned up. And that time when Glorie was sure she'd smelled gas in the house, Louisa had told her she was imagining things. "We don't have any gas in this house, Ma, you know that. Everything is electric."

But Blanche's boys were visiting and Louisa shouldn't have been taking chances. "There's gas in the neighborhood, isn't there?" Glorie asked. "It could have leaked in. Maybe you should call someone."

"I don't smell anything, Ma, nothing at all. Do you have gas up your nose?" she asked, trying to joke Glorie out of worrying. For the rest of the day Michael would turn to his brother and say, "You have gas up your nose!" and Jeremy, the littler one, would say, "No, *you* have gas up your nose," then together they would say, "Grandma G. has gas up her nose!" and collapse on the floor laughing.

"Come on, you two," Louisa said. "That was funny the first ten times. Give Great-Grandma a break. As soon as I put this roast in the oven I'll tell you a story, OK?"

"Once there was a monster," Michael began in a creepy voice, "who had gas up his nose!"

Louisa tried not to laugh.

Louisa was always doing three things at once, and Glorie was afraid that one day all that busyness would catch up with her.

Louisa went so fast, she might not even notice if her boiler blew up underneath her or some greasy rag on Patrick's workbench caught on fire. There would be a small glow in the basement. Glorie would be able to see it from her window. The flames would spread up. Where was Louisa? Glorie would phone the fire department first, then Louisa, but there was no answer. She raced across the street in the cold wind, but she'd forgotten her keys, so she rang and rang the bell and pounded on the door until she finally had to go back to her own unlocked house, get her keys and let herself in just as Louisa was coming out of the bathroom in her robe, still wet from the shower, coughing in the smoke that was filling the house. Glorie got two wet facecloths to put over their mouths and led her daughter across the street to fresh air and safety. Then she collapsed on her own front steps in tears, because what would she have done if she hadn't gotten there in time? What would she ever do if she lost her daughter, too?

Her heart was racing and tears were running down her cheeks as she stood in the TV room. She wiped her cheeks and hoped no one was looking in the window. She felt much better, though, sort of refreshed. She was only a little bothered that she had upset herself again for nothing.

I hope Patrick doesn't start about the house tonight, she thought as she put on her coat. If I live to be 110 I might get to like him.

"He took you in without complaining." Jack reminded her of this a lot.

"He complains. Believe me."

"You know what I mean, Glorie."

Jack used to say, "He'll grow on you," when Louisa first brought Patrick home.

"So if I live to be a hundred ten I might get to like him," she'd answer.

"A hundred ten. I'm almost there," she told Jack now. "Why isn't he growing on me?"

"He is, you're too stubborn to admit it."

"He isn't! He's more stubborn than I am, he's more stubborn than ever and he's still the Italian Patrick!"

"Patrick Mariano?" Glorie had asked when Louisa first mentioned his name. "He's part Irish?"

"No, he's full-blooded Italian," Louisa told her. "His real name is Pasquale and his nickname was Pat, so some of the other kids started calling him Patrick and it stuck. He likes it."

"He *likes* it?" Glorie whispered to Jack in bed that night. "Because it *stuck*? It sounds ridiculous."

"You changed my name, Glorie."

"That was different, that made sense," she said. "Who ever heard of an Italian Patrick? I think this is a very bad sign. He must have no spine."

"Give this boy a chance," Jack said, and Patrick became the son he never had. But to Glorie, being the Italian Patrick said everything.

"The son you never had. He's the son you never would have had," Glorie told Jack now. "He's spineless and pigheaded, nothing like you."

"He's trying to take care of you. He's just not doing a very good job."

"I'm tired of arguing with him about it, that's all," she said.

She counted back and realized she had been putting up a fight for almost a year. "It's paid for, it's my money that keeps it up, I don't want to hear another word about it," she would say, as sternly as she could, as if that settled things. "I will not sell my house."

But Patrick kept pressing. Sometimes Louisa would explain to Glorie patiently, "We're only thinking about you, Ma." Sometimes Louisa would say to Patrick, "Let it go, we don't have to decide this right now." But Glorie knew he would never let it go. He wasn't a tax accountant for nothing. He did the numbers and said they didn't lie, as if something had to be right because the whole world thought it.

Ever since Glorie was a girl she had heard the whole world say, "Who does she think she is?" Jack never let her feel that way. "I'm going to spoil you," he had promised, and he kept his word.

As soon as they could afford it, she hired help for the spring and fall cleaning. When they could afford more, she got a mink jacket. "It's not a mink, it's a gopher," Jack said when he surprised her with it. "I wouldn't want you to feel too spoiled." She had other fur coats after that one, but the latest was always called "the gopher." She had a house so comfortable and safe she was happy to stay in it for days at a time, and when she left it she felt so luxurious she wore her gopher to the PTA.

Once at a PTA meeting, a mother she hardly knew looked in her direction and muttered loud enough for her to hear, "Who needs that snob?" When she told Jack about it, he said matter-of-factly, "But, Glorie, you *are* a snob." He said this with love and even a hint of pride, as if he had been saying, "But, Glorie, you *have* blue eyes. I like blue eyes." Whatever sting she had felt from the other mother's comment vanished forever.

Jack would not have said she was wrong to keep a house she used only during the daytime, only on weekdays. She could stand up to Louisa and Patrick, to her neighbors and her in-laws, to anyone who called her spoiled like it was some disease.

She began to wish Jack were here to defend her, then pushed the thought away, as if he could hear and might feel bad about leaving her alone.

"I wish you were here to call me Glorie," she said. That one sentimental wish she allowed herself. It might make him feel good to know that no one would ever call her that again.

She took a deep breath as she walked down her well-lighted front steps and headed across the street.

I'm doing what he would want, she thought. I can take care of myself.

Chapter 2

ADA WAS TRYING to drive and talk at the same time. So far she was doing OK. Now and then she ran a red light, but generally she was doing OK. Glorie took some credit for this, because she was purposely not distracting Ada with interesting comments. Maybe she could drive and talk, but drive and think was something else.

"I says, 'Anthony, the least you could do is load the dishwasher,' which is what *she* wanted, right?" Ada said. "She nags and nags and then when I open my mouth to help her, she turns around and tells me to mind my own business. So I'm in the doghouse with the both of them. Honest-n-God, I can't win."

"Can't win," said Glorie.

"But I sit and watch TV with them anyways, cause I'm still sociable even if they treat me like dirt."

"After all you've done for them," Glorie said. She could carry on this conversation while thinking of plenty of other things. Ada probably did butt into her son's life too much. Glorie wanted to say, "Leave it alone, are they asking *you* to do the dishes?" but didn't dare, because Ada was already zooming along as if she were on the freeway instead of Charles Avenue with cars parked on both sides. She snuck a look at her watch to make sure they were on schedule and could beat Louisa home from the hairdresser's. "I know what you mean," Glorie said as she was thinking, This might be our last trip ever. She always thought that and it was always a possibility, because Louisa had forbidden her mother to drive with Aunt Ada.

"Ma, she's dizzy," Louisa said the first time she'd heard about the cemetery dates.

"So? She was always dizzy. She was born dizzy."

"You know what I *mean,* Ma. She aims the car and hopes she doesn't hit anything. She should have been off the road years ago." Louisa sounded very impatient and sure of herself; she sounded like her father when he said, "We've been through this, Glorie. You don't need to know how to drive. I'll take you wherever you want to go." He had said that for twenty years before Glorie gave up. And where was she now? Strapped into this flimsy shoulder harness, clutching the armrest, nearly sideswiping cars with Ada.

Every time Louisa heard about another trip to the grave, she'd say something like "You were lucky this time. I'm warning you, don't call me from East Egypt someplace and expect me to come pick you up when she gets lost. You know Aunt Ada's done that, I don't know how many times." Louisa ended in her I'm-ordering-my-mother-around voice, "I do *not* want you to get in a car with her again."

But would she drive her own mother to her own father's grave? "No, Ma. You get too upset. That's it," Louisa said. Just because the first few times Glorie had sobbed for an hour, maybe two, after she came back. Because she had fallen to her knees and put her arms around the stone and cried, "Jack, I wish I was with you. Come get me."

If Louisa had bothered to ask, Glorie might have admitted she was being dramatic. "Oh, that jump-in-the-grave feeling was a passing phase," she would have told Louisa. "Some people might call it an emotional relief." But Louisa never brought it up. She refused to give her mother another chance.

So Glorie put on a sad face during Louisa's threats about Ada — what was Louisa going to do, ground her? — and did what she wanted, which turned out to be visiting the grave and eating greasy pizza with someone she had called dim-witted most of her adult life. Glorie didn't feel bad about that. She knew that when she had first come into the family Ada had called her a Portagee until she got to know her better. Then she called her the Queen of Portugal. And now Ada was the one who knew how to drive, so who turned out to be dim-witted?

Ada parked crooked, partly up on the grass, but there was no one around to yell at them. Glorie had been telling herself for a while that she would take Ada shopping downtown sometime, maybe help her pick out some things. If she wore jackets or heavier sweaters they would hide the old-lady hunch Ada had developed. Ada didn't know that you shouldn't tuck a blouse into pull-on slacks, especially with her waistline, and apparently she didn't think pink plastic pearls looked tacky. She did keep her hair black, Glorie had to give her that, even if it was what Blanche called Helmet Hair, chopped off at the neck. Sometimes Glorie felt she was letting Ada down by not giving her advice, but then she figured what Ada didn't know couldn't hurt either one of them. "Relax," she told herself as she got out of the car. "Have a good time."

And she had actually learned something from her sister-in-law at this cemetery. Jack was only a few rows from Anthony, and their parents and one of their sisters were buried together in sections not far away. After their first visit, as they got out of the car, Glorie had said with some genuine feeling and a lot more duty and guilt, "Don't you think we should pay a visit to Mama and Papa?"

"Are you kidding? I seen enough of them when they was alive," Ada said.

Glorie chuckled. "I'm not going to argue," she said. "We agree on that."

Glorie stood at Jack's grave and forced herself to concentrate. There were no silly vases of plastic flowers here, no weeds or candy wrappers anywhere. Out of the corner of her eye she saw Ada get to Anthony's grave, kneel, put her head down and cross herself with her rosary. When Glorie noticed this she began to pray, "Dear God. Please, please, don't let her say the whole rosary while I stand here." It seemed too chilly for that, but in warmer weather she had seen Ada do it. One hot day Glorie had watched for a good five minutes and Ada's beads didn't move at all. Her head was lowered, and Glorie was pretty sure she had fallen asleep on her knees, but didn't want to wake her in case she was in the middle of some religious trance. She let Ada catch some beauty sleep. That day they didn't even beat the lunchtime rush at the mall. Glorie didn't mind the times when Ada sang "Ave Maria." At least it was shorter.

Glorie looked down at the stone again. The salesman had tried to get her to put her own name on in advance, to save money, but nothing was worth looking down at your own gravestone. At first coming to Jack's grave had been like getting slapped in the face. Now she hardly felt the slaps at all. She felt hollow and transparent, like a ghost with the wind blowing through her. But she couldn't risk staying away from any place Jack might be.

Here I am, standing over his bones, she thought. No, that didn't work.

I'll never see him again, she told herself. Big surprise.

She couldn't stand to think of dust and ashes and worse things, so she simply wished him to be in a better place, hoped he'd been right all the years he had gone to church only on Christmas and Easter, all the decades he had refused to go to confession, grumbling, "Why should I tell my sins to some crook who's no better than me?" And if he were wrong it shouldn't count for much, weighed against the fact that he was a good man.

OK, I'm praying, I really mean it this time. She started: Why did you take my husband and where did you put him? That came out too angry and sort of funny, as if Jack were being held hostage somewhere.

Maybe I could buy him out! she thought. Bring a barrel of money next trip and trade it to get him back. It made as much sense as anything.

She tried again. I never gave up faith, not when Manny's baby died, not when Frank Jr. was killed in Korea. But I do not understand this.

It was all she could do to handle small questions. Why go to Mass with Louisa and Patrick every week? Because they might be right, she thought. Because there were people in church who were amusing to watch, looking dressed up or as if they'd come from washing the car, poking each other and whispering. Because it was easier to go than to explain to Patrick and Louisa why she wasn't.

All right, once more, she thought. I don't have to be sure, I just have to be hopeful. I'm praying: Dear God, please rest Jack's soul.

But she didn't want it rested. She wanted it active and fluttering around her.

This was useless.

"Ada is saying her beads in this weather," she told Jack, looking at the polished stone and the neat grass. He didn't seem interested and she started to get mad at him. Maybe he couldn't help it that he died, but he didn't have to be as distant as he acted at this place. When she first saw his casket, still closed at Manfredi's before the wake, she fell to the floor. That was when it all seemed real. She had visualized the wake, the funeral, but not the shock of that heavy casket. He's in there, she thought, and she knew that saying good-bye would be even worse than she was prepared for. At the cemetery, they had left the casket in the chapel instead of going to the grave. So how did she even know the coffin was buried here under her feet? She had walked out the door and left him there. She cried out loud, "Good-bye, Jack," as Louisa led her to the car.

"Always an actress, even today," she heard one of the sister-in-laws say behind her as they walked out. She didn't know which one and didn't care.

Fuck them, she thought, shocking herself. Where did that word come from? Was she losing her mind or her soul or both?

"I want to see Josie," she told Jack now, but it was like talking into the windy air. It was a dumb idea, too. If Louisa wouldn't go to see her own father, why would she go to see her Aunt Josie and Uncle Al in a cemetery two towns away?

"I don't know why, but I miss my sister all of a sudden, I've been thinking of her. I know I never missed her much when she was alive, but I do now. I don't *know* why."

The wind must have got to Ada. After about fifteen minutes, only a few Hail Marys for her, she wandered over to Glorie. "Are you ready, hon?" she said sadly. These were the only times Glorie knew her to be calm, when Ada was barely back from praying at the grave, still quiet and mournful. Glorie liked her better that way.

"How's your digestion?" Ada asked as she swerved into the mall parking lot.

"Fine."

"Pizza, here we come. Might as well live it up, right?"

Ada wasted quite a bit of gas circling around the lot looking for a spot close to Papa Gino's. "We can drive around to the wishing well later," she said. "I wish they'd put a well in this section, too."

If their stomachs were up to it, they ate pizza then drove to another entrance, tossed a few pennies in a wishing well and headed home. If one of them wanted something bland, they went to Roy Rogers. The food wasn't so tasty, but it was near the wishing well and they might even have time to shop. Today Glorie was willing to skip the well, but she only suggested it once. "No way," said Ada. "Everybody needs luck. I'm taking no chances and don't even ask me what I'm wishing for. Even if you guess right, I'm not telling you."

Glorie didn't guess, but she saw the use of throwing some change in the well just in case.

At 11:30 the lunch crowd wasn't jamming the floor yet, but there were plenty of people — mothers with strollers, teenagers who should have been in school — racing past them. Ada linked her arm through Glorie's, and Glorie checked around in case she saw anyone she knew. Couples walked arm-in-arm; old people too feeble to keep their balance walked arm-in-arm; dignified ladies did not walk arm-in-arm. But what did Ada care? She was the one who had danced with Margaret at their nephew's wedding, two old widowed sister-in-laws doing a slow-motion jitterbug in the center of the floor. "Aren't they great?" Louisa had said. "Look at them." Everyone thought they were so cute and spunky. Glorie didn't open her mouth to say, "They're making asses out of themselves." She just threw Louisa a withering look across the table.

"I'm not saying *you* should do it, Ma. God forbid," said Louisa. "I'm saying they're having fun, good for them."

And here Glorie was, trapped arm-in-arm with Ada at the mall. She seemed to hear an annoyed sigh or catch a dirty look when people passed, as if she and Ada, side by side, were taking up too much space.

As they settled down at the table, Ada took a Kleenex out of a hideous-looking homemade case: blue cotton with two lopsided white daisies embroidered on it. Ada caught her staring. "That's eye-catching," said Glorie.

"You like it?" Ada asked. "I made it at sewing club. Why don't you ever come when I ask you? You sew so beautiful! You always did. You could teach us a couple of things."

Glorie was glad Ada had ways to distract herself, but she wasn't planning to clutter up Louisa's living room with stupid pillows that said "God Bless This House" and only proved Grandma could still move her fingers. In the privacy of her own sewing room she could design her own clothes, do something practical, at least have pretty new things to wear to church or the hairdresser's.

But why hurt Ada's feelings with the truth? "Maybe. I'll surprise you someday," she said.

"So what have you got better to do?" Ada asked. "You running around with a millionaire on the sly? You going skydiving in your spare time? Come on."

"Yes, I'm running around with a millionaire. Donald Trump loves me," Glorie said. "We're going scuba diving next week.

Besides, I'm happy in my sewing room. I have my machine, my dress form, all my things there, I'm settled in."

"You're so lucky to have your own house," said Ada. "You have the best of both worlds. Don't get me wrong, I love my childrens, but sometimes — I don't know, it's hard to live with them. Like the other night."

A young waitress came to the table. "I think I'll have myself a *tiny* glass of red wine," Ada said, holding her thumb and forefinger an inch apart. "Just a tiny one."

"We only have one size," the girl said.

"Then bring it to us," Glorie snapped. "And I'll have one too."

Ada looked confused as the waitress turned away.

"I'm old but I'm not stupid and I'm not going to put up with insults," Glorie said.

"That's right," Ada said, catching on. "The nerve! That girl will get a man and he'll be miserable and leave her and it'll serve her right. Where was I? Oh, yeah, the other night." She leaned across the table, looked around to make sure no one was listening, lowered her voice like a mischievous kid. "I couldn't sleep, it was about twelve-thirty, one o'clock in the morning. And I hear noise from Anthony and Barbara's room, and it's not the first time I hear that bed creak, you know what I mean? I felt like throwing something at the wall."

Glorie had no idea what she was supposed to say, but she guessed she should be shocked and embarrassed. An image flashed through her mind of the time Jack had piled blankets and pillows on the floor when Louisa was a child, restless with the flu and the right age to notice a creaky bed. She shook her head at Ada and frowned. "How embarrassing for you," she said.

"Embarrassed? I was jealous!" Ada was practically yelling. She picked up her fork and banged it down. "What I wouldn't give for some fun, you know? Not that I want to have sex with anybody, but I wouldn't mind cuddling up with someone now and then! There must be some nice man out there who wants a nice round body like mine to snuggle up with! The last time I tried that, it was my friend Rose's older brother and he fell asleep on my shoulder, but I think that was bad luck, don't you? So what do you think? Should I give him another chance?" She raised her eyebrows. "I could think of ways to keep him alert," she said, laughing extra loud. And the wine hadn't even come yet.

"Why not," said Glorie, trying not to giggle. "What's the worst that can happen? You listen to him snore?"

"I done enough of that already in my lifetime. That's what I mean. I'm not putting up with any more snores. The next man, no snores!"

"Is he a quiet snorer? Cause a quiet one might be OK, but if he snorts like a pig or sounds like a train, that would be hard to take."

"I didn't wait to find out," Ada said. "I pulled the hair on the back of his neck to wake him up. I was very sneaky. When he woke up I said, 'No snores!' "

"No snores!" They were both laughing so hard, saying "No snores!" that they forgot to glare at the rude waitress when she brought their wine.

"Salut," said Ada.

"To your health," said Glorie.

Ada offered Glorie a Kleenex from the ugly blue case and took one for herself. "I never had another man and I never wanted one," said Glorie as they both wiped laugh-tears from their eyes.

"You're lucky, very lucky."

Glorie couldn't explain how the next words slipped out. "And I wouldn't know how to get one anyway."

"Oh, honey, there's nothing to that," Ada said. She straightened up as if she were suddenly in control. "You're still pretty, you got that red hair, you get out and meet people and men will fall at your feet. They won't be young. Come to think of it, they might be so old they'll *have* to fall at your feet." Ada was grinning and shaking her head at her own joke, though Glorie thought the time for comedy had passed. "That doesn't matter," Ada was saying. "What you have to watch out for is that they all want one thing." She paused to let the importance of this sink in. "Your money. You may not be rich, but your husband owned his own business, he did pretty good, you got your own house." Glorie rolled her eyes but Ada didn't stop long enough for her to explain that her home was being stolen out from under her. "You don't mention that, you hear me, not at first. You want him to like you for yourself. There are men out there who would give a lot to live in a good home, believe me. You know, I'm thinking. Rose has another brother. His health isn't so good, but he's very quiet and dignified. He might be the type for you."

"Maybe he's not dignified," Glorie said. "Maybe he's in a coma."

"At least he wouldn't snore. Come on, give it a try, flirt a little."

"No, I'm not interested. It was so easy with Jack, when we met it was instant. I never had to try. I always wondered about women who could go after any man that comes along. You know what I mean? Women who could wrap men around their little finger, they didn't even care who it was? I was never like that."

"Like who? You know some women like that?"

"No, I don't *know* any. I *wish* I knew some." Glorie took a sip of wine. She'd had enough wine to talk and Ada had had enough so she probably wouldn't remember this conversation in an hour. Maybe Ada wouldn't get any of this, but it was worth a try. "I wish I knew what women like that knew," Glorie said, trying to sound casual and not as if she were about to reveal one of her deep, secret longings. "Even now I just wish I knew. Women like, I don't know who, like the Duchess of Windsor. She wasn't young, she wasn't pretty, she gets a king. What secret did she know that we don't know?"

"Oh, her," said Ada, making a face. She shrugged. "A slut. I think she knew a few bedroom secrets, that's what. Must of."

"You think he would have married her for that? He didn't have to. You know that saying about the cow."

"He liked cows?"

"Why buy the cow when . . . Never mind."

"I don't know how dukes think, Gloria, I never knew a duke. He might as well be a duck as far as I'm concerned. I never even kept up with Princess Diana, but I know that the Duchess of Windsor was never a nun. I remember that whole thing when it happened. She was a slut, everybody knew it."

Glorie sighed. It was hopeless. She had said enough. Ada would laugh so hard she'd cry again if Glorie told her that back in 1936 she had actually cut out newspaper articles about the king giving up his throne for a common American, stashing the old clippings in an envelope in the kitchen drawer. Glorie read every word of every article, studied Wallis Simpson's hair and clothes and heavy jewels. She didn't exactly want to imitate her. Glorie wasn't even thirty yet; Wallis was middle-aged and no beauty. No, Glorie pored over the Simpson story like a detective looking for clues. She wasn't sure what she was searching for, but she filed away clues that might come in handy someday. They never did make sense, not yet anyway. You could read those articles over and over and there was always something missing, something Glorie was afraid everyone could see except her.

She stopped clipping soon after the king gave up his throne — she wasn't obsessed, just mystified — until the Duchess died. It was some kind of eerie sign that she died three months after Jack, as if Glorie wouldn't be needing her anymore so she might as well pass on. That was when she'd started her scrapbook, the one no one knew about.

She had bought a big burgundy leather photo album for Jack's obituary, and for all the sympathy cards and pressed flowers from the funeral. When the Duchess died she started a new book, a matching green one, beginning with Wallis's death notice. The paper even printed some of the Duke and Duchess's old love letters. HE WAS HER KING, SHE WAS HIS QUEEN, the headline said. Glorie read, "Darling Sweetheart, I couldn't bear hearing you cry." It seemed the most romantic letter ever, until she realized it was Wallis writing to the King. That gave her the creeps, but she put the write-up in her scrapbook anyway. It proved Jack was stronger than the King of England.

She kept the scrapbook going with birthday cards and postcards and clippings of things that caught her eye: an article from the paper about how swans mate for life and die together; a magazine article she didn't know what to do with but was scared to throw away, about how old women have strokes when they're tipped backward over the hairdresser's sink; Lucy Ball's death notice.

That big envelope of clippings from '36 had disappeared long ago. But every now and then Glorie could see herself walking in a garden with Wallis through rows of rosebushes and pink gladiolus in the sparkling sun. The Duchess laughed with quiet elegance. "Oh, Gloria, it's so simple," she said. "The key to holding a man is . . ." something, something, something. Glorie couldn't imagine what.

Ada was still talking.

"So Elizabeth Taylor gets a young man. Money. Wake up, honey, life's not that complicated."

But it was, it was. Jack had never betrayed her, not that she knew of. If he had, how would she ever have known how to get him back?

She had only been suspicious once, and she blamed it all on that picture *The Seven Year Itch.* Glorie didn't care about some Marilyn Monroe movie, but Jack wanted to go and that was fine with her. He wasn't much of a movie type. Glorie figured the photographs of Marilyn with her white dress blowing up over her waist was what did it. As long as Marilyn Monroe wasn't going to follow them home, let him drool all he wanted.

When he came home for supper and canceled the movie plans she was disappointed; it would have been a night out. "We'll do it another time, maybe even over the weekend," he said. "I've got to go measure a job tonight, these people both work during the day and I've got to get started." Of course she understood. It happened often enough.

A few minutes after he left the house, the phone rang and a voice that sounded young, pretty, breathless and almost familiar asked, "Is Jack there?"

"No, this is his wife. Who's calling, please?"

"Oh, no," the pretty young woman said. "He was coming to measure the bathroom tonight and it's not such a good time, I was hoping to catch him before he left. But if he's on his way."

"He just left," said Glorie.

"All right, then. Thank you," the woman said, hanging up and leaving Glorie to her misery. Where did she know that voice from? Why didn't the woman give her name? Why the last-minute change? Whoever she was, she didn't want Glorie to have much information. Whoever she was, she sounded not much older than Louisa, who at this very minute must be singing Patrick Jr. a lullaby.

Glorie went on clearing the supper dishes, and when they were done she kept pacing around the kitchen. Maybe she was wrong and the voice wasn't familiar. Maybe she was wrong and Jack wasn't tired of her just because he wanted to see a Marilyn Monroe picture about a man who wants a sexy, trampy young blonde.

She sat at the kitchen table and thought, I'm not a stupid person. Am I really jealous of Marilyn Monroe?

She wasn't. She thought back and hated to admit it, but she was still upset at how Jack had looked at Patrick's secretary. She was no hot blonde, but she was attractive, her brown hair in a chic French twist, her eyelashes fluttering at Jack.

Matchmaking, Patrick and Louisa had invited the secretary to dinner with another accountant from the office. At the last minute, Glorie got a frantic call. "Can you and Dad come and help me with the baby?" Louisa asked. "He's so cranky today, I can't keep him quiet and have a dinner party too. Come for dinner with us."

Glorie was jumping up and down from the table, changing the baby, rocking him. Louisa was jumping up and down serving dinner. Carol was paying no attention to her blind date, and Glorie couldn't blame her. The guy was so nervous his foot tapped constantly and he gulped loudly before talking, which made his Adam's apple race up and down his throat like one of the baby's toys. Whenever Glorie got back to the table, Carol was batting her eyelashes at Jack, saying things like "I can't believe you started your own company from nothing. You must have a great mind for business."

And when it was time to go, the nervous guy said good-bye, shot out the door and drove away as if Carol wasn't even there. Gallant Jack saved the moment, saying, "Do you need a ride home? Our car is across the street. I'll drive you."

He was back in fifteen minutes; Glorie didn't mean to time it, but she did. He walked in the door and said, "She's something, isn't she? A lot of ambition for a girl. She wants to start her own accounting company someday." Then he went into the bathroom and closed the door.

Glorie got into bed and tried not to tremble. Why was he treating her like some sister he might confide in? In those fifteen minutes she had decided not to say anything about the ride. She had heard about monkey business starting out that way, with an innocent ride, but nothing had happened yet. Maybe it never would.

That was the voice on the phone, it was Carol, she was almost sure. She got up and started pacing around the kitchen again. Or maybe not. In the past two weeks she could have forgotten what the secretary's voice sounded like. How could she find out? She didn't know Carol's last name, so she couldn't find her in the phone book. She couldn't call Louisa and say, "I'm checking up on your father, what's Carol's phone number?"

Panicky, she paced, looking at her round stomach and wrinkling hands. She had been married a lot more than seven years. It's not my fault I'm forty-seven, it's not fair, she thought. But it was all her fault, it must be. There was no one else to blame.

Other women, even women who looked nothing like Marilyn Monroe, must have all sorts of tricks for getting men and keeping them. The Duchess of Windsor crossed her mind. How could Glorie even guess what they were? She tried to push her imagination as she walked back and forth between the stove and refrigerator.

All she knew about sex was what Jack had taught her. She could move underneath him. Sometimes he would take her hand and put it where he liked. She instinctively held him in her hand, not too hard, and moved her hand slowly. But there must be other things she had no idea existed. She would do anything to please him if she only knew what that could be. He still seemed to want her, from time to time, but they weren't kids anymore. They had settled in.

I could sob and beg, she thought.

Then he might pity her, but it wouldn't make him want her.

I could threaten to leave.

That was something she would never do; she would die if he let her go. And even if she had known someone with all those flirty feminine wiles she read about in magazines, what could she have said to such a woman? I feel old and ugly and helpless? No one could change that. While Jack was out doing God knew what, she could look forward to hot flashes.

She kept pacing and crying, keeping an eye on the clock over the stove. She thought Jack should be home by 9:30. At 9:00 she went into the bathroom, splashed cold water on her puffy eyes and looked in the mirror. She fixed her hair, put on lipstick. She looked like herself, so she started to cry again.

She went to bed at 10:30 and heard him come in an hour later. Her back was turned to him when he got into bed, and he didn't smell different. The next day she mentioned nothing. She was afraid she wouldn't be able to bring up the phone call without sounding jealous or suspicious, the very things that would make her even less attractive. So she said nothing, ever.

He worked a few more nights that month. The mystery woman never called to confirm another appointment. Glorie decided that *The Seven Year Itch* had planted the thought in her mind and made her get carried away. She could have imagined the whole thing. She would behave as if she *had* imagined the whole thing. But for months after, a weird dream wouldn't let her go. She was alone in a forest at night. She was tied to a tree, with wolves howling around her. In one version of the dream her mother came to untie her, and Glorie held her grown mother in her lap and told her a story:

Once upon a time there was a young queen who loved her husband very much. One day he took his bow and arrow to hunt and wandered into a part of the woods where no one had gone before. A woman appeared. She looked like Marilyn Monroe in a sparkly, sheer good-fairy's gown, and she said that anyone who passed through that part of the forest would forever stay the same age they had been when they entered it. The king returned and soon the young queen seemed as old as her husband. Before long, her hair turned gray, her face wrinkled, but the king looked as handsome and young as he had on their wedding day. The queen refused to see him and stayed in a tower, weeping and wondering what she had done wrong.

"Tell me the story again," Glorie's mother said, looking up at her and shrinking down to a child's size. "Tell me again."

"Don't cry, honey," said Ada, grabbing Glorie's hand across the table. "We all get lonely sometimes."

Glorie jumped, pulled her hand back and wiped her eyes fast. Was she crying in public? Had she talked out loud?

"I'm fine," she said quickly, sitting up extra straight. "I'm fine."

"You want to talk about it, honey?" said Ada.

"No, let's eat," said Glorie and turned her head to look around. "Where's our food?" Her eyes were beginning to fill up again and she couldn't turn back to Ada this way unless she was ready to talk heart to heart.

"You know, I was telling Barbara the other day," Ada said kindly, "Glorie seems so odd sometimes and everyone always says she's so stuck up, but she's really not bad when you get to know her."

Glorie was about to think Ada wasn't so bad herself. Then she had to say that. At least it made Glorie's eyes turn dry.

She spent the rest of lunch trying not to be mad at Ada for calling her stuck up — she meant well, Glorie knew — but it was tough.

"Do you lie about your age?" Ada asked. "Cause you could, you know. You could get away with it easy."

"No, I don't," Glorie lied, cutting off any age talk.

Neither of them had much appetite, and they each took a quarter of the pizza home.

"I don't think we should tip that insulting waitress too much, do you?" Ada asked.

"I agree," said Glorie.

"I have an idea! Let's take a lot of sugar and Sweet'n Low to get back at her."

"You do that, I have another idea," said Glorie, looking around to make sure the waitress was nowhere in sight. Then she quickly screwed off the tops of the salt and pepper shakers and left them loose so they'd fall off when the next person used them. That waitress would have one mess to clean up.

"I knew you had it in you," Ada said. "Do you mind if we skip the wishing well today, honey? I'm feeling kind of beat."

"Me too," said Glorie. "I don't know why you throw money into that well, anyway. Why don't you just do the Evil Eye?"

Ada froze halfway out of the booth, which left her in a weird hunched-over position. She looked fierce. "I do *not* do the Evil Eye, Gloria, I don't care what anybody says about me. I only do that spell that wards *off* the Evil Eye, it's a total different thing. I tell everybody that, they don't have to believe me, but it's the God's honest truth," she said, making a cross over her heart.

"All right, I'm sorry, I was teasing. I believe you, I was joking." She didn't mention that now they were even, one snob remark for one Evil Eye.

"Let's go," Glorie said. "We want to make sure to beat Louisa home."

When they got to the corner of Jasmine Street, they looked in Louisa's driveway. Her car wasn't there, so it was safe for Ada to drop Glorie off in her own driveway instead of leaving her at the corner. The car behind them honked and Ada made the turn. Glorie's house keys were already in her hand when she kissed Ada on the cheek and got out of the car. As she was closing the car door she felt bad about something but didn't think she had anything to be sorry for.

"Thanks again," Glorie said. "You take care and stay in touch."

"Don't worry, I will, honey. And you take care, too. You need to get out more. I'm going to call and ask you to my sewing club next time, and I want you to come."

"We'll see. Good-bye." She stood on the porch waving until Ada drove away.

Glorie dropped her coat on the couch and got a Tums out of her bag. She hardly managed to chew it, sit in the soft armchair Jack liked and put her feet up on the footstool before her eyes closed. She couldn't keep them open but wasn't quite asleep.

"What a relief," she told Jack. "She has a good heart, but a little of her goes a long way."

Glorie was nearly dozing when her leg twitched and she opened her eyes for a second. She was in the TV room, her feet up on Jack's footstool; her eyes drooped again and she saw the small back bedroom she shared with Josie when they were girls and lived at the top of the triple-decker. There were the windows on Josie's side, with pink, frilly curtains. On Glorie's was the wall covered with her fabric cutouts: green and blue cotton stars with silver spangles sewn on to make them sparkle, a ruby-red velvet heart, daisies made from white organza and pasted against sapphire-blue cotton. "We're not rich but we'll always have good material," her mother used to say when she brought these jewel-colored scraps and bits of fancy trim home from the mill. Her mother had made some of the cutouts to start, but Glorie had made most of them, and she couldn't bear to part with any. They crept across the wall beside her bed: a big pink flower, one of the first, that was supposed to look like a rose but didn't quite; a mustard-yellow half-moon.

Then Glorie started to make her rainbow. She had been saving the longest pieces of material for almost a year, waiting until she had the real rainbow colors. She put a big purple crescent close to the edge of the wall. Josie said, "Don't think that stuff is coming on my half of the room." She was sixteen and felt too grown-up for cutouts; that's what Glorie guessed. Their mother said maybe Josie didn't want to spend all night looking at the same material she cut in the mill all day.

Glorie was only eight, but she thought it was Josie who was being a baby. These were the kind of decorations any adult might make. They weren't balloons or kiddie things. Grown-ups made lovely decorations like this; they went places and they had complicated, serious conversations after the kids went to bed. Grown-ups were interesting, which proved to Glorie that Josie was still a baby.

"Josie could sew but she never made anything pretty," she told Jack. "She was always more practical than me."

He started laughing.

"Well, you're right," Glorie said, chuckling and half asleep. "I know the day you're thinking about. I can just see your face when you walked into the kitchen."

"I never cheated on you, you know. If you had asked I would have told you that."

"I know that now," she said. "It was only that one time I worried."

"It was nothing."

"We never did see *The Seven Year Itch.*"

"I wonder if Al ever saw it," said Jack. "Maybe that's what gave him the idea to cheat on Josie. It was about that time."

"Oh, as if he needed help."

She was chuckling louder now, though she still couldn't keep her eyes open. She was remembering how confused Jack looked when he walked into the kitchen of this very house all those years ago and found Josie sobbing at the table. Glorie looked up but before she could eyeball Jack to leave them alone, Josie raised her head and explained to Jack between sobs, "I didn't mean to set his pants on fire."

Glorie's heart had almost stopped when she'd seen a taxi pull up in front of the house. Something like that had to mean bad news. When her sister got out, Glorie realized someone must be dead. As Josie came up the walk, Glorie was stunned at how old she looked. By then Josie's hair was mostly gray, her features round like their father's, her figure very full.

A dozen years before, Josie had been the one to call and tell Glorie their father was gone. He had died in Josie's house, though he had hardly had time to unpack since moving in with her. "I can't even take care of myself," he complained, though his health was perfectly good. "I have to take charity from my own daughter." A few months later he passed on.

And now Josie was at the front door looking hysterical. This news must be even worse. Josie fell into Glorie's arms and sobbed. "Al's gone, he's gone. I didn't mean to set his pants on fire."

Glorie led Josie into the house. They sat on the couch while Glorie patted her sister's back and Josie kept sobbing, "He's gone."

"Tell me what happened," Glorie said. The only story she could put together from this couldn't possibly be true: Al had dropped dead and her sister had gone crazy and set the poor man on fire. Josie was on the run from the police.

"Is he dead?" Glorie asked as gently as she could.

Josie stopped crying and pulled back to look at Glorie. "No, the sonofabitch, I wish he was. He walked out. For someone else. Another woman." And Josie started bawling again.

They went into the kitchen so Glorie could make tea, and Josie had moments when she was calm enough to talk.

"He planned this for lunchtime, so he'd have to go straight back to work after he told me," she said. "The coward. And I didn't even know anything was wrong. He comes in and tells me he's been fooling around. Can you believe it, at his age? What does he want with that anymore? He tells me he's come home to get his clothes. And I'm thinking, Who is she? This isn't happening. And then he says, 'I'm confused, but I have to do this. You don't know what I've been through deciding this.' That's when I threw the frying pan at him. Cause, how dare he tell me what *he's* been through! I couldn't help it, I picked up the pan with the pork chop for his lunch and threw it against the wall. I threw the coffeepot and the salt and pepper, everything on top of the stove I threw on the floor. I couldn't stop. So he ran into the bedroom to get his clothes. I thought I was going to be sick, and I'm thinking, How can I stop him? And I noticed the pilot light was out, so automatically I get a match. Then he comes out holding a pair of work pants, he's holding out this pair of pants that just yesterday I was wondering whether they needed to be patched or not . . ." This made Josie sob some more, so Glorie went around to her side of the table, stood behind the chair and put her arm around her sister.

Josie sniffled. "He's holding out the pants and he says, 'Josie!' so loud he scared me and I accidentally dropped the match and it hit the cuff of his pants and he started jumping around."

"The pants he was holding?" Glorie asked.

"The pants he was wearing," Josie sobbed. She was crying so much she could hardly talk. "He starts jumping around cause there's a little fire on his cuffs and he's pulling up his pants legs and trying to beat the cuffs with the other pair of pants in his hand."

"Was he hurt?" Glorie asked. Because if he wasn't she might have to laugh. She had this image of Al dancing a jig on one foot, holding up his pants leg and swatting his cuffs with green work pants.

"No, he put it out very fast," Josie said calmly. "You know his brother Joe is the volunteer fireman, so he knew what to do. He's OK, but he started screaming. He ran out of the house and all the time he's screaming, 'I'll divorce you! You're crazy. She tried to kill me. She set me on fire!' so all the neighbors could hear. And then he was gone and then I came here." Josie sighed.

"He'll be back, don't worry," Glorie said in a soothing voice. It was probably the stupidest thing she had ever said in her life, but what else *could* she say? She felt awful letting Josie down like this, offering useless sympathy instead of smart, practical advice. When had Josie ever needed her for anything like this? When had Josie ever needed her for anything except a little help with the boys' tuition? And this was the best she could do. "He'll be back," she said, helplessly.

Josie brightened up. "Do you think so?" she asked, looking at Glorie with the expression of a five-year-old.

"Of course," Glorie said, as if she'd stumbled across some solution. "He loves you, he loves the family. He's just gone nutty for a while. Who else would he want but you after all these years? Don't you think he wants a real home?" she asked, hoping something she said might turn out to be true. "He'll come back before you know it."

And while Josie was sipping her tea and Glorie was patting her hand, Jack came in the door. Glorie noticed that it was turning dark outside. Jack stood in the doorway, baffled, and before Glorie could say anything, Josie saw him and started up again. "I didn't mean to set his pants on fire," she bawled to Jack.

Josie stayed in their spare room that night. Whether she was too exhausted to go to any of her children or too embarrassed, Glorie never asked. She was glad she could help her sister for once, make her feel safe and protected, though she knew Josie's life was falling apart. She remembered how she snuggled into Jack's arms in their soft bed that night and had trouble sleeping.

"No one ever made me feel as safe as you," she told Jack now, her arms folded for warmth as she dozed in the chair. "No one ever understood me like you," she whispered.

Then she was back in the triple-decker, watching her mother make dress patterns out of newspaper at the kitchen table. It seemed magical, the way she could find pictures she liked in newspaper ads for the department stores, cut out the picture, then turn the newspaper itself into a dress pattern. Her mother's bun of dark graying hair was bent over the table; pins stuck out of her mouth. She seemed old and wrinkled to Glorie, though she wasn't forty yet, would not live past forty at all. She pinned the newspaper to the cloth, cut and basted and sewed, and in a few hours turned a remnant of cotton she had been allowed to buy cheap at work into a beautiful flowered dress. She taught Glorie to do that.

Josie was always complaining that she wanted to buy the clothes she saw in the paper. There were huge screaming fights in the house about how much of her pay from the mill Josie should turn over to the family. Her mother pleaded, "She's sixteen, let her keep something," but her father yelled, "I'm the head of this family and I take care of the money. Have you gone hungry yet?"

Glorie didn't understand why Josie didn't like their mother's homemade clothes best. When she was seven, she was already helping sew buttons on clothes for the rest of them. While they sewed on Saturday afternoons, her mother would tell her stories about fairy godmothers and donkeys who could sing and witches who turned grapes into gold. There were frog kings in castles, and beanstalks that grew through the clouds. She was calm and talked slowly as she taught Glorie how to measure and mark the cloth with chalk. Her mother always talked fast when she got upset. "Josie," she would say, "come put on the water and peel the potatoes, I can't do this all myself, I got home late." But she never talked fast when she sewed or told stories. Softly, she told Glorie how ladies behaved. "A lady doesn't have dirty fingernails," she would say. "A lady never chews with her mouth open like those girls at the mill." Josie worked at the mill and she didn't chew with her mouth open. Glorie figured that was because their family was special.

But they weren't. The family was eating breakfast one ordinary morning. Josie and Manny were set to go to work with their parents, Frank to the junior high, Glorie to grade school. Their father said, "Frank, leave your books here. It's time you came to work with us. I fixed it for you, but if anybody asks, you tell them you're Manny Rodriguez's son and you say you're sixteen." Just like that.

Glorie felt sick. Her turn would come next, in three years, faster than she could stand. Her mother was looking down at her plate, not saying anything. Josie started clearing half-eaten dishes of eggs. Manny, who had been at the mill even longer than Josie, said, "Come on, kid, it won't be so bad. You can come with me." Glorie sat and stared, wondering why no one was yelling at her father, or crying about their brother. Why weren't they more upset? It was years before she realized everyone must have known except her and Frankie. Their mother must have known.

"If anybody asks, remember you're sixteen, but nobody will," their father said.

Then Frank jumped up from the table and ran out the door without his coat. He hadn't said a thing. Glorie didn't know whether to be afraid he had run away for good or to hope he had.

After supper he came back. Glorie never found out where he had been all day or who he might have talked to. He walked silently in the door and straight to his and Manny's room. Glorie snuck in the room. Frank was lying on the bed looking at the ceiling. "What are you going to do?" she asked, ready to pack his bag or sneak him food or even run away with him.

"What choice do I have?" he said. He rolled onto his side and looked at Glorie. "I never liked school anyway. Don't worry about me. Worry about yourself." He seemed like he was going to start crying, but instead he rolled on his back facing the ceiling again and closed his eyes. Glorie snuck out.

When her mother came to her room and kissed her good night, Glorie asked, "Do I have to go to work, too?" Her mother held her very tight and whispered, "It's too late for the rest of us, but there's time for you. I promise." Glorie didn't understand.

"But do I have to go to work soon? Do we need money?"

Her mother kissed her. "You don't have to go to work. You have to go to sleep so you won't be tired at school tomorrow." Her mother left and Glorie closed her eyes tight. The spangled stars on her wall made bright fuzzy shapes behind her eyelids, but she couldn't help seeing the big ugly brick building where all these beautiful scraps had come from. The mill floated back and forth in space, behind the starry light, like an angry monster with coal-black eyes and a giant mouth of wolves' teeth getting ready to leap at her. Then it fell to earth in its real spot on Narragansett Avenue, disguised as a regular building, waiting.

Sometimes she and Frank had met their mother and Josie after work and walked them home. Her mother and sister looked like all the other women rushing down the front stairs, wearing kerchiefs and thick stockings and shabby coats in winter, dresses and aprons in summer, carrying crumpled bags with leftover fruit from lunch.

Glorie had seen the inside of this place once, when Frank lifted her to look in a low window. There were rows of big machines and sawdust all over the floor. She tried to spot someone she knew, to wave, but everyone's face was hidden behind the machines and no one was looking out the window.

That was where she was going to end up, with a kerchief on her head, grease on her dress, sawdust on her shoes, tired and cranky. What did her mother mean, there was time? Maybe the man from the boat would come to their door. He would climb the stairs and stand in the dark hall holding a bushel basket filled with ten-dollar bills. "For the little red-haired girl," he would say. "So she doesn't have to go to the mill."

After Frank went to work, Glorie became quieter than ever. She even gave up nagging her mother to take her to the library so she could find books with pictures like she had seen in school. She tried to explain about the day Mrs. Silva was sick and a substitute teacher came in carrying heavy books. During English time she passed the books around, with slips of paper marking the pages that had the best pictures. They were by famous painters, the new teacher said, named Fra Angelico and Leonardo da Vinci, and they painted the Annunciation or the Blessed Virgin and Christ Child with all different kinds of angels and halos.

The teacher was talking about Fra Angelico. He was a priest and an artist at the same time because the Pope gave him permission. But Glorie kept staring at the picture of the Virgin sitting outdoors someplace strange, with blue and brown mountains in the background. The beautiful angel next to her was even more glamorous. It had curly hair and wings you could barely see, and it wasn't even looking at Mary or Jesus or the baby John the Baptist with a halo. It was pointing at one of the babies, but it was looking at something more interesting far away. Glorie kept staring at the picture for a long time, until Pauline Andrade poked her from behind and whispered, "Pass it on. It's my turn."

But Glorie noticed that the new teacher's books had library numbers on them, and she was sure she could find some herself at the library and take them home. "I don't have time to go looking for pictures," her mother said. "Read your schoolbooks."

Maybe there was no connection, but one Saturday morning, a few weeks after Frank started at the mill, Glorie's mother said they could take the streetcar downtown to the big library on North Main. "That's the one you want, isn't it?" she asked.

Glorie put on a church dress, but her mother looked like she was going to work, in an old dress with a kerchief around her head. She talked fast and acted as if she were mad at Glorie, but Glorie couldn't figure out why.

When they got to the library, they stood in the middle of a giant room and her mother looked around in a circle. There was a card catalog and a desk where a woman was stamping books. In another section a man with a cart was putting books on a shelf.

They stood in line waiting for the woman stamping books, and when it was their turn Glorie's mother said, "Can you help my daughter find some picture books?"

The woman sent them upstairs to the children's room, where another woman sat behind a desk. She asked Glorie what grade she was in and what kinds of stories she liked. "Sixth grade. I like Fra Angelico," Glorie said and the lady smiled.

"We don't have any books by Fra Angelico, but we have lots of stories for your age, right over here," she said, walking to a shelf and picking out a few. They were the most boring books Glorie had ever seen. *Treasure Island* had black-and-white drawings of pirates. *Sally's Summer* had black-and-white drawings of a farm. A tiny pamphlet called "The Life of Saint Maria Goretti" had no drawings at all. This was not what Glorie was after, but she didn't see anything like the picture books the substitute teacher had, so she supposed she must have been wrong to come here. Or maybe only grown-ups could get those books. Glorie didn't know what else to say. She didn't want to sound stupid, so she picked *Treasure Island* and *Sally's Summer* and said, "Thank you."

"Do you have your library card with you?" the woman asked. Her mother looked madder than ever as they went back downstairs to the front desk to get Glorie a card. The woman at that desk wrote down the information her mother gave her, then handed Glorie a card with her name on it. They took it upstairs to the other lady with the stamp, so Glorie could take out the books she already knew she'd hate.

"Did you get what you were looking for?" her mother asked on the streetcar.

"I guess," Glorie said.

"Well, they must be good books or the lady wouldn't have picked them out for you," her mother told her.

Two weeks later, Manny took her downtown and she returned the books, without looking around any more. When she figured out how to find the books she wanted, maybe she'd try again.

But before she could, in less than a year, her mother got sick. For weeks she stayed in bed and Glorie was only let into her room for a few minutes a day. Her mother's hair was more gray than black now, and she looked very tired, though she slept all the time. Glorie talked fast then, as fast as her mother used to when she was upset, because she only had a little time to spend. She thought hard before she went in to see her mother every day so she wouldn't forget anything. She told her mother she wanted to learn to make dresses from the newspapers, and save up to buy a watch, and find the picture books in the library and maybe go to Italy, where she thought there were whole palaces full of real paintings.

"Don't make yourself sad," her mother said slowly. "You marry a good man, not somebody from the mill. You find a gentleman who'll take care of you like a lady. That will be good enough." Her mother, Glorie knew, must be very sick to say that.

Glorie came home from school one day and found a black car on the narrow street in front of the house. No one in their neighborhood had a car, and children were crowded around it looking in the windows. Upstairs, her father and brothers were sitting at the kitchen table talking to a man in a suit. Josie came out of their parents' bedroom and closed the door behind her. She hugged Glorie and said that Mama would be laid out at home for two days, then there would be the funeral. "You can wear your navy blue dress," she said.

"I'm not going," Glorie said right away, and she wouldn't change her mind or tell what she was thinking: If all they can worry about is what to wear, I won't have any part of it. As if a stupid dress mattered.

Then she went to her room and slammed the door.

Josie came in after a while. "I'm going to the undertaker's with Papa and Manny. Frank will stay here with you. They'll bring Mama back tomorrow for the wake."

"I'm staying in here till it's over," Glorie said.

When Josie was gone she took the navy blue dress and hid it under the mattress, then went to bed.

The next day she got dressed in school clothes and sat on her bed. No matter how many times her father yelled, she wouldn't come out. Relatives she hardly knew knocked on the door. "Don't you want to see your mama?" they asked. "Don't you want to make her proud of you?" She ignored them. Frank brought her food and said, "It'll be over soon," but for two days and nights she heard people come and go. She heard the priest pray and everybody answer. She heard one of the women who knocked on the door say, "Tsk, tsk, tsk. I always said Jacquelina babied that one too much. She'll find out now." She heard Josie come to the door and say, "Leave her be," and explain that Glorie refused to go to their mother's funeral because she didn't have a proper black dress. "Gloria's a very nervous child," Josie said, which only made Glorie more angry and quiet.

She wouldn't give them the satisfaction of explaining. She did not say that her sister was a hypocrite, that their mother was dead and she wanted to be left alone to cry and wear anything she wanted. That she wasn't going to act polite and serve food to a lot of people she didn't know or care about. Let them think what they wanted. Let them think she would rather sit in her room than respect her own mother. Let them think she couldn't stand to see her mother dead. Let them think she didn't know she was really all alone.

From the parlor she heard women sobbing. "Jacquelina, Jacquelina, so young!" they sobbed. Glorie put her fingers to her ears and cried and told herself her mother would understand.

Then everyone went to church and left her by herself. She went into the parlor, where two men from Costa's were folding up wooden chairs. The furniture was all pushed to one side and there was a long wooden platform at the front of the room where the casket must have been. There were coffee cups and wineglasses on the floor as if there had been a party. Flower petals had fallen on the floor and the whole room smelled of rotten flowers.

When Glorie woke she could still smell flowers, and thought it must have been the smell that awakened her; then she heard the phone ringing. She sat up in the armchair in the TV room and saw that it was already dark. It must be Louisa calling, wondering why she wasn't back. She let it ring, picked up her coat from the couch and headed for the door. She remembered, on the night Josie had slept in the spare room, how bad she felt that she had spent so many years after the funeral angry at Josie, how silly it seemed after all. She remembered snuggling against Jack that night and asking if he thought Al would come back. She wanted to know more than that — would you ever do the same? do you want a younger woman? — but all she could ask was, "Do you think he'll come back?"

"He's a goddamn fool if he doesn't," Jack said. "Who wants two families to support?" Then he rolled over and softly started to snore.

Chapter 3

PATRICK WAS IN THE BASEMENT family room watching the six o'clock news.

Glorie was on her way from the kitchen to the dining room table — a few steps, really — carrying three plates to set the table when Louisa raced by and grabbed them out of her hands. "We're late," she said. "Please, hurry up, get the napkins and the silverware. Please."

"Louisa, can I help you get anything up there?" Patrick called from the cellar. "We've only got forty-five minutes."

"No, nothing, we're almost ready."

"I don't want to be late for that lesson, Louisa."

"All right, all right, don't worry, Patrick. Jesus!" she yelled. "Besides, it's the fox-trot tonight, we already know that one."

"Well, we're paying for it, we don't want to lose out."

For once, Glorie thought, Louisa was annoyed at her husband and not her mother.

"So what if you're a little late for your tango lesson?" Glorie asked. "You'll catch up fast. You both went to college."

"It's not tango, Ma, it's the fox-trot, you know that. And you *know* how he is about being on time."

"I wish I didn't," Glorie mumbled.

"Huh?"

"Can I do anything else?"

"No, Ma, just sit down. Let's try to have a calm, relaxing dinner. We have plenty of time now," she said, though the way she looked at the clock said something different. "Patrick," she called sweetly down the stairs. "Come up."

"Twinkletoes," Glorie whispered in a singsong. "Come on up."

"What?" said Louisa. "Honest, I can't hear a word you say tonight, I must be going deaf."

"I'm just going to wash my hands first," Glorie said.

"Ma! We're ready to eat."

"Don't wait for me," she said, using her innocent voice. "You don't have to wait for me."

In the bathroom she ran her clean hands under warm water and rolled her eyes at her reflection in the mirror. Patrick hated being late, he got too wound up about it. It might do him good to be late, force him to be looser, deal with life's problems.

"Ma?" Louisa called.

"Coming!" She dried her hands extremely well and shook her head in the mirror, disappointed again at the way her daughter followed every dumb new hobby her husband cooked up. Now it was dancing and Glorie knew Patrick was serious about it because he was willing to do two things he usually avoided: spend money and make an ass of himself. Just last Saturday Glorie had gone downstairs to get a bottle of grape juice from the storeroom and caught Patrick marching from one end of the den to the other, learning some line dance from The Nashville Network. "Shitkicker music," Jack had always called it, and though Patrick had never played it before, it figured that this kind of bad taste would come out sooner or later. He was smiling like a kid at Halloween until he saw Glorie standing at the bottom of the stairs. Then he stopped and pointed at the television — "Slap that leather," the announcer was saying — and Patrick explained, "Do you know how much we'd have to pay for lessons like these? We already pay for ballroom, so you add this it's like getting two for the price of one."

"You're missing your slap," Glorie said as she headed toward the storeroom. In the time it took her to walk past Patrick's desk, into the room with the shelves of food, and out again with the bottle of juice, Patrick had put the coffee table back in front of the sofa where it belonged and changed the channel to CNN.

Glorie shook her head and walked by. The only thing stupider than line dancing to The Nashville Network was stopping because your mother-in-law caught you at it.

"Ma, did you fall in?" Louisa called again from the dining room.

In the bathroom Glorie was putting on hand lotion. She folded the towel neatly, walked to the table and took her place across from Louisa.

"I thought we'd eat light, since we'll be jumping around," Louisa said, passing a plate of broiled chicken to Patrick. "There's a big salad, too."

Patrick glanced at Glorie, she was sure of it. She tried to smile mysteriously, as if to say, "Yes, *I* made the salad and maybe I put a few pebbles in it to choke you." She passed the dressing to Patrick.

"So, Ma," Louisa said. "What did you do today?"

I didn't see Ada, if that's what you're thinking, crossed her mind, but she was too smart to say so. She chewed her lettuce for a long time, putting together a foolproof answer. "Oh, I puttered around, I dusted, I watched Oprah and Sally Jessy," she said. Louisa never watched Oprah or Sally Jessy and Glorie could fake a show if she had to. Something about cross-dressers and how they broke their mothers' hearts or cross-dressers and the terrible problems they had getting panty hose to fit.

She decided to change the subject. "I was flipping channels and I saw this program about barbers," she said, staring at her plate. "There's a shortage of barbers in the country."

Patrick's fork dropped against his plate. "There is? What program was that?"

"I couldn't say. I just caught the end of it, it was on one of those high-number cable channels."

"Have some more chicken, Ma," Louisa said, putting the platter under her nose and forcing Glorie to look at her. "Stop it!" she mouthed.

Louisa always said Glorie was picking on Patrick, poor baby, but he deserved it. For someone who hated to look like an idiot, he acted foolish quite a bit. Before ballroom dancing he was crazy about woodworking, and everybody got handmade shoehorns for Christmas, the kind with the extra long handle so you didn't have to bend over. It came in handy, Glorie had to admit, but it wasn't much of a present. Before that it was Chinese cooking, and on birthdays everybody got fortune cookies with sayings like, "The IRS will smile on your return," and a smiley face. Glorie couldn't keep track of all his hobbies. Jack would remember the craziest one, about twelve years ago. She tried not to giggle thinking about it.

Patrick had started acting worried, preoccupied. He walked around with a frown for months. Whenever Jack and Glorie visited he would be sitting at the kitchen table hunched over papers covered with numbers. When he finished agonizing, he decided it was his dream in life to go to barber school. "Even if I don't use it," he had told Louisa. "Even if I just do the family." He hadn't been so excited in years.

Louisa confided this to her mother, looking pretty worried. "He wants to do something creative, he says, and barber school would be his dream come true."

"What the hell kind of dream is that?" Glorie asked.

"Ma," Louisa snapped. "It's his *dream*." All of a sudden she looked mad. "I was just preparing you, that's all. He's going to tell everyone at Easter dinner." And she stomped out of Glorie's kitchen and back across the street.

Glorie felt bad that she hadn't thought before opening her mouth, but even if she had she probably couldn't have stopped herself. She didn't mention anything to Jack, hoping it would pass before he had to know such a thing.

At Easter, the whole family was together around Louisa's dining room table. Pat Jr. had passed the bar exam and gotten engaged to Emily. Blanche was working on her master's degree in English education and wouldn't shut up about it. And all Patrick could talk about was finding the barber school that was right for him. He was almost jumping out of his chair. "Even if I never use it," he said. "Even if I just do the family!"

"This family?" said Pat Jr. "Do me a favor, Dad, make sure you're set for your old age first, OK? I don't want to see you on a street corner wearing a sign, 'Will Cut Hair for Food.' "

Patrick glared at his son as if he had raised a moron. "Well, I won't give up accounting," he said. "Not completely."

"Unless you have to cram for an exam," said Blanche, making very fast scissor motions with her hands. Glorie and Jack stayed out of it.

"This," she told Jack when they were back home. "This is the barber you never had."

He shook his head, as if Patrick had finally gone too far for Jack to defend him.

The dream petered out, but not before Glorie noticed that

Patrick's hair was gradually getting shorter and shorter, and his ears looked like they were two different sizes.

"What shoes should I wear?" Patrick was asking Louisa now. "Good looking or comfortable?"

So typical, Glorie thought. Sometimes he would say things that made her skin itch, even if she couldn't figure out why. Sometimes she knew why, like when he named Patrick Jr. and Blanche after himself and his mother.

"I saw another program today," she said, "about Chinese food."

"That's nice, Ma," Louisa cut her off.

"Didn't the man come to fix your washer today?" Patrick asked.

"He's coming Monday," Glorie said, adding for protection, "it's not a big leak, and I have my own money to pay for it, don't worry."

"You're so paranoid, Ma. We know you're paying," Louisa said. "That's not the point. He was only asking a question." Louisa threw a warning look at her husband.

"But now that we're on the subject," he said.

"We are not on the subject, Patrick," Louisa said.

"No time like the present." He ignored her. "You know how worried we are about all the money you're spending on the house, Mom."

Here we go again, she told Jack.

"Think about it, think about it logically now, think about the facts. Taxes went up," Patrick said, sticking his thumb in the air. "Winter's coming and you'll have big oil bills," he went on, sticking his index finger in the air.

"He's so boring he should be in the *Guinness Book of World Records*," Glorie told Jack. "What's more boring than Ivory Soap? Whatever it is, that's what he's turned into."

"And let's face it," Patrick was saying, adding his third finger. "The roof wasn't in great shape when Dad was alive."

She ate her salad, pretended to listen and planned her strategy. He thought she didn't know what was going on. He thought she was so old her hearing must be gone, but he'd be surprised what she could hear by leaving her bedroom door open a crack. Sound traveled very well down the hall from the living room. She heard him talking to his friend Tom the real estate agent, about what her house would sell for.

"We thought maybe you could find someone to rent it, at least cover the expenses," Patrick had said.

"Sure, I can do that," said Tom. "If you're willing to keep putting in major repair money. I can get you a good price if you want to sell, too, let me know when you're ready."

"Will you two keep your voices down?" Louisa had whispered.

"Your mother's asleep, her light's off," said Patrick.

"Yeah, sure," said Louisa, so softly Glorie had to put her ear near the crack to hear. "Maybe she hears better in the dark. I can't believe I'm letting you have this conversation. It will kill my mother to move out of that house. Rent, sell, either way it will kill her."

"It won't kill her," said Patrick. "It will be good for her."

"You don't know my mother," said Louisa.

"After all these years?" he asked.

El stupido, thought Glorie. You know nothing.

She wanted to run out of the room and stop them right away, but thought better of it. She wouldn't let on she knew anything. Let him think she was in the dark, the better to prepare her sneak attack. "You see what he's like when you're not around?" she'd told Jack.

The next time Louisa went out for the day Glorie crossed back from her own house and snuck into Patrick's office. If Louisa caught her she would pretend to be going to the storeroom to pick up a can of soup for lunch. She went to the fireproof filing cabinet, found a whole section marked "MOM" and inside it a manila folder marked "DEED." There were advantages to Patrick being overorganized. She carried the manila folder back home. In a few days she went downtown, carrying the deed in a Shepherd's shopping bag; it looked like she was going to exchange something at the store, but she went to the bank and got a safety deposit box for the deed instead. She hid the receipt for the box in her recipe book in the kitchen.

One of these days when he tried to sell her house out from under her, he would notice the deed was missing. He would look everywhere, turn his neat filing cabinet inside out, then ask Glorie if she knew where it was.

"How would I know?" she'd ask innocently. "*You* took away all my papers. Do you mean you don't have it? Do you mean you *lost* it? How could you be so irresponsible?" She could hardly wait. She smiled as she took a slice of bread and passed the basket down the dinner table to Patrick.

"Dad's insurance, a pittance from Social Security, and no additional income," he was saying. "No additional income whatsoever."

"What do you want me to do?" Glorie said. She could jump back into this conversation anywhere at all, no problem. "You want me to take in boarders?" she asked.

"That's an idea," he said.

"Patrick, be serious!" said Louisa. "Could we please change the subject?"

"No, let him finish," Glorie said. I'm not paying attention anyway.

She was working out the perfect fallback plan. "Gloria, tell us, how did your son-in-law steal your home out from under you?"

Oprah was asking. Glorie was sitting in the center of a row of older women. Maybe one of them could be a multiple personality or a drug addict, to keep Oprah interested. Glorie couldn't be the only person with this house problem, but she would be the best dressed and the smartest one on the show. She was the one smart enough to write to Oprah in the first place.

"My husband, my late husband, left my son-in-law in charge of his marble business when he died," she explained to Oprah. "He's a CPA, he's supposed to know about money, but he bankrupted me. He said he couldn't keep the business going because it was too small and business was too bad. He said he couldn't even sell it, because it was just a pastime for my husband at the end. Not that I would ever have let him sell it," she said, getting choked up. Showing some emotion was good on TV. "He called it worthless and a pastime. Can you imagine? A man's life's work." She dabbed at her eyes prettily as the audience sighed "Aww!" in sympathy.

Oprah's eyes were beginning to fill too. "What have you learned from this terrible experience, Gloria?"

"Never trust a man who looks like Ivory Soap," she would say. Wait. What if Ivory was a sponsor? She'd have to notice next time she watched. She needed some snappy lines like that, though. She didn't want to seem pathetic; she only wanted to save other, genuinely pathetic people from losing their homes too. That should be her attitude: helpful.

"What are the warning signs?" Oprah might ask.

"He used to dance by himself in the basement," Glorie would say, making Patrick look like an idiot on national TV. He'd hate that. She would raise her eyebrows to suggest all kinds of craziness. "And he still had power over my money." The camera would close in on a few tears welling up in Glorie's blue eyes. She couldn't cry more than that because her nose would turn red.

Maybe she should practice crying one lonely tear. That could be useful around the house, too. She looked toward Patrick at the head of the table for inspiration.

"If you keep dipping into that money for repairs, there will be nothing left," he was saying. "How much more can you afford to sink into that house? Be practical."

"I'll sink as much as it takes," she said, and Patrick rolled his eyes, pushed his chair away from the table.

"You don't have it," he said, raising his voice. "We've been through this a million times. You don't have it. Talk to her, Louisa, tell her she doesn't have it."

"So where did it go? Aren't you supposed to be taking care of it for me? Is it my fault you're bankrupting me? Dad left you in charge and you're ruining me. A man's life's work you call worthless and a pastime. Can you imagine?"

"I never said that!" Patrick yelled. "Where did you get that?"

"Ma, calm down," Louisa said. "We're not going through this again right now. Patrick, shut up."

"What do you want from me?" Glorie said, not meaning to sob. This was supposed to be her time to practice crying prettily for TV, but that wasn't working out. "Do you want me to live here and pay room and board? Is that what you want?"

"Ma, don't be silly and don't get upset," Louisa said. "We just don't want you to throw all your money down the drain."

"My house is not a drain! Don't you ever call it that."

"Ma, don't you feel comfortable here?" Louisa said softly. "Listen, we want you to think of this as your home. You can watch TV with us at night. You can bring your own sewing machine over, we'll find space for it. You don't have to do anything you don't want to. It's not good for you to be alone so much."

"Maybe I'll take a trip with Aunt Ada. Visit Hollywood," Glorie said.

"Louisa," Patrick said, lifting his nose from his plate and looking confused. "Where would we put that sewing machine? I don't care if it comes over, but I don't see where it would go."

"Patrick," Louisa said, still with her soothing voice. "Imagine that fox-trot we're going to learn. One-two-three-four, there you go. Imagine you're dancing now, put your mind somewhere else," she said, then screamed, *"And let me talk to my mother! Or else take this chicken leg and stuff it in your ear!"*

"Why is it whenever you talk to your mother we end up fighting?"

"This isn't a fight. You want a fight — wait! And you sit down, Ma," she said, turning to Glorie. "Don't you dare try to sneak away."

"I have to go to the bathroom."

"I'll wait for you."

Glorie settled back into her chair instead, folded her hands in her lap and stared into space over her daughter's head.

"Put on a long puss if you want, Ma, but you have to face the facts. We've considered every possibility. Sooner or later you won't be able to afford the house. And the worse shape it gets into, the less you can sell it for. That's all we've been saying. We're worried about *you.* After the holidays, we have to do something."

"How long can I live on what I've got?"

"That's not the point — "

"A year," said Patrick. "Then you'll be broke. You'll be dependent on us in one year. I've done the numbers."

"Can I go to the bathroom now?" Tomorrow she would look up Oprah's address for sure.

* * *

Glorie sat in her room with the door partway open, waiting for them to get back from the tango lesson, so she could pretend nothing was bothering her. She would act like she was so interested in her program that she didn't hear them come in. There was a documentary on Channel 2 about ants; a giant ant crawled up a giant blade of grass. Glorie would bet these ants did not leave any sexy, musty smell behind. She flipped channels with the remote, not noticing what was on.

Could be they're trying to scare me, make me more careful, she thought. Next they'll be telling me some other cock-and-bull story. "The tooth fairy took your money. There are toothless old ladies in China who need it more than you." They think I'm an idiot, but I know I can't be broke.

Patrick wasn't the only CPA in the state. She could get a second opinion. She would make him turn over every piece of paper, not just the ones in the filing cabinet, but the second set of books and all the other crooked things he must have hidden, too.

"I want to see everything," she would order him. "Every single bank record. They're mine." Then she would go to someone who could explain it to her. She would look someone up in the phone book.

Glorie could see her face reflected on the TV screen; she looked furious. "I don't want to fight about money," she told Jack. "I don't even know how."

She hadn't known how much money Jack made, not for years, not since they were young and poor. She was used to signing "Mrs. John Carcieri" on charge slips and never seeing a bill. Now every dollar she spent meant a fight.

She was ashamed to remember how she had screamed at Louisa about a year ago when this whole fuss started. Glorie had come into the house at dusk, hung up her coat and asked Louisa to take five hundred dollars from the money market and put it into her checking account. Louisa said, "Why don't we make it three?"

Glorie looked at her the way she used to when Louisa had talked back as a child. She almost said, "I told you to make it five, young lady." Instead, she asked, "Why?"

"Because you're going through your money too fast. What do you need that much money for, Ma?"

"Charge accounts. Christmas presents. Things," Glorie said. "Do I have to get permission from you now? Do I have to account for myself? I never had to do that with your father."

"You had more money when Dad was alive. He took care of everything." Louisa was beginning to sound annoyed. "You never asked how, either. I never once heard you ask if you could afford something."

"What does that have to do with anything? And he would have told me if we couldn't afford something."

"I doubt that, Ma. I doubt it very much. You never thought about money and now you have to think about it."

"It's my money!" Glorie hollered. "It's not up to you. I know what I'm doing."

"I don't think you do, Ma." Louisa was calmer. "But if you want to do your own banking from now on, go ahead. Do it all yourself. You can do it by phone these days. And don't come complaining to me when your checks bounce."

"I won't complain."

"Well, they'll bounce."

"You're treating me like a child."

"You're acting like one."

They were both screaming again. "If your father was here . . ."

"It is not my fault my father died!" Louisa shrieked, glaring at her mother. They stared at each other for a second, then

Louisa put her arms around Glorie and they both tried not to cry.

"Let me look at the charge bills," Louisa said. "We'll figure it out. Come make the salad for me, OK?"

A year later, Louisa was on *his* side, and Glorie was forced to eavesdrop to protect her property. Even her own granddaughter had turned against her now.

Blanche was visiting, sitting where all Glorie's guests sat, on the edge of the bed next to her chair. Glorie had turned off television, which she didn't do for everyone. She was trying to explain why her house meant so much to her.

"Oh, Grandma," Blanche had said, as if Glorie had just told the cutest joke. "You're living in *The Cherry Orchard.*"

"What?"

"You remind me of a character in a play, that's all. She says something like" — and Blanche looked into the air like an actress — " 'I love this house. I can't conceive of living without the cherry orchard. If it must be sold, then sell me along with the orchard.' "

"Stop that, Blanche," Louisa said, eavesdropping as she passed by the door. "Stop that book talk right now. You know you're showing off.' "

The orchard line sounded useful to Glorie, like something she could save up and say to Patrick at the right moment. But she agreed with Louisa. It wasn't worth encouraging Blanche to be any sillier than she already was. Just like her father.

"It's all Patrick's fault," she told Jack, still clicking past the giant ants on TV. "He's a no-good CPA who can't even juggle a few numbers."

"It's not his fault, Glorie," Jack said.

"It's not his fault he's nothing like you, that's true."

"I think he did his best to help you," said Jack.

"I hear them talk about me when I'm not there," she said. "They talk about me when I *am* there as if I don't exist. He has no manners, I think he was raised by wolves."

"That's a new one," said Jack.

"Well I always thought it, I just never told you. It's the only explanation, he was raised by wolves. You should have listened to me when I said he was bad news, the day Louisa brought him home."

"I didn't know about the wolf idea then. That would have changed everything."

"Sure. As if you would have told her no."

Louisa was so popular at college, she went to shows with her girlfriends, she had the best dates for dances and brought the handsomest boys home to dinner. But how she had cried, as if everyone dear to her had died, when the handsomest one got engaged to someone else.

A few weeks later she came home with this dull, predictable, safe accounting student, this Italian Patrick.

"Take your time," Glorie told her, but would she listen? By then she had probably forgotten crying on her mother's shoulder.

Jack insisted there was no connection between Louisa's new love and her broken heart. He thought Patrick would be a good match. "Be nice. Louisa picked him," he told Glorie. But he hadn't seen those tears.

In bed at night they whispered. "Patrick has no features, none at all," Glorie said. "What will their kids look like?"

"They'll look like you, Glorie. They'll look like you and their mother. Now go to sleep."

She swatted his back. "Roll over. Look at me. What if they don't?"

"Then they don't."

"I think that boy has no passion," Glorie whispered. "He's too quiet. She chose him after that good-looking Bill because he's safe."

"He's what Louisa wants. And what's wrong with wanting to be safe?" he asked. "Besides, you never know about those things." Glorie had a feeling, though.

Jack defended Patrick through everything, even when Jack himself was slapped in the face. The whole family knew he hoped Patrick would take over the marble business, keep the Carcieri name going for generations. But whenever he mentioned it Patrick changed the subject. Glorie could see things coming. When Patrick became vice president at the accounting firm, Jack gave up the plan for good.

"Pat Jr. will take over," Glorie said, though their grandson was fourteen at the time. "You'll have to keep it going yourself until he's ready."

"I don't want to talk about it anymore," Jack told her. "Patrick has a good job, it's good money, it's secure. It's a step ahead, Glorie. That's the end of it."

She found it harder to forgive.

The ants on TV had turned red and were running in and out of an anthill and Glorie still had time to roam around the house before Louisa and Patrick got back. Usually when they were out she would poke in the kitchen closets to see what was new, look at the pictures of the great-grandkids on the living room mantel, rummage around awhile — very neatly — on Patrick's desk and in his filing cabinet to see if there were any new papers with her name on them.

This time she went to the refrigerator, then put a slice of turkey on a paper towel and carried it back to her room, standing and looking out the window, nibbling, flipping channels, too jumpy to settle down. One of Patrick's idiot line dance programs was on again. People with cowboy boots and tight jeans and big bellies were marching around.

They're all so fat. I guess this kind of dancing isn't very good exercise, she thought.

"It might be good enough for *you,*" Jack said.

Maybe, Glorie thought. Maybe she would just do the feet part, taking baby steps so she wouldn't have to march around the furniture. She turned right and took three steps back, she faced front and took three steps ahead. She twirled and turned her back on the TV, and discovered she could see the dancers in the mirror. She reached out in front of her to join hands with her partner, and had to laugh when she saw herself in the mirror, reaching out with half a slice of turkey in one hand and a paper towel in the other. She stepped back again. This wasn't hard, an idiot could do it. But it was new, which was probably why she missed hearing the car in the driveway. The next thing she knew the side door was creaking open.

She crumpled the paper towel, flipped the channel and sat down fast, taking air in and out of her lungs slowly so she wouldn't seem out of breath. Louisa arrived at the open doorway to Glorie's room and stood there as if she were waiting to be invited in. "Do you want anything before you go to bed, Ma? You didn't eat much."

"No, I'm fine," Glorie said coldly, still trying to control her breathing. She kept her eyes on the giant anthill. "I'm watching my educational show."

"OK, good night." Louisa went away as quietly as she had come.

"I wish I could be dead in a year — no more, no less," she said.

"You don't mean that, Glorie. You just want to keep the house."

Lying next to her in the tiny twin bed, Jack put his arm around her.

"No, I mean it. I want to use up the money, and the day before they put the house on the market I want to go to sleep and never wake up. Maybe I'll go to sleep over there. Maybe I can haunt the place after. We can haunt it together."

"Patrick didn't mean exactly a year, you know. It's about a year. Let's see what happens."

"Why couldn't he keep the business going? You did."

"I'm sorry," Jack said. "I thought I took care of you." Oh no, she thought, now he feels bad. "You don't have to decide anything tonight. Get some rest. Get some sleep, Glorie," he said, one arm around her and the other hand stroking her hair.

She was wide awake and alone in this small bed she hated. The house was quiet and dark. The bed seemed to shrink all around her; she could feel it shrinking, as fast as a cartoon, until it was just big enough to contain her body, and she felt dizzy lying here. She opened her eyes and felt paralyzed as she lay on her back, arms by her side, staring at the ceiling. Her back ached, her neck felt sore, and she felt like a woman in a monster movie, her eyes locked open as if she were afraid of someone coming to take her away while she slept. What was that movie Pat Jr. watched at her house when he was about ten, when he got so scared he actually came to the kitchen and watched her cook dinner? Something about Ray Milland buried alive in a coffin, and when they found him his fingertips were all bloody from pushing up on the lid. That's what she felt like.

"Why do I take it out on Louisa when Patrick makes me mad?" she asked, arms still frozen by her side. "What am I going to do?" Her voice echoed around the room, she saw it traveling; it looked like a green neon tube racing around the ceiling in circles. She felt dizzy hearing it and watching it.

"Do you think she's just trying to scare me?"

"I think you have to pay attention, Glorie."

I have to pay attention.

"Maybe I was wrong to protect you so much," he said.

"No, no, it's only that I want things back the way they were."

But he can't do that, she thought. He can't do that, Glorie, she told herself firmly. You have to remember that he can't.

I'll make myself think about what I spend, every penny. I'll do it right now. It will be like counting sheep. It will make me stop inventing conversations with Jack. It will make the room stop spinning. It will make me sleep.

$25 a week for the hairdresser.

$40 for groceries.

$20 for rides in bad weather from the teenage kid down the street. She saw his gray jalopy leap over a fence in her mind like a sheep. One jalopy, two jalopies, three.

She saw her house leap over the fence, and she saw Patrick chasing it. He was wearing one of those Spanish dancers' outfits, with big frilly sleeves and toreador pants over those skinny legs of his. He was clicking his fingers over his head as he tangoed over the fence, chasing her house. But he caught a heel of his shoe on the fence and did a belly flop over the top.

Then Ada came by and said, "Why don't you find you some sugar daddy, honey? It's easy."

Sure. She'd need a hundred-year-old millionaire; to him she'd be a younger woman. She saw herself lying on her side in a harem outfit, the kind with chiffon pants and a veil, like *I Dream of Jeannie.* It was pale green, with a brocade vest that matched the living room furniture. A man walked over to her. He was a skinny, scrawny old coot with a cane, a black suit and a gloomy face. He was barely able to stand, and when he tried to bend over to kiss her she pulled a piece of paper out from under her elbow. She meant to wave it in front of him with an exotic flair, but it turned out more like rattling it under his nose. "Sign this," she said, handing him the new will that left all his millions to her. "Go ahead," Jack whispered over her shoulder, "marry him. You can hide me in the guesthouse."

Jack was a comfort, but sometimes he was no help.

Chapter 4

GLORIE WOKE from these dreams feeling wise, and in the daylight ruthlessly sized up her situation: Jack was out of bright ideas; Louisa was treating her as if she were one step out of the old folks' home; Ada wanted her to flirt.

OK, she'd flirt. Marriage was out of the question, of course. She would turn down any offers.

But I'll show them I can get offers, she thought. I'll show them all.

Deciding to flirt was hard; choosing a man to flirt with was tougher. He had to be single, dignified, not effeminate. He had to be old. He had to cross Glorie's path. Finding him became a major project.

She mulled it over for days as she did her morning burglar sweep and made afternoon tea. She went through her address book, but wasn't willing to call business associates of Jack's and hope they were still around.

She sat at the kitchen table and made a list of the men she might see without trying too hard. She could flirt with Larry, who came to rake her leaves, but he only showed up twice a year. The mailman was in his twenties and not even good looking.

Once a week she saw delivery kids from the market. Twice a week she took the bus downtown, on Fridays to have her hair done at Gilda's old place and on Tuesdays to shop. Steve, the bus driver, was always so friendly; he had salt-and-pepper hair but he couldn't be much over sixty and she was pretty sure he wore a wedding ring. There was Mr. Harris, who owned the fabric store. He must be more than seventy, polite and still handsome with curly gray hair. He believed in serving his best customers himself, though whenever Glorie stopped by she seemed to be the only one he paid attention to. And — where had her mind been? — his wife had just died. Why hadn't she thought of him first thing?

Because I'm not that way, she told herself.

A fast woman would have jumped in before the body was cold. It hadn't occurred to her to do more than send a sympathy card to him at the store.

When exactly had his wife passed on? It wouldn't do to move too quickly and look like some desperate gold digger.

It must be six months, she realized, a perfectly respectable period of time. She circled Mr. Harris's name then tore up her list.

I have to go through with this, Glorie told herself. It's real life. It's important for me to be in real life. If not, Louisa will drag me back to live with her and I might as well be in a cage.

Walking around her house planning an intrigue with a new man brought on that crazy-old-lady fear, but having Patrick and Louisa on her case was scarier.

"Oh, there's nothing to flirting, honey," Ada had promised. "It's easy." Easy for Ada, who had so little pride she probably prowled the supermarket hunting for single old men, ready to crash her cart into theirs on purpose. She couldn't turn to Ada for pointers. She couldn't turn to anyone for advice on this harebrained scheme. It would be like asking someone to teach her how to tie her shoes.

She had known Mr. Harris for nearly thirty years, though. How could she hint she had taken an interest in him now? A mild interest, so that if he didn't respond she could still show her face and shop there? She could start calling him Victor instead of Mr. Harris, but somehow that didn't seem to be enough.

"Oh, Victor, call me Gloria," she might say. "Are we flirting yet?"

What I need is a practice flirt, she realized. Steve will be my guinea pig. If I make a fool of myself with the bus driver, no one will have to know.

Best of all, Steve expected her at 9:15 every Friday and most Tuesdays. He would have to come to her.

Once or twice he had waited, putting himself behind schedule a minute or two, when he saw her walking up Jasmine Street to the corner. Last winter, when she'd been sick with the flu for three weeks, he said he'd been worried about her. So he was on the young side; she couldn't be too fussy. So he wore a wedding ring; he could be a widower, alone and too sentimental to take the ring off. Maybe he wouldn't even mind being flirted with. Still, she felt as if she were planning to break into Steve's house while he was sleeping.

She was awake and exhausted very late Monday night, trying not to chicken out. She couldn't let Jack in on this, of course, so she lay in bed alone, tossing around, telling herself she better relax her muscles and get some sleep. But she kept pumping energy into her body with pep talks.

She had picked up a copy of a teenage girls' magazine at the market. The cover promised "How to Get Him to Notice You!" and it was worth a few dollars to find out. It would be good for a laugh. Now she practically had it memorized, and it kept coming back to her, keeping her awake. *Ask him to join you for a soda with the gang,* it advised. *Join an after-school activity he enjoys. Look him in the eye and give him a great big smile. The most important rule is: Be Yourself!*

If Glorie had been a teenager, this useless advice would have made her mad. The girl doesn't want to see him with the group. Besides, Glorie wouldn't find some replacement for Mr. Harris or Steve in the junior high glee club. Look him in the eye? Instead of looking him in the nose, maybe? She had wasted her money on this. And how are those teenage girls supposed to be themselves when they're too young to know who they are?

I know *exactly* who I am, she thought. I am not a flirt.

But this, this is my big chance to be one! It's time to be Wallis Simpson, Scarlett O'Hara, Elizabeth Taylor, all those women a lot less fussy than me. I should think of this as an adventure.

As if she were suddenly an adventurous type. She knew better. But being stubborn had taken her a long way in life. By Tuesday morning she was determined that flirting would be fun. Her watchwords became, "What would Wallis do?"

She got to the bus stop at the corner of Jasmine early, wearing a new pair of stockings and a winter coat that hit the bottom of her knees. Her heart started racing and she felt herself blush as soon as she saw the bus come down the street. What if he wasn't there? She knew that in an emergency she was supposed to flirt with any driver at all, think like the Duchess, get in every bit of practice she could, but she wasn't prepared for that. How silly, he'd be there.

The bus stopped and she climbed the steps slowly and deliberately, taking time to raise her coat almost above her knees, to show a little leg. Lucky they were the last things to go and didn't look bad, if she said so herself. She had worn pumps to show them off instead of her rubber-soled walking shoes. The trick, she had decided, was to move slowly enough to be seductive but not so slow that she seemed feeble.

She had her coins ready in her pocket, but she held them in her hand while she looked Steve straight in the eye and gave him an enormous smile. "How are you today? Good to see you," she said, smiling wider, flushing and almost giggling with nerves. The blood was pounding in her ears, the sun was blindingly bright through the windshield and she felt light-headed. She was actually doing this, it was happening right now. She dropped her coins steadily in the box and Steve said, "Good to see you, too. Glad you're dressed for the weather in that pretty blue coat. It's getting nippy out."

Then she sat a few rows behind him — no need to be too obvious — and looked out the window, trying to calm herself down.

He said pretty. Does that mean something? she thought.

What did a bus driver do at lunchtime? What if she went wild and invited him over? A naughty grin appeared on her face; she saw it reflected in the window.

His bus was pulling into her driveway. He was coming to the door with a bunch of flowers in his hand, sitting down at her table. She had set the places so that Jack's usual spot was empty. "This is great, a real treat," Steve said. "Sometimes I'd make it home for lunch when my wife was alive, but she's been gone for ten years." What a relief; no competition.

She knew better than to offer him a real drink while he was on the job. "Would you like some juice, or soda, or something else to drink?" she asked.

"I don't suppose you'd have some hot chocolate?"

"I do, I keep it for the great — " She almost slipped and aged herself, a great-grandmother. "I keep it for those great cold days," she said.

"I know it's a kids' drink, but you know what? I feel like a kid," he told her.

Probably he was a bus driver by accident. Maybe he had been going to law school or medical school and had to drop out to help his family. Or maybe he came from a long line of bus drivers. His family had owned their own bus company until it fell on hard times.

Glorie felt the bus head down the steep hill that signaled they were downtown, near the end of the line, and she felt flushed all over again. What was she supposed to say getting off? She had meant to use the ride to figure out her next move, depending on how he'd reacted to the first one. Here they were, already pulling into her downtown stop, and she had no plan. She pretended to fish for something in her bag, stalling for time while she let everyone else head down the aisle in front of her. What could she say? Lunch might be too much right away. But she should say something personal. The soda strategy! Ask him for coffee. As she got to the front of the aisle, the last person on the bus, Steve looked at her, tipped his finger to his hat, then turned to check his watch. She hurried off the bus the best she could without stumbling, gripping the handrail tight as she walked down the steps. He had treated her like any paying customer. She was an idiot. He would never come to lunch.

She wandered through Shepherd's as if she were lost, circling through the ground floor again and again, by the same cosmetics counters, until one of the saleswomen leaned across her counter and asked, "Can I help you, ma'am? Are you looking for anything special? Are you all right?" Glorie turned and headed toward the escalator, humiliated. She wasn't thinking about shopping, she was examining her morning as if it were a seam that had come undone. She was searching for flaws, weaknesses, something she must have done wrong. Ada would have known what to do. Even Ada would have known.

This is what I get for having one man my whole life, she thought. But it doesn't matter. Nobody knows.

Steve probably didn't notice anything different.

That's how bad I was, a failure as a flirt. If he noticed, he's probably forgotten already. And what do I care what he thinks? What did I want from him? Nothing. It was a game. It was a trial run.

But going to Harris's today would be more than she could handle; she had a feeling the trial run would be the end of it. She headed toward the ladies' department. She had wanted to start Christmas shopping, to begin with Louisa, who was always the hardest. If she was lucky she would find some small, exquisite thing her daughter would never have thought of for herself. Some Tuesdays she bought nothing at all, simply wandered through the stores looking for treasures that were bound to turn up sooner or later. Once she found a red silk scarf with embroidered flowers and golden threads, and saved it from July till December. Louisa seemed to love it when she opened the box, though she never wore it.

Glorie had wandered into the shoe department and happened to be standing in front of a pair of maroon velveteen wedgies. "Can I find you a size in that?" a salesman asked, as if she would *think* of buying such trash for her only child. She ignored him and walked away.

She glanced at racks of dresses, all too expensive. She looked at blouses, too plain for Christmas gifts. The loudspeaker was playing some song she knew. Something by Dolly Parton or Kenny Rogers; if they'd had the words she would have recognized it. "Shitkicker music," she heard Jack complain. She had to get away from it. “We're leaving, don't worry,” she told him.

Glorie took the elevator to the tearoom. To calm herself, she ordered a cup of tea and a blueberry muffin, toasted with butter and jam.

She found a scrap of paper in her purse, an ad she had torn out of the newspaper. She could write her Christmas list in the margins.

I'll be OK, she thought. I have to try very hard to be OK.

But the list depressed her. What could she afford? Shouldn't she put every penny into her house? She looked around the nearly empty tearoom, with its heavy tables and old-fashioned gilt mirrors. There was a mother and grown daughter — they must be, they looked exactly alike — surrounded by shopping bags. There were two middle-aged women. What did these people think she was doing here, alone? Did they feel sorry for her? Did they even notice her? She had to go home.

She called for the check and tried to be OK again. She could buy wrapping paper and ribbon. Glorie always wrapped the most beautiful Christmas presents. It was her trademark, every year a different style but always gleaming foil paper and wide velvet ribbon and trinkets — tiny trees or berries or angels — to decorate the top. Everyone said her gifts were so beautiful they hated to open them. She could at least buy paper.

No. She had to get back on that bus and she might as well get it over with. She left three dollars on the table to cover the bill and tip.

If I don't buy fancy paper, I can take a taxi home, she thought.

But the last thing she needed was for Louisa to see her getting out of a cab.

How stupid she was, never to notice the drivers' schedules going back. Waiting at the bus stop, she wondered why her heart was racing more than it had been this morning; there was no reason. She knew how to handle this part. If she got Steve as a driver she wouldn't look at him, would keep her eyes on the coin box and keep walking.

When the bus pulled up she could see right away that the driver was a young guy with a lot of curly blond hair. She was out of danger.

She sat down for the ride home, exhausted.

What was I doing? What did I want?

What she wanted, of course, was Jack.

"I didn't mean anything by it," she told him, struggling to sound lighthearted. "I thought I'd have an adventure."

Her head was crowded enough to explode as she struggled to push aside the memory of the morning, the way she could push aside thoughts of her house. Her heart felt as if it had been pumped full of hot air. She was a fake, she was a failure, she was a fool.

What was I thinking? she asked herself.

Maybe she had been trying to make Jack jealous.

Or it could be she was a bad flirt because she was betraying him. That idea cheered her right up. If she could feel guilty, it meant she still belonged to him. The morning was slipping away. She would leave it downtown in the dust and get back to her ordinary life.

The wind was fierce, making the bus windows rattle, but Glorie felt the sweltering June morning when Jack had rung the doorbell of the triple-decker. She had belonged to him from that first swoony day, when she had done the most flirtatious thing that came to mind and pretended to like barnyard animals.

"I never pretended to you again," she told him.

Before Jack turned up, everyone felt low. In those days Josie was the only one in the family with any reason to be happy.

Josie had decided to marry Al, the plumber's helper. They would have a small wedding in six months, enough time to save for Josie's dress and the rings. The night Josie and Al told the family their plans, Glorie sat on the bed in the room she still shared with Josie, the fading scraps of fabric still on the wall. She talked nonstop as Josie got ready for bed, trying desperately to convince her sister to have a long engagement and a big wedding, the kind that would take a couple of years to save for, the kind that wouldn't impress Josie at all. "You deserve the best," Glorie tried anyway. "You only get married once, do it right."

Josie looked at her as if Glorie had lost her mind. "I have to do this my own way," she said. "It's what Al wants too. Why throw money away on a fancy wedding when we need so many things?" Always practical, Josie seemed baffled, then kind. "I'll still see you all the time," she told her sister. "We won't move far. Probably right in the neighborhood."

No one had bothered to mention what would happen to Glorie after Josie got married. She was sixteen. They didn't have to.

A month before Josie's wedding, when the school year was almost over, Glorie sat at the supper table, stared into space in her father's direction and said out of nowhere, "I'll keep house all summer but in the fall I'm going back to school."

Her father lifted his head from his soup dish but didn't stop eating.

"You will not," he said, slurping up broth. "You will pick up where your sister left off. You have to pull your weight around here."

"Pull your weight" was one of his new expressions. He thought they made him American. He learned new words, but Glorie could see they didn't make any difference. His ideas were still old and foreign, stupid and stubborn. And since her mother died, her father was tougher, more stupid, more stubborn than ever.

"Be thankful you're not going to the mill like you used to cry about," he said. "Learn to do something useful for a girl, Gloria. Someday you'll be getting married, too."

"I can go to school *and* keep house, I have the schedule figured—"

Before she could finish, her father yelled, "You'll be married someday, too, I said. Don't be jealous and ruin things for your sister. That's the end of it."

Josie stayed out of the argument. She was escaping, she was saving herself, and Glorie couldn't blame her. There was no arguing with their father unless they were ready to go out on their own like pitiful orphans or streetwalkers.

Glorie cried in her room, she cried in the bathroom at school, she tried to be grateful for escaping the mill. She talked to her English teacher, a young woman Glorie thought would understand. "Maybe you could go to night school," the teacher said, as if she hardly knew who Glorie was.

The insult! She didn't belong in night school with a lot of worn-out immigrants trying to learn how to speak English, people who would be satisfied with a few cents more an hour. She still wanted to find those library books with the paintings, to look at pictures besides the ones on the free calendar from the hardware store. She wanted to eat in restaurants where every place was set with a lot of forks and spoons and glasses. She wanted to understand books like *Great Expectations.* The language was old and hard to understand, but she was pushing herself through it because she knew this was what it meant to be educated. If she could say she had read it, that would count for something. For all she knew, half the people who read it didn't understand it either. There must be a way to find out all these things, and she knew it wasn't at night school.

When fall came, she hardly spoke to her father and he didn't seem to notice. She went on shopping and cooking and cleaning. She stomped around the house furious at her brothers for leaving dirty socks and underwear on the floor for her to pick up. Being mad was the most she could do.

Then things got worse.

Two years later, Manny's girlfriend got pregnant. "Thank God your mother's not alive to see this," their father screamed. "You had your fun, now you pay the price." Right after Manny got married, Glorie's father took the small ground-floor apartment in the back of the triple-decker for himself and Glorie and Frank. Her father would be the building handyman. This would save in rent and improve their lives, he said, but it made Glorie feel like a servant, coming down in the world instead of moving up. She was sure they had hit bottom.

But she didn't know what bottom was until her father got the chickens. A friend from the mill had promised, "They're moneymakers." You could sell eggs, sell chickens, eat eggs and chicken, start up your own business right in the backyard. So far her father hadn't turned out anything you could sell and not much to eat. He passed the evenings cooing at the animals and clucking at them, talking to them and fussing over them as if they were human, or better.

He had a special technique for feeding them. Most mornings he or Frank left grain in their trough. But on Sundays and at night he played: he walked into the pen, tossed grain neatly from his wrist, scattering it just far enough so the chickens would come and scratch the ground at his feet. It was disgusting. They were the most overfed chickens in the country.

When her father and Frank had to go to work early for overtime, it was Glorie's job to feed the chickens. *She* had a technique, too. She refused to walk across the pen, picking her steps through chicken shit to get to the trough. Instead, she crept quietly into the pen, staying near the wire gate. She would squat near the ground, hold her fist at arm's length, dribble the feed in a pile on the ground, then back away as fast as she could and be outside the gate again before the chickens got there. That way the grain didn't scatter on her shoes and the chickens couldn't touch her.

This took more time than she would have liked. She couldn't dribble much grain before they came toward her, so she waited until they had finished and were pecking their way toward the other side of the pen near the barn. Then she would creep in and leave another handful or two. Each time she would have to move faster and risk being near some of the clever chickens who lingered near the gate, waiting for her. Some winter mornings they only got what she could dribble the first time, too bad if they stayed hungry. As long as she didn't have to feed them too many days in a row she figured they wouldn't starve.

She prayed that some terrible contagious chicken disease would wipe them out all at once, and every time she stuck her hand in the grain sack she envisioned a pen full of peacefully dead chickens, lying on the ground, gone on to some pig-and-fowl heaven.

The day her father ran out of grain she was as happy as she had been in months. Let them starve, she hoped. Instead, he got Carcieri's to make an emergency delivery the next day.

She answered the doorbell and saw a tall, thin young man with thick wavy black hair. He had a strong nose and a serious expression that made his handsome face look distinguished.

"Miss Rodriguez? You expecting some chicken feed?" he said.

She nodded. "Would you bring it around back?"

He put his cap on, far back on his head, the way he would wear his hats for the rest of his life. He lifted the large sack over his shoulder and followed her around the side of the house to the yard. As she led the way she tried hard to think of something alluring to say about chickens.

"Would you like me to open the sack for you?" he asked, as he put it down outside the pen. "I hear these chickens are pretty hungry."

"Would you? Please? I'm trying to get better at this, but so far they seem happier when someone else feeds them. I don't know why."

"Don't waste your time, they're filthy animals, I hate them," he said, pouring grain in the trough and tossing a handful on the ground as if he were a king passing out coins to the peasants. "I'm working for my father until I can manage something better."

She laughed. For the first time he heard that low chuckle that always slipped out when she said forbidden things. "They *are* filthy. And noisy."

"And they're ugly!" he said. "The only place for them is in soup, that's what I say."

"Maybe so, but I can't stand to cook chicken anymore," Glorie said, "no matter who raised them."

"Eat these rotten things? Who could do that?" and he smiled at her as he tied up the sack. "I'll bet you're a good cook, though. I'll bet I could even eat chicken if you cooked it." It was so clumsy, it was so easy to see through. It was, she thought, the most romantic thing she had ever heard.

"If you'd like to come over for supper one night, I promise I won't cook chicken."

She said it before she could think about it. Nothing was ever easier.

She had to warn her father and Frank not to make a big fuss about this. "Don't tell him I've never invited a boy over for supper before, please."

"What do you think, we're stupid, Gloria?" Frank asked. He glanced at his father. "I'm only speaking for myself."

"What's the matter? You afraid I'll embarrass you?" their father asked. "In front of some Italiano? The grain man's kid?"

"Please, Dad, don't do anything to scare him off," Glorie said.

"Yeah, Dad, or you'll never get rid of her," Frank said, smiling at his sister.

"What's his name again?" her father asked Glorie.

"Giovanni."

He snorted. "Italiano."

Glorie got an Italian neighbor to teach her to make lasagna for Jack's visit. Ten minutes before he should have been there the kitchen of the apartment was so hot it felt like it was on fire.

"We don't even get our own kind of food tonight?" her father asked, sniffing around.

Glorie had been trying to look cool, fanning herself and running to the bathroom mirror every few minutes to pin back wisps of stray hair between cooking and setting the table. "Frank," she said, fanning herself and sitting down. "Make him behave."

"How?"

In ten minutes the doorbell rang. Glorie jumped up but her father beat her to the screen door. He opened it and said, "You the grain man's kid?"

Glorie froze.

"Yes, sir," Jack said, holding out his hand, "Giovanni Carcieri." And as he shook hands with her father he looked ahead at Glorie, smiled and winked.

No one talked much during supper, but her father managed to get Jack to say that he was thinking of buying a grocery with his cousin, or maybe starting some other company on their own. "I want to be my own boss," he said, and Mr. Rodriguez snorted.

"People go broke that way. I was my own boss on the farm in the old country, what am I doing now?"

"Good food, Gloria," said Frank. "What is this, chorizo lasagna?" Frank was trying, he was always on her side.

By July, Jack was taking Glorie for long walks in the park at dusk. The first time he came in the black pickup truck, with CARCIERI AND SONS GRAIN written in bright blue on the side, he thought they'd take the trolley to the park. He couldn't ask her to hop into the pickup. But she didn't mind, so she suggested it. Jack, Glorie and Frank crammed into the cab. After that first night they dropped Frank off as soon as they turned the corner and her father couldn't see.

They took every path through the elaborate flower gardens, circling often by the giant red roses that Glorie liked best. For a joke they visited the zoo. "That camel is the ugliest animal I've ever seen," Jack decided. "Even uglier than a chicken."

"Uglier than that anteater over there?" Glorie asked.

"Good question. I say uglier."

"Uglier than that porcupine?"

"Much uglier."

"Uglier than my cousin Lucy?"

"Now you've got me stumped."

Most nights he would buy her ice cream and they would walk around the lake, stopping to sit on benches and watch the rowboats go by. She wore her prettiest dresses and he wore Sunday clothes — a white shirt buttoned up high — every night.

One warm evening they passed an older couple — a heavy

woman in a housedress and a man in dusty work clothes—walking arm-in-arm around the lake too. "Giovanni!" the woman said, kissing him on the cheek. "*Come stai?*" and her husband answered for him, looking at Glorie and saying, "*Molto bene! Guarda la bella signorina!*"

Glorie understood he was calling her pretty, but didn't catch what Jack answered in Italian before he waved to the couple and started pulling her away fast. "They're neighbors," he told her. "I would have introduced you but you don't want to waste a minute talking to them."

"Do you speak Italian at home?" she asked.

"When I have to. My mother's lazy about speaking English. Do you speak Portuguese when I'm not around?"

"Never. No one in the family does at home. My father thinks he wants to be American, but then he never bothers with anyone except the Portuguese, so he ends up speaking Portuguese to them. I don't understand him."

"His English is good, though," Jack said. "My parents came here just after they were married. They don't speak good English. But I was born here, I have no excuse. No one gets ahead acting like a greenhorn." He was matter-of-fact about this, not angry or embarrassed the way Glorie had heard other men sound.

"I know what you mean. It marks you to speak a foreign language."

"It's bad enough I'm stuck being Giovanni. At least you have an American-sounding name. Do you read the newspapers? I always read the papers. That's a good way to learn how things operate."

"I look at the paper," she said. "And I try to read books, too."

"What do you mean? What kind of books?"

"Novels. Stories about a different time. People in England and other places."

"Why?"

"To learn things, I suppose," she said, hesitating. Was that the right answer? "To know different things." She shrugged. "I like them." Suddenly she didn't know why she was trying to read *Great Expectations.* It wasn't the best way to learn things. Why would she need to know about England in the 1800s anyway? Maybe it was a silly idea.

"I get a lot about business out of the papers," Jack said.

He knew what he was talking about. Boys from the mill, friends of Manny and Frank, talked like morons. One of them came to supper and spent the whole time talking to Frank about a poker hand he had won — not even a game, Glorie realized, just one hand. He told the story at least three times. "So then I says, 'I see you,' and I look real worried, but *what* I'm holding in my *hand*!"

She didn't care that Jack didn't read books, didn't plan to travel places. She understood how much he wanted things. She could see him as a businessman, she could imagine herself in his arms; she would never see anyone from the mill again.

The lake was so big you couldn't see to the other side, but they never got tired of strolling around it. They passed by posters for Saturday night dances and movies, and talked about going, but rarely made it. They preferred to be alone and walking, saying things they could never say to anyone else.

"My father thinks I have to stay with him, inherit the grain business, help run it while my brothers and sisters are growing up. But I've had enough. I'm not going to tell him about the grocery until it's settled, but we're close. I think we can do it soon."

"I think you can, too," she said. "You've got a good mind. I think you can do whatever you want. You can start your own business anytime."

"My cousin wants to call it Carcieri Cousins, can you believe that? I want a real American name, to bring in everybody. Don't you think that's better?"

"Definitely. You could call it the American Grocery Store."

"Not bad."

"You could call it No Chickens Sold Here."

"Even better."

"You could name it for the street it's on."

"We could, whatever that turns out to be. We looked at a place on Angelo Street. That wouldn't help much."

"How about Giovanni's Grocery?" she said. "I like that. It should have your name on it."

"Giovanni Carcieri's Grocery?" he said. "We might as well be in the old country."

"So if you don't like your name you could change it. You can do anything."

He looked as if she had suggested they dive in the lake with their clothes on and it sounded like a good idea. "Would you want me to do that?" he asked. "Change my name?"

"Not your family name, your first name. You said you don't like Giovanni. You can make it American. You can be John."

"Right. Translate it to English."

"I'll call you Jack, that sounds even more American."

He smiled at her as if she were a genius. "Smart and pretty, too. I can't believe it," he said.

He liked the idea so much he made everyone call him Jack, and Glorie got the blame. His three sisters spread the rumor that it was that Portagee girl who didn't like his name. She was ashamed to be associated with a Carcieri, they said; she made him change his name. When Glorie heard this through a nasty neighbor she was in tears. If that were true, why wouldn't she have changed Carcieri? Why would she dream of marrying a Carcieri, of becoming one?

"Ignore them," Jack said. "We know the truth." He insisted to his family that the name change was his idea. They never believed him.

Her family was no better. Her father and Manny were suspicious of the Italiano with big dreams and no money, but Glorie was almost twenty-one. So when Jack sat down at the kitchen table, Glorie standing behind him, and told Mr. Rodriguez that they wanted to get married, her father agreed right away. He seemed more relieved to be getting this unsociable daughter off his hands than he was annoyed at losing his housekeeper.

The Carcieris thought Jack was disgracing them by marrying the poor Portuguese girl, but they insisted on having the tiny wedding reception in their house. Anything other than that cramped Rodriguez cellar, they said.

Glorie finally thought she understood why Josie had been so impatient to get married. She and Jack could have waited until he started the grocery. They could wait and save for a house. Or they could be together in the apartment above his sister Delia while he went on with the grain business for a while. As a wedding present, her father offered them some of his most prized chickens and a brand-new rooster. They couldn't afford to say no. "When we get ahead I'll wring every chicken's neck myself and throw them in the trash," Jack promised. "It won't be so bad living over Delia. She won't bother us." Like Josie, Glorie would be free in six months.

Josie tried to be helpful. When Glorie visited, Josie sat at her own kitchen table feeding baby William and keeping an eye on his older brother. "Make sure you know what you're doing," she told Glorie. "An Italian, it will be like moving to a foreign country."

Glorie bit her tongue to keep from saying, "Just what I've always wanted."

Josie, it turned out, was wrong a lot. She was expecting her third child, but she made sex sound like something she'd only heard about from other people. "It's better than the old ladies make you think," she told Glorie, sounding embarrassed but determined to have this talk. "Sometimes it's better than others. Sometimes the man wants to get it over with fast and that's all right."

"But what should I know?" Glorie wasn't even sure what she was asking, but Josie had brought the subject up, so she should have something more to say.

"Don't worry," Josie told her. "He'll teach you."

He did.

The day before the wedding, he surprised her with an elegant, narrow gold wedding band. "It's beautiful, it's perfect," she said. "But how could you manage this?"

"Don't worry about it," he told her. "We can afford it. Just don't ask me where it came from." It was engraved with her new initials and their wedding date: "GC 6-15-29."

She had her picture taken in the wedding dress she had made, with its long silk sash, a wreath of flowers and a lace veil down to her feet.

There were only two dozen or so relatives and neighbors in church that Saturday morning as her father walked her down the aisle. When she saw Jack standing there, looking stiff in his high-collared shirt, she wondered why anyone else was there at all. This should be a private moment between her and Jack. And why were they facing the priest when they should be looking at each other?

He took her hand, he led her out of church. For the rest of the day — as the relatives drank wine and ate sandwiches and cake, the Italian and Portuguese families sitting on opposite sides of the Carcieris' parlor — Jack and Glorie kept looking at each other and the clock.

Before it was dark they traveled in a borrowed car the few streets to the new apartment, with Josie and Al to help them settle in. Josie pinched Glorie's cheek as she left her there and whispered, "Don't worry. Relax. Whatever you do, relax." Then they were alone.

Glorie had searched until she found a long, silky white nightgown and robe — "Oh, yes, you want what they call a neg-li-jee set," the saleslady said — and she had sewn on it beautiful white lace left over from her veil. Jack went into the bathroom to put on his pajamas. Glorie knew she was supposed to change while he was gone, but she had on so many more clothes than he did and she had so little time. She was so nervous. She fumbled with hooks, couldn't get her garters undone and was terrified he would come out of the bathroom too soon. She didn't want him to see her in her ugly corset, so she slipped the nightgown on over it, just in case. Then she lifted the nightgown, which got all tangled up as she tried to reach back and unhook her bra. She managed to get her underwear off and was heading toward the bed when she heard the bathroom door at the other end of the apartment open. "Glorie? Can I come in now?" he asked, standing at the bedroom door.

He kept the hall light on, and turned the bedroom lights off. They could barely see each other in the shadowy darkness as he put an arm around her and led her to the bed. He held her; he stroked her arms, her waist, her legs, slowly; he moved his hands gently beneath her nightgown. Though his hands were moving slowly, everything was going so fast she hardly had time to be shocked. She noticed that her breasts were tingling and his hand was on the inside of her thigh. He was above her, raising her nightgown to her waist, looking into her eyes as if he would never look anywhere else, and her hands were running up and down his back though she couldn't remember deciding to do that. "Don't be afraid," he whispered.

"I'm not," she said. "I've never been afraid of you."

She was ready to do whatever he wanted, happily. Then she gasped because his hand was on her breast, then it happened. He felt huge and strange, but it didn't hurt. He moved inside her. It crossed her mind that those women Josie mentioned, the ones who were relieved that their husbands got it over with fast, didn't know what they were talking about.

The bus came to a quick stop in traffic, jolting Glorie forward. She looked around, surprised to be here. And as the bus moved on slowly, from the window Glorie saw a heavyset old woman sitting on a bench at a stop just ahead. She had short, straight white hair, and was wearing a camel-hair jacket. In her lap she held a large white canvas tote bag with brightly colored balloons all over it, like a child's. As the bus approached she stood up, leaning on a metal cane, then held her cane out toward the street to hail the bus. She squinted and looked up at the route number on the front, then sat down again, the balloon-covered tote clutched in her lap. She looked healthy, not poor, not sad. Her face showed no emotion other than disappointment that her bus hadn't come. As Glorie rode away she knew what she should have thought: Good for her, still out and around.

Why was that woman so heartbreaking?

Chapter 5

"*One morning a rooster woke up and said, 'Kerk-a-lerk-a-lerk, I'm going to go fight with the king.'* That was my favorite of all the stories Grandpa used to tell us," Pat Jr. said.

Glorie sat royally in her armchair, wearing the new midnight blue silk dress she had made for tonight. Her grandson sat on the side of the bed in her room, and from down the hall they heard Louisa, Blanche and Emily in the last stages of making Christmas Eve dinner.

Glorie had been watching holiday *Jeopardy* when everyone arrived. During commercials she glanced up and saw the Three Wise Men trotting across the top of the TV set as if they were walking to her house. Each of the ceramic figures was almost a foot tall, though the one carrying the chest of gold seemed stooped over with the weight. There wasn't room for more of the old Nativity set here. In her religious days Glorie might have made the proper choice and put the crib and Baby Jesus and Mary and Joseph here on the TV. Instead she amused herself with the idea that the Wise Men were heading in the right direction, aiming straight for the treasure that was her house.

From her chair near the bedroom window she saw Pat Jr. and

Emily and their adorable Lily pull into the driveway just ahead of Blanche and awful Bob and their two boys. But she didn't hit the mute button until her grandson settled in to visit. As he talked she thought he looked as good as any television lawyer, with his grandfather's wavy dark hair and narrow-rimmed glasses that made him look smart and handsome at the same time.

It was cozy here with all the family and only the family. While Emily and Blanche helped Louisa, Lily played with her cousins downstairs. Patrick and Bob were around somewhere, but who cared as long as she didn't have to hear them?

"I loved that story," Pat Jr. was saying. "You remember it? On the way to the castle the rooster met all the animals in the forest. Turkey Lurkey would say, 'Where are you going, Rooster?' and the rooster would say, 'Kerk-a-lerk-a-lerk, I'm going to go fight with the king.' And Turkey Lurkey would say, 'I hate that rotten king, I'll go fight him too.' One by one all the animals joined up. Grandpa used to tell a long version on Christmas Eve, with extra animals. On Christmas Eve animals like the Greased Wildebeest joined up."

"He got the wildebeest from Marlin Perkins on *Wild Kingdom.*"

"I always wondered about that. Then at the end . . ."

Glorie rolled her eyes.

"You always hated this ending, didn't you?" Her grandson laughed. "At the end the king would go into an outhouse and all the bees would swarm out of the hole and sting him on the ass!"

"Very nice story," Glorie said, though she was chuckling. Of course she remembered this story. Maybe Pat Jr. thought her memory was fading, but she would bet he was just being kind, bringing back Jack's voice for her like a special Christmas present.

"It *was* a nice story," Pat Jr. said. "You know, Dad tells it to all the grandkids now. Of course, he changes the ending."

Glorie didn't know that. It wasn't so bad an ending. A little earthiness never hurt a child.

"I've been thinking lately, Grandpa was kind of hostile toward authority, wasn't he?" Pat Jr. asked. "I mean, in that story, sometimes he called the king King Roosevelt." He got up and peeped out the window. "Your house looks good, all decorated."

Glorie hadn't dared ask anyone to help her put up a Christmas tree at home this year, but she had asked Patrick Sr. to string blue and green lights around the biggest windows and to hang a large green wreath with a red velvet bow on the front door. "It's not for me, it's for neighborhood beauty," she had told him.

"When I was a kid I really loved Christmas Eve and Christmas at your house," Pat Jr. said, sitting back on the bed.

"Your grandfather used to make a big fuss about you and your sister."

"You did, too. I had a client the other day who reminded me of Grandpa. He was about seventy, retired, lives on a nice, quiet street. He wants to sue the city because one of the Parks Department crews came during work hours and hauled away some dead trees from his neighbor's backyard as a personal favor. He said it was corruption and a misuse of his tax money and he had time on his hands to sue the bastards."

"What did you tell him?"

"He couldn't prove anything. I told him to take pictures next time and go to the newspaper."

"Your grandfather never would have gone to court. He always minded his own business. But he would have liked the idea."

"He used to warn me not to grow up to be a politician, remember? I was about six, I still wanted to be a fireman and he was telling me politicians are corrupt sons of bitches and

I should be a doctor because there would always be sick people."

"He hated politicians cause he had to give them money."

"You mean kickbacks?"

"No, no, nothing like that. It was just a smart thing to do if you gave them an envelope now and then, if you wanted your street plowed and a police car to go by at night to keep an eye on the shop, that kind of thing."

Lily came running into Glorie's room, looking like no one else in the family, her long, silky golden hair flying. She was grinning and held both hands behind her back. She stood in front of Glorie's chair and held out a paper angel cut from a magazine and glued to cardboard, with an ornament hanger attached to the top. "I made this for you, Grandma G," she said, "for your tree."

Glorie hugged Lily. "An angel, my favorite. Just like you. This is the most beautiful ornament I ever got, and I know right where we can hang it. Come here." She took Lily's hand and they walked a few steps to Glorie's dresser. A three-foot artificial green tree stood on top, overloaded with exquisite ornaments: hand-blown glass balls with ruby-colored swirls inside, delicate golden harps and violins. They were the loveliest of the ornaments Glorie had accumulated over fifty years, and you could hardly see the cheap tree beneath them. Next to the tree was the round music box she had always put on the mantel in the living room: three golden cherubs moving in a circle as "Hark! The Herald Angels Sing" played. On the floor between the bed and the dresser was a pile of packages in thick, shiny emerald paper, tied with red velvet ribbons, each with a gold or silver name tag.

"Look," Glorie said to Lily. Hanging on the front of the tree was a construction-paper angel, a funnel of yellowed-white paper with an angel's face and wings drawn in crayon by a very small child. “Your daddy made that one for me, and we can hang yours right next to it,” she said, taking away a violin to make room. “Right here in front where it will be the first one people see.” Pat Jr. lifted his daughter so she could hang her present.

“I have to help Mom with the fish now,” Lily said. “I have to hold my nose while I do it cause it smells too fishy. See you later.” She held her nose and ran out of the bedroom toward the kitchen.

“She’s so beautiful, your grandfather would have loved to see her,” Glorie told Pat Jr. “Stay and talk a while longer.”

“I wasn’t going anywhere,” he said, sitting down. They heard a pan thud onto the counter (“Be careful, that’s hot coming out of the microwave,” Louisa said) and smelled a mix of spicy tomato sauce and fish that made Glorie feel it was finally Christmas.

“This is nice. All the family and only the family. Before you were born we used to have very big Christmases, with all your grandfather’s brothers and sisters. Those were in the days when the Italian custom was to have a dozen different kinds of fish on Christmas Eve because you couldn’t eat meat.”

“We still have fish.”

“But nothing like the old days. That was a feast! Smelts, eel, scallops, shrimp, everything you could imagine. Baccalà in the sauce. It took me two days to soak the codfish. Your grandfather always said, ‘More Catholic foolishness. They make a rule that you can’t eat meat to punish yourself, so what happens? Instead you have an even better meal of fish. What’s the point?’ I argued at the time but now I think he was right. He was so smart.” Glorie shook her head.

Pat Jr. nodded.

“His family, they were another story,” she told him. “The

food was great, but I have to say I was glad when you grandchildren came along and we could have our own Christmas. Your grandfather's family was tough to deal with."

"You mean Aunt Margaret? She's an old gossip. Didn't she start a rumor that Aunt Delia was really the mailman's daughter?"

"No, Aunt Delia started that one herself. She was mad at her father for something. I think he wouldn't let her go to a dance. Everyone knew it wasn't true. She *looked* like your great-grandfather, he couldn't deny her. He was a decent man, he was always nice to me. But your great-grandmother was no honey pie, let me tell you. When I was first married she used to speak Italian to me on purpose so I wouldn't understand. She could speak some English but she didn't bother, then she'd stop and say, 'Oh, I forgot. You're Portuguese.' She didn't know that I was picking up a word here, a word there. Italian's not so different from Portuguese, you know. Then one day I was ready." Glorie was chuckling and getting flushed, laughing at the end of her story before it was in sight. "We were bringing extra chairs to the table, and your great-grandmother says in Italian, 'How many chairs do we need?' and I answered, *in Italian,* 'We need three more,' or whatever the number was. You should have seen her face. The funny thing was, I didn't know half of what she was saying most of the time. She could have gone on fooling me a lot longer, but she spoke English to me from then on."

"You always had a mischievous side, Grandma, I could see it."

"You could?" She laughed. "Well don't tell anyone, you'll ruin my reputation."

"Mom knows."

"True, I can't fool her."

"You didn't ever start any rumors, did you?"

"Me? Are you kidding? I always minded my own business."

Lily ran into the room. "Daddy, Grandpa's looking for you. He wants you to go with him to pick up the Aunts."

"Be right there," he said. "We'll be back in about half an hour," he told Glorie, kissing her on the cheek and leaving the room.

She turned back to the television and automatically hit the mute button to bring back the sound, but she was looking outside at her house, at Patrick and Pat Jr. as they drove off, at the tree on the dresser reflected back at her in the window.

"Pat Jr. turned out so good he even laughs at my jokes," she told Jack. "And Lily. She turned out so pretty. We found her a very nice present, too."

Blanche walked into the room. "Grandma, why don't you turn off television and come talk to us? It's Christmas Eve."

"I'm waiting for Midnight Mass from Rome."

"That's not for six hours. Come on, please. We won't let you miss it."

"There are other Christmas shows on first."

Blanche had it coming. When she had brought her family to dinner last week, Glorie had tried to join in the conversation. Blanche was complaining as usual, about teaching, and chauffeuring her kids around, and not having time to herself. Then she sighed and said, "I wish I were in my condo." Did Blanche have a new house? Had she moved without anyone telling Glorie?

"You have a condo?" Glorie asked. "Since when?"

Blanche laughed for about ten minutes and said, "Not my condo. *Macondo.* It's the name of a village in a book. I wish I were someplace else, someplace magical, like on vacation."

Now how the hell was Glorie supposed to know that? Here she was trying to express interest, to be part of the conversation the way everyone was always nagging her to.

And I get laughed at, she thought.

She became very quiet for the rest of dinner. It was no fun feeling as dumb as Ada. She went to her room early, while Blanche was still helping Louisa finish the dishes. But soon after, through the crack in her door, she heard them talking as they sat at the kitchen counter. "Grandma was so funny. My condo. That's priceless."

"You shouldn't have laughed at her, you did wrong, honey," said Louisa. "You do it all the time."

"I wasn't laughing *at* her. I couldn't help it."

"Well, I think she was hurt."

"Mom, you're overly sensitive about her, you protect her too much. And what do you get back? She runs you ragged."

"What do you mean? I do some shopping, some banking, laundry, it's what I'd do anyway. Besides, she's my mother, what do you want me to do? Leave her in the street? I hate to think what you'll do with me."

"I would think you'd be more reasonable about the house, for one thing. Dad told me all about that, it's ridiculous."

"That house means a lot to your grandmother, you don't understand."

"When did you become a bleeding heart for Grandma? You always say she was awful when you were growing up, she gave all her attention to Grandpa and none to you."

"I never said that!"

"You did, too, Mom, I've heard it all my life."

"I didn't. And if I did, you misunderstood — that's been known to happen, Blanche. She was a wonderful mother, what are you talking about?" Louisa kept her voice low, but Glorie could hear how mad she was.

"We're as dysfunctional as any family in a case history," Blanche said. "You think it makes sense for her to have a pied-à-terre across the street? I know you don't want to hear this, but there are a lot of unresolved conflicts between you and Grandma that come from fighting for Grandpa's attention all those years. You don't want to face it."

Louisa had a good laugh. "Stop it with that mumbo jumbo, Blanche," she said. "Don't make me tell you how ridiculous you sound, honey."

Glorie heard Blanche swat the dish towel down on the counter. "I'm trying to be realistic, Mom. What are we going to do? She stays in her room. She lives in a dream world."

"She does not," Louisa hissed. "And she's not deaf. Quiet down or she'll hear you."

Dream world. At least I know the difference between real life and books, Glorie thought.

She felt chilled at what Blanche had said. Considering the source, she tried to ignore it, but the words crept back. "Gave all her attention to Grandpa and none to you . . ." Could that possibly be true? Could Louisa even have thought it?

Of course not, Glorie decided by dawn, or Louisa wouldn't have been so mad at Blanche. She didn't know Glorie was listening, and she was telling the truth. Blanche, on the other hand, knew nothing. Maybe one day her granddaughter would grow up, but until she did Glorie would rather watch holiday *Jeopardy* than talk to her.

The doorbell rang and Glorie jumped as if she had been shot. Blanche ran to the door faster than you could say "traitor."

"They're here," she called. "Dad's back with the Aunts." She went to the cellar door to call down to her husband and the children. "The Aunts are here. Come on up, guys."

From her armchair, Glorie could see Louisa and Emily putting foil over the fish to keep it warm and wiping their hands on dish towels so they could rush to the front door to make a big fuss over the Aunts too.

"Here they come," she told Jack. "Flopsie, Mopsie and Cottontail." In public she called them the Aunts like everyone else. In private, she thought of them as the Cottontails, or the Ooo-*maas*. Patrick's widowed aunts had always been goofy, but they were getting worse every year.

"Auntie Stella, Merry Christmas," she heard Louisa say.

Blanche and the kids and the Aunts were all talking at once.

"Auntie Gemma! Merry Christmas!"

"Merry Christmas, Auntie Toni."

"Ooo-*maa,* how big he *got,*" said Toni. "Look at the little boy, Gemma."

"Ooo-*maa,* how big you *go-o-t,*" said Gemma. "Stella, look!"

"Come in, Aunties, don't stand in the hall," Louisa said.

"What the hell is that ooo-maa business?" Jack had asked her once. "Where did they get that? That's all they say, ooo-maa, ooo-maa."

Glorie had never thought about it much, but in the past few years she'd had plenty of time to figure things out. It must have come from "Oh, my" or "Oh, my God," or maybe "Oh, Mama." Last year she'd invented a Christmas Eve joke for herself. She had greeted the Aunts in the living room and said, very distinctly, "*Oh, my,* how nice to see you." No one noticed, not even Louisa, but Jack laughed and it made Glorie feel better.

"Here comes the circus! Elephants, trapeze artists, and performing old people. Gray-haired women with the amazing ability to tell the same story over and over till you beg for mercy! Women with three pairs of glasses around their necks and one on their heads."

"Come on, Glorie, be nice," Jack told her. "It's Christmas Eve. You can stand the Aunts once a year."

"OK, I'm being mean. I can stand it once a year," she said.

But how could she stand it when Christmas had been stolen from her?

She sat in her room, knowing exactly what would happen this night. They would hear the Aunts' old-age story, and the whole family would act as if they hadn't heard it a million times: about how lucky these three widows were to be together, how much they owed their sweet nephew Patrick, how much they loved their own apartments in a building for senior citizens downtown.

"Could you believe it?" Toni was probably saying already, not five minutes in the door. "We were first-grade friends, Gemma and me. Then I got to know Stella and Blanche, God rest her soul, cause they were Gemma's sisters."

Good thing you mentioned that, Glorie thought. There might be someone here who didn't *know* they were sisters.

"Then we lost track of each other. Sixty years later, could you believe it, we run into one another in the laundry room of our same building. It's a be-you-tee-ful new building, too, practically a skyscraper. Now it's like we're all real sisters. We're a family," Toni said.

You didn't need this story to see that Toni was an afterthought as an Aunt. Stella was intelligent and tasteful. She wore dresses with matching jackets, and her thin gray hair was always perfectly set in bubbly curls. Gemma talked and thought in slow motion, and wore several pairs of glasses slung around her neck. They were all the same prescription. She had a habit of taking her glasses off, cord and all, and putting them down all around the house. So now every morning Gemma put a pair of glasses on her nose and a couple of spares around her neck.

"Aren't they heavy around your neck?" Patrick had asked her once.

"Oh, I'm used to it," Gemma said. "At least I can see when I want to. I need to see to find my glasses, don't I?"

"I think it's a fashion statement, Aunt Gemma," said Louisa.

"Oh yeah," Gemma laughed slowly. "A fashion statement, that's good."

Glorie had always liked the sisters, even Patrick's mother when she was alive, until they hooked up with Toni. She was loud and silly, and the others followed right along. Toni had oversized glasses that made her eyes bug out and oversized dentures with bright red lipstick smeared on them. She wore hideous vests that she said she crocheted herself but Glorie suspected were old doilies sewn together. Everyone thought she was a riot. The three Aunts were never apart now, and each year they were more alike, with identical bubble-headed gray hair, and the never-ending story about how incredible it was that they had ended up together in their old age.

For these three, my own family has abandoned me, Glorie thought. She had turned the TV off and was sitting quietly by her window while everyone was still fussing in the living room, hanging up the Aunts' coats, getting them drinks.

The furniture had been rearranged to make space for the seven-foot tree near the picture window. Now the heavy, flowered couch was facing the fireplace, and the matching armchairs placed on either side formed a big circle. The Aunts poked around Louisa's living room. There were fir boughs decorated with red balls on the mantel, and little tables everywhere with Christmas candles, trays of cookies, musical angels.

The Aunts inspected every corner. "Ooo-*maa,* look at that tree, how big it *is!*" said Stella.

"Those angels over there, how cute," Gemma drawled.

"Home-baked cookies," Toni said, swallowing. "Bee-yoo-tee-ful."

"Oh, look, even the coffee table has a garland around the edge," said Stella. "How cute it looks."

And where did they think Louisa learned to make a Christmas like this?

"Be happy, Glorie, be glad they appreciate it," Jack told her.

"But they're taking over in my house," she said.

"This is your house now?"

"Well, compared to them it's my house."

"Where's Gloria?" said Stella near the bedroom doorway. "There you are," she said, coming in, kissing her Merry Christmas, sitting in Pat Jr.'s place on the side of the bed. "Ooo, what a cute Christmas tree."

"Lily just gave me that cutout angel there. She made it," Glorie said, pointing. "And the one next to it her father made for me when he was her age."

"It's so nice you saved everything."

"There's a lot more at my house that I don't have room for here. I have part of my Nativity set here, and the rest I put up at home."

"I'd like to see that," Stella said. "Maybe one day we can all take a walk over there, Gemma and Toni and me, we'll come for a visit."

Did they always travel in a pack?

"Anytime," Glorie said.

"You know, Gemma's daughter invited all of us out to California for Christmas this year, even Toni cause she's one of us now, but we said we'd go visit later on. I said, 'You can go, Gemma, but we always have Christmas with Patrick and Louisa and Gloria, so I'm gonna stay here.' And Gemma didn't want us to be split up, so we all stayed. It wouldn't be Christmas without being here."

"I know how you feel. I wouldn't want to be away either."

Stella was being nice and Glorie decided to say something nice back.

God forgive me for lying, she thought, then said to Stella, "You're very lucky to have Patrick. He was in the kitchen helping Louisa all afternoon, then he went to the Knights of Columbus to play Santa at their kids' party. He's very helpful to everyone." Well, why not? Stella was her guest.

Stella glanced toward the open doorway to see if anyone was listening, then whispered to Glorie, "I hate to say it, cause he *is* my nephew, and we'd be lost without him, but don't you think he's too good sometimes? Not that Louisa doesn't deserve help, don't get me wrong, you know I love her like my own. But the Church, the Knights, sometimes I want to grab him by the shoulders and shake him. 'Patrick, go out, get drunk, do something!' Don't ever tell them I said that, please!"

"My lips are sealed."

"Ooo-*maa,* they'd kill me."

Stella and Glorie were giggling when Glorie heard Toni say loudly from the living room, "Where's Gloria? What, is she hiding in her room again?" Gemma said, "Shhh!" almost as loud as Toni was talking. Gemma was slow, but she'd been raised right.

Stella didn't turn around, so maybe she didn't hear. She said, "I think we should go out and join the rest of the family. They're probably waiting for us. Just don't make me laugh anymore, Gloria."

Smiling, Glorie followed Stella, trying to sneak into the living room behind her without making a grand entrance. "There she is!" Toni yelled, then, as if realizing what she had said, she started singing, "*There* she is! Miss A-*mer*-i-ca."

"You should see me in a bathing suit," Glorie said. No one was going to throw her tonight. She could keep up if she had to.

Gemma got out of one of the comfortable armchairs, kissed Glorie on the cheek and said, "Take my seat. I have to go in the kitchen and put the final touches on my appetizer."

Every year Gemma made her traditional Christmas appetizer and if Glorie had known about this family ritual she might have tried to stop the marriage. The appetizer was deviled ham on Ritz crackers and right now Gemma was adding her special holiday touch. She took half the deviled ham and mixed in green food coloring, and came back to the living room passing around a platter that alternated Christmas colors, or colors as close as she could manage: pink ham on Ritz next to purplish green ham on Ritz. Glorie took a pink one. She knew from experience it didn't taste as bad as it should, though she had tried to get Louisa to sneak better crackers onto the platter. "Maybe unsalted melba toast," she suggested, "so we don't have to drink a gallon of water after dinner."

"Ma, it's her appetizer," Louisa said, in the same tone she had used during Patrick's barber days when she'd insisted, "Ma, it's his dream."

Bob took two. "Yum, I can't resist these, Aunt Gemma. But" — he wrinkled his forehead in a fake gesture of thinking — "they remind me of something. I know. Did you ever see that episode of *The Honeymooners* when Ralph invents a special appetizer? 'Kranmar's' he called it."

"It's dog food!" Toni yelled, laughing. "It was dog food and Ralph didn't know it! We saw that one."

"We saw that," said Gemma, laughing too. "That was a funny one. Yeah, *The Honeymooners,* it's on every night, eleven o'clock, channel five. Sometimes we stay up for it."

"I like that Norton," said Stella.

"But Kranmar's tasted good, right?" said Bob. "Maybe Aunt Gemma could make some money on this recipe."

"This isn't dog food," said Gemma, looking worried.

"He knows that," Stella said. "Bob's teasing you, Gemma."

"Oh-h-h," said Gemma, catching on. "Yeah, Blanche's husband. He's the one that likes to tease."

Glorie would have liked to smack him.

"Bob's the dentist," yelled Toni. "After dinner I'm gonna have him check what's left of my teeth."

Louisa called them to the dining room for soup. Patrick sat at one end of the long table and Louisa at the other, so she could jump up and down fast for trips to the kitchen. The Aunts sat in a row on one side: Toni, Stella then Gemma across from Glorie. Bob made sure he sat next to Toni, and by the time they were passing around the platters of fish he had drunk enough wine to start teasing the Aunts for real.

"So, Toni," he said, "who's your latest boyfriend?" Toni and Gemma leapt before anyone could swallow another bite.

"He means Phil!" Gemma squealed.

"He does not. I don't have no boyfriend," said Toni. "I was married to a good man. And if I did have a man friend it wouldn't be Phil. I don't think he takes a bath too often."

"He waits for you around the mailbox, Toni," Gemma said.

"Oh, he hangs out there. I talk to him. I talk to everybody, I don't care who they are."

"I don't kno-o-ow," Stella sang. "I think you kind of li-i-ke him."

"Oh, he likes that Florence. He's always taking her food shopping. If that's what he wants, he can have her. She always has some man to take her around, cause she looks like a floozy in those see-through blouses and that dyed red hair — no offense, Gloria."

"And her slacks are too tight," Gemma drawled.

"You look at her and think she's no good," Toni yelled at Bob. "If you saw her you'd right away think, she's no good."

"Calm down, Toni," said Stella, but she was laughing with everyone else.

"I'll take Phil if you don't want him," said Gemma. She sounded serious. "He can always take a bath."

"He can take a bath in your apartment," Toni screamed, laughing almost too hard to talk now.

"No, no, in his own."

"No, in yours!"

"I wouldn't know how to tell him he smells, so I'm out of the picture," said Stella.

"Do you think Phil pays for that Florence's groceries?" Bob asked Toni.

Glorie would have smacked him so hard his teeth would have rolled on the floor.

"Ooo, I never thought of that," said Toni. "Maybe he does. Maybe they have some trade going on, a business deal."

"You think he's getting some action?" said Bob.

Stella was blushing. "Toni, come on, don't talk about those kinds of things at the dinner table."

"Why not? We've all done them. We were all married. Of course, that was a long time ago. Too long for me," and she started fanning herself with her napkin. "Is it hot in here or have I been alone too long?"

By now the whole table was roaring, even Pat Jr. and Emily. Blanche was wiping her eyes with her napkin, Louisa was smiling and shaking her head. To Glorie, the Aunts looked like three organ grinder's monkeys lined up across the table, dressed alike in red jackets with red hats over their bubbly gray hair. Maybe Stella had a split personality, because she was one of the monkeys too.

"We have each other. We don't need nobody else," Toni said, getting serious, nodding her head as if she had settled every problem on earth. "We were girlhood friends. We lost track of each other, then we found each other again in the laundry room. I didn't see them for sixty years, and there they are, cleaning a lint trap in the laundry room of my same building. Now I'm like their real sister."

Ooo-maa, thought Glorie, what a surprise.

"And we have such nice apartments, ooo-*maa,*" said Gemma. "We each have our own. We have our own kitchen, our own bathroom, our own living room, our own bedroom."

"And we have bingo, right in the building, twice a week," said Toni. "We don't even have to go out to get a game. We have a laundry room in the basement. We're one big family. We look after one another, everybody looks after everybody else."

Everybody knows your business, thought Glorie.

"You'd love it there, Gloria," said Gemma. "It's so neat and clean."

"You should come visit," said Stella. "Next time you're downtown shopping, call me up and come over for lunch."

"We can all have lunch," said Toni. "And we can fix you up with a blind date. Not Phil. Somebody high-class. We'll find somebody who takes a bath."

"Toni, Gloria doesn't want a blind date," said Stella. "She just wants to come to lunch."

I do? thought Glorie. Do I have a say in this? But she smiled and said, "Someday I'll surprise you."

"That's a good idea, Aunt Gemma," Patrick said as soon as he could get a word in — which wasn't as soon as usual. "I think Mom would like it there. I've been thinking that myself. You know, her house is very expensive to keep up."

"Patrick," Louisa whispered. "Not on Christmas Eve."

"I was just saying—"

"Not on Christmas Eve."

"What's going on?" said Bob.

"Nothing," said his mother-in-law."

"Stella, would you pass me the bread?" Glorie asked. "Don't you think Louisa did a great job on the smelts this year?"

"Dee-licious!" yelled Toni. "Bee-you-tee-ful!"

It was just like Patrick to put his aunts up to this. Was everyone in on it?

I'm smarter than they are, she told Jack. They can't fool me.

Patrick took the Aunts home around 10:30, all of them shouting from the driveway, "See you tomorrow." Blanche and Bob, Pat Jr. and Emily were packing up their families. Glorie got some water and an Advil and settled down in front of TV to wait for Midnight Mass. For years the whole family had gone to Midnight Mass together, even Jack. It was like going to a party in the middle of the night — the singing, the church filled with flowers and crowded with people. Now the great-grandkids had to get home and Glorie herself would have been too sleepy to leave the house. Besides, she got a better view and a bigger show on TV.

Blanche and her boys came in to say good night.

"What are you watching?" Michael asked.

"Midnight Mass," said Glorie. "From Rome, with the Pope and lot of music."

"It's the Late Show, starring the Pope!" he yelled like a TV announcer. "The Pope's guests tonight: altar boys, holy singers and Da-a-vid Letterman." He was only ten; they let that kid stay up too late.

"Don't make fun of the Pope," Glorie said. "He's a very smart and very good man."

Michael ran from the room, yelling, "Great-Grandma has a crush on the Pope."

Everyone laughed and Glorie flushed. I could do a lot worse, she thought. I could be flirting with a dirty old man named Phil.

He's just a little boy with idiot parents, he's not being mean, she reminded herself.

She had been so worried about the boys' presents, too. She trusted herself to find the perfect gift for Lily: a jewelry box with a ballerina on top that played the theme from the movie *Sleeping Beauty.* But she didn't know what boys liked these days, so she had given Louisa money to buy them toys.

"It's too much, Ma," Louisa said. "They don't need expensive presents from you, get them something small, they don't know the difference." But Glorie wanted to give them something big, something they would play with all year, something that would make them think of her. She wouldn't take the money back. Louisa came home with two walking, talking robots, with no price tags on them anywhere. "Did I give you enough? Do I need to add to it?" Glorie asked.

"No, it was enough, there was a sale," Louisa said.

But Glorie was crafty. She kept her eye on ads in the paper until she found those robots. They were advertised at a special price that was twenty dollars more than Glorie had given Louisa. "Well, they're her grandchildren, she wants to spoil them," she told Jack. But she felt as if her presents didn't count anymore; they weren't really from her.

And now everyone was in the living room laughing at her. Michael was still saying, "I'm not kidding, Great-Grandma has a crush on the Pope." It didn't matter though.

Even at my age I can learn things, she reminded herself. I can learn not to open my mouth.

Soon the house was empty and Glorie was drowsy, but she didn't want to miss anything. She looked at the Wise Men trotting across the top of the TV.

"Do you remember Julia and Baby Jesus?" she asked Jack.

The year she got the idea to move the ceramic set from under the tree in the Christmas Room to the top of the television in the den, it drove Jack crazy.

"I want to look at the program, not a lot of statues in dresses on top of it. It takes my attention away," he said. "What do we need all this stuff for, anyway?"

"It's only once a year," Glorie said. "Why put it where we never see it? You want to put it in that green room you hate?"

"Yes."

"You'll get used to it."

While they were sitting on the couch watching Julia Child make roast duck and plum pudding, Jack poked her in the side and said, "Isn't she wearing the same dress as that Wise Guy in the middle?" It was a remarkably similar shade of royal blue.

"Oh, her neckline is entirely different," Glorie said.

"The Christ Child and Julia Child — you think they're related?" Jack asked.

"I never thought. They have the same last name," she said. "Same initials — J.C."

"I told you putting those statues on the TV was distracting," Jack said. "Now I'll never know how to make that plum pudding."

She had laughed at the idea of him cooking. They had laughed at each other's bad jokes with all the warmth of their lifetime together. Glorie had no jokes to make anymore.

From Rome, music was playing while everyone in St. Peter's waited for the Pope to march down the aisle. To kill time the TV toured other parts of the Vatican. They were showing close-ups of the ceiling Michelangelo painted in the Sistine Chapel, while the choir sang "Adeste Fideles." Glorie would have liked to be there; she would have liked to go to Rome with Jack. They would have gone to Mass at the Sistine Chapel, and the Pope would notice her and nod as he passed by their pew. She would sit close by Jack, their arms touching, the way they did at Midnight Mass at home. They would whisper to each other and point out interesting people.

The Pope had reached the altar and was praying in Italian. Glorie started to chuckle. She saw herself and Jack lying on the floor of the Sistine Chapel, alone, his arm around her. They were looking up at the ceiling.

"I think that devil looks like your brother Manny," Jack said.

Glorie smiled. "I think you're right. I don't want to guess where Manny ended up."

"Where's the angel from the living room?" he asked.

"That was a different painter. Do I have to keep track of everything?" she teased him.

"You have to keep track of me."

Glorie's head had been dropping as she sat in her bedroom chair, but she lifted it fast, listening. It felt as if Jack had really been in the room, telling her, "You have to keep track of me." This wasn't her imagination.

She listened.

She held her breath.

She waited.

She heard nothing.

Goddamn fool, she told herself. If you don't watch out you'll be hearing reindeer on the roof.

She brushed away the few tears she couldn't keep back and decided she should get some sleep.

I'm not going to cry over crazy ideas.

Chapter 6

GLORIE'S ELBOW WAS HOOKED around the green metal pole that held up a No Parking sign. She was trying to keep her balance, to keep her feet firm on the snowy sidewalk, while the wind kept pushing her forward, doubling her over. The snow created a curtain in front of her eyes, as if she were looking at the downtown street through white sheers. All she could make out were the fuzzy shapes of cars and buses creeping and sliding along Williams Street in the distance.

Her knit hat blew off her head, but that was the last thing she was worried about. She didn't dare let go of the pole; she knew better than to try to make it the few feet from the curb to the door of the brick office building. No one was coming out of that building. There was hardly anyone left on Williams, never mind this narrow side street, whatever it was called. The streetlights burst on above her, hitting her face as if she were a spy about to be questioned. She had walked out of Shepherd's at 11:30 and headed down Williams toward the bus stop, but didn't make it halfway before the wind came up and carried her off, trapping her alone in this daytime darkness.

The snow wasn't supposed to start until late afternoon. When she had left Louisa's to head home that morning, Louisa had warned, "Don't get too comfortable. I'm coming across to get you as soon as I see that first snowflake." But Glorie figured there was plenty of time to get downtown, exchange the horrible quilted robe Blanche had given her for Christmas and get back — to her own house or Louisa's, depending on the weather.

When she reached Shepherd's a little after 11:00 the streets were still dry but the store was practically empty, and a guard at the front door was telling customers they would be closing at 1:00. He had a portable radio on the stool beside him: the storm had suddenly picked up speed, they were predicting the fastest-moving blizzard in years, and the announcer was telling everyone to stay off the roads. Schools were on Christmas break, but offices were letting out early.

Always the last to know, Glorie told herself. Well, there's no point in leaving the store now.

If she did she would have to wait a half hour in the chilly bus shelter. So she wandered to the sleepwear department but kept checking her watch, figuring how much extra time she would need to walk to the bus, wondering if the snow had started. The department was deserted except for one saleswoman, on the phone to her baby-sitter, it sounded like. All the robes looked ugly, designed for a farmer's wife.

I better go now, Glorie thought after fifteen minutes. Better to freeze on the street than miss that bus.

The second she walked out the door she knew something terrible was going to happen to her. There was already an inch of snow on the ground; cars had their headlights on, and the few people who walked by her had their heads down. The world was so quiet, for a second she thought she had lost her hearing.

Stay calm, she told herself. Thank God I'm wearing the rubber-soled shoes. I can walk in them, I'll make it if I walk very slowly. I can drop the shopping bag and leave it if I have to. If I have to, I can ask for help.

She took tiny steps. She made it across the empty side street next to Shepherd's and all the way to the corner of the next long block where she stood, wondering if the length of one red light would give her time to get across the street. From there it would be straight ahead to the bus stop; in clear weather you could see it from here. Then she noticed that the traffic lights were hardly visible in the storm and the cars weren't paying attention to them. They were moving in slow motion, crawling through the intersection, sliding and finding paths wherever they could. Even if she were fifty years younger she couldn't dodge those cars. She would have to go back to Shepherd's while it was still open and call Louisa to come get her.

She'll be furious, Glorie thought. I'll never live it down.

Then as she reached the side street the wind caught her and pushed her onto it, as if a giant arm had grabbed her around the shoulders and started running down the empty sidewalk, sweeping her along. As the giant arm pushed her, her feet raced to keep up; if she didn't run she would fall. She saw the signpost flying toward her. She dropped the shopping bag and clutched the pole, throwing her weight into it, hanging on tight.

She had no idea how long she had been standing there, maybe half an hour, maybe longer. Her eyes were watering, her fingers were getting stiff, her ears felt frozen, and every time the wind bent her forward she thought her back would crack in two, but none of that would kill her. No, she was going to die because no one who passed on Williams Street would be able to spot her. Even with her red hair flying in the wind, no one could see her through this curtain of snow. The wind doubled her over again and she was losing the strength to hang on. She would have to sit down, she would have to die like one of those Eskimos who were set out to sea on a block of ice when they got too old. She would freeze to death, alone.

She heard a voice from above.

"Hey lady, you need some help?" a young man yelled. She looked up and thought she saw a blurry face stuck out a window several stories high. She tried to say yes but no sound came out of her mouth.

"I'll come down," he shouted.

She held the pole so fiercely she thought her arms would break. In a few minutes a tall, thin man in a shabby ski parka and knit cap had his arm around her waist and was sheltering her from the wind, half-carrying her toward the doorway of the office building. He pulled up a wooden chair for her next to a small table in the lobby.

"You look frozen, lady, how long you been out there? There's a coffee machine down the hall, you want some?"

Glorie nodded.

"Use that phone if you like. Dial nine for outside," he said.

The phone was inches away from her on the table, but all she could do was sit and shiver, too numb to move. She would wait for the young man to come back and hand her the phone.

In a minute he was putting a cup of black coffee in her gloved hands. He wore heavy work shoes and had a long, graying brown ponytail that stuck out from under his cap. He wasn't rich; she thought she should pay him for this coffee but didn't know how to bring it up.

"You gonna be OK? You want me to make a call for you?"

The bitter, lukewarm coffee brought enough of her voice

back so Glorie could say, "Will you dial a number for me? My daughter will come get me."

"Sure, what's the number? I hope she's not coming from far."

Louisa answered on one ring.

"Louisa," Glorie whispered.

"Where are you? My God, I searched your house up and down, I called Aunt Ada, I called the Aunts. Where are you?"

"I got caught downtown in the storm. I'm in a building at . . ."

"One-forty-five Hopkins Street, right off Williams," the man said and she repeated it to Louisa.

"I can't make it down there, Ma, the streets aren't plowed, no one is getting around," Louisa told her. "Emily will have to come get you with the four-wheel drive. Give me your number there and I'll call you back after I've talked to her."

Glorie started to cry softly. It wouldn't be all right after all. "I'm afraid to hang up," she said quietly, trying not to let Louisa hear her cry.

"Are you at a pay phone, Ma?"

"No, I'm in a lobby."

"So I can call you right back. Don't worry. Give me the number and if I don't call you in three minutes, you call me, OK?"

Glorie got the number from the young man, gave it to Louisa and hung up to wait.

"I'd take you upstairs but the heat's out all over the building," the man said. "I was locking some offices up there and I kept my jacket and hat and gloves on the whole time, it was so cold. Your daughter coming?"

"I think so. My granddaughter probably."

In five minutes the phone rang. Emily would have to leave Lily with a neighbor and drive downtown. On the way, she would pick up Pat Jr. at his office, then they would get Glorie and take her home. "But remember, Ma, she's twenty minutes away in good weather, so this could take a while. Try to stay calm until she gets there. Call if you need to talk to me."

Glorie explained this to the man. "Am I keeping you?" she asked. "Do you have work to do?"

"No," he said. "Almost everybody got out of here early. I can stay here till your relatives come." He sat in a chair facing hers across the lobby and pulled a Walkman out of his pocket. "Let's see what the news is saying," he told her and put the earphones on. He lifted them in a few minutes and said, "Two feet by three o'clock."

She nodded.

"Yeah, pretty bad out there," he said.

She nodded again, staring at him. She didn't want to talk, but she knew she ought to make conversation, pass the time, be polite. "So, you work here," she said, surprised at how feeble and hoarse she sounded.

"Yeah, it's a job," the man said. He must have noticed the tears in her eyes because he put the earphones back in place for good.

Glorie sat there holding her half cup of cold coffee, staring at the snow as it raced by the glass doors. Outside it looked like midnight. She couldn't phone Louisa because then she would fall apart.

I can't think about anything sentimental, she told herself. I have to be tough and not let myself go.

So she tried to run through yesterday's *Oprah* in her mind, something about reformed bulimics counseling schoolkids. What was Oprah wearing? What did the bulimics look like? One was a fat man with a plaid jacket and slicked back hair. Could he have been bulimic? There was a skinny young girl with long stringy hair and tight blue jeans. Somehow Glorie thought they were a couple.

She wanted to close her eyes and put her head in her hands, she wanted to curl up on the floor. Her head ached and her back was beyond help. But if she sat straight and looked ahead, if she concentrated hard enough she would keep control, the time would pass, Pat Jr. would walk through that door.

The man with the ponytail kept fiddling with the radio dial of his Walkman; now and then his foot tapped and his head bounced. Glorie kept repeating to herself, "It will be all right, it will be all right," kept forcing her mind back to cold-blooded things. She made herself imagine the shelves at the grocery store, running through the aisles. Where was the Minute Rice, where was the Campbell's? As long as she kept her mind busy she wouldn't have to worry about what to do if nobody showed up to rescue her.

The man caught her eye and lifted his headphones. "You OK?" he asked loudly.

"Yes, thank you."

"You want to listen awhile?" he asked, holding the earphones out toward her.

"No, thank you very much. You keep them. You're very good to ask."

He reminded her of someone. She tried to picture him without the ponytail, and he looked like a stranger again. Maybe the ponytail was what did it. Who did she know with a ponytail? That was it. He reminded her of Josie's grandson David, the first man she had ever seen with hair to his shoulders. Josie had been scared to death. "He'll turn into a drug addict and die on the street, I know what's coming," she had worried, even though he was an A student at college studying computers. He got married a few years back; that was the last time Glorie had seen him. His hair was short and somebody said he made a lot of money. Josie would have been so proud. "I'm glad to be wrong," she would have said. Glorie could see her sitting at their table at the wedding, wearing a pale blue gown, her white hair beautiful around her face. "I'm glad to be wrong," she would have said.

Glorie sat straighter in the wooden chair. No thinking about family, she warned herself.

After an hour she took off her watch and put it in her bag to keep herself from checking it every half minute, then she was sorry. The young man was looking at her, as if he thought she was afraid he would steal it. She glanced toward the glass door. No one was passing by. She tried to remember all the words to the theme song from *Cheers* but as she was singing "everybody knows your name" in her head, she kept seeing herself sitting on a giant ice cube in the middle of the sea. She tried to list the ingredients in her favorite cookie recipe, but she saw herself putting a cookie sheet in an oven in an igloo. She would die alone, her soul as frozen as her body. She saw herself treading water in an icy ocean as the sky grew black, and hours must have passed before she heard pounding on the glass doors and saw Pat Jr. walk in. She was too stiff to jump out of the chair by then, so she sat there and stretched her arms out for help, like a baby who wants to be held.

"Grandma, you OK?" he asked. His face was bright red. "Emily's got the Jeep over on Williams but we didn't want to risk coming down here because it's not plowed at all. I'm going to have to carry you to the car. It's only half a block. I'm going to give you a fireman's carry cause it's the only way I can make sure to keep my balance."

He helped her stand up. He lifted her gently and tossed her over his shoulder with a small grunt. She felt him squirming and fishing under his coat. He reached into his pocket and handed the young man some money, Glorie couldn't see how much. "I appreciate this," Pat Jr. said.

"Thanks, buddy, no problem," said the man. "I'll get the door for you."

"Thank you," Glorie wanted to say. "I didn't mean anything by the watch." But she was already looking down at the snow on the sidewalk and at her handbag dangling from her left hand. The blood was rushing to her head. The wind had died down but the sky was still dark and the streets bright white and empty.

Emily was waiting to open the door and help her into the backseat of the Jeep. She sat next to Glorie and wrapped a blanket around her.

"Are you OK?" Emily said, and Glorie nodded.

"If it looks like we can't make it home we're going to the Aunts', " Pat Jr. said. "Mom already called them." Glorie was too tired to argue. She heard Emily say, "Let's see if we can get her home and then get to Lily." Glorie tried to open her eyes. She felt Emily rubbing her hands, putting another blanket over her legs.

Then Emily was softly shaking her awake. "We're here, Grandma. Grandma?"

Louisa had cleared a short path to the front door. Pat Jr. carried her to her own room.

"I'm sorry," Glorie mumbled as Pat laid her on the bed. "I'm sorry."

Louisa put her in a heavy nightgown and robe, gave her aspirin and cough medicine and tea. She checked her mother's fingers and toes and ears for frostbite. It was four in the afternoon, the sky was almost back to normal now, but Glorie could feel herself falling asleep in the very center of her bones, falling into the kind of sleep so deep that dreams never surface. Her neck was tilted at an odd angle but she was too exhausted to move her head. She saw herself curled up on the ground while snow piled on top of her. She was hidden under a mound of snow and she didn't care.

When she woke at 9:00 the next morning, abruptly, she remembered every humiliating detail of the day before. Her left arm felt sore, and when she pulled up the sleeve of her nightgown she saw a huge black-and-blue mark where she had been clinging to the metal pole.

They'll want me locked up, she thought. I might as well face the worst before Louisa makes me. They'll say I'm too crazy to be on the loose.

She had to find some good excuse for being downtown, some emergency that had sent her there, something so convincing she wouldn't seem loony. She had to find this excuse before Louisa came in, because Louisa would know she was awake; Louisa would know everything. Glorie couldn't pretend today. Maybe she could never pretend again.

But instead of excuses that might save her, she kept seeing that sharp, sudden moment when the wind grabbed her by the shoulders and she was blown down the street, alone. She saw herself almost carried off her feet, flying toward the green pole. The image came back and came back, and while she fought it and worried about her excuse, in some deep, shadowy, scary part of her mind she kept wondering, Where was Jack yesterday when I was too alone and frightened to remember him?

Where did he go to when real life forced him from her thoughts?

She lay there feeling woozy and confused until Louisa slowly opened the door. Glorie told her daughter she was fine.

"My voice is scratchy, that's all," she said, but Louisa was already putting a thermometer in her mouth. Glorie didn't say "I told you so" when it turned out to be normal.

"Good," said Louisa. "The doctor said if you don't have a temperature there's no need to see him. But I'm making you stay in bed for the rest of the day." She brought tea and toast and a boiled egg on a tray and sat with Glorie while they pretended to watch the news. Louisa didn't ask any questions.

"I feel like a fool," Glorie said after a while. "I should have known better. I'm sorry I put Pat and Emily to all that trouble."

"They didn't mind, honest. You can call them up, they'll tell you."

"I will. Is Lily all right? Was she OK at the neighbor's yesterday?"

"She's fine," Louisa said. "You weren't the only person who got caught by surprise, you know. That storm came up very fast. But, Ma, you have to let me know where you're going from now on. Promise me that."

This was the nightmare happening. Louisa would never let her out on her own again. "I'll be more careful from now on," Glorie said.

"Promise you'll let me know when you're going out."

"I promise I'll be careful," she said calmly.

Louisa looked ready to argue, then changed her mind. "You're lucky that man helped you. A stranger like that. That's unusual."

"Very much so. He reminded me of your cousin David. Have we heard from him lately?"

"No, I haven't heard anything."

"The way he yelled to me on the street reminded me of somebody else too," Glorie said. "I can't quite get who it was." She closed her eyes for a minute, then smiled. "Oh, my God," she told Louisa. "It was when I was a little girl. Somebody took me to meet my mother after work at the mill, I'm not sure who. I was standing alone next to the side entrance, by that stream of water between the two mill buildings, sudsy water. Every time I went by there I thought it smelled like egg salad. I was looking into the water, and I heard a woman yell, 'Hey, little girl, how about some necks?' I looked up and two women were leaning out a window from the mill next door to my mother's."

"How about some necks?" asked Louisa.

"That's right. I didn't know what they meant, either. Then they threw down a handful of plastic necklaces. Red plastic necklaces, I can see them. They were junky, even for a kid, you could see the string through the plastic beads they were so cheap. I guess they were going to be thrown away or something. I don't remember what I did with them. I wasn't scared at all, I just didn't know what they meant by 'How about some necks?' What a strange thing to come back to me."

Louisa was laughing. "Necks. That old jewelry factory was there for so many years. I remember that smell too. It was from the dye the mills used to dump in the water. Those were the days before ecology."

"I'm sorry," Glorie said. "I'm really sorry about yesterday. I know it was foolish. It won't happen again."

"Don't worry about it so much, Ma, it's over. You were scared. It was dangerous, but you're OK. It's over."

Glorie wanted to laugh it off and say, "I'll be up and around tomorrow," but instead she could only grab Louisa's hands. "You saved me," she said softly, in wonder, as if she had never imagined living so long that she would have to say such words. "You and Pat Jr. and Emily saved me."

"Oh come on, Ma," Louisa said. She sounded cheerful. "It wasn't that bad. You saved me plenty of times. Remember when you saved me and Cathy from the mad dog?"

"Was he really mad?"

"I don't know, but we thought he was at the time."

"I'll be fine by tomorrow," Glorie said. "I'll be up and around. I'm just tired right now."

"Well, see how you feel, Ma. You can't cross the street in this weather anyhow. And I made you a doctor's appointment for the day after New Year's. I'll feel better if he checks you."

"Fine," Glorie said.

Louisa smiled. "The things that come back to you. I even remember Dad's face when he looked at the omelette on his plate that night. He said, 'What's this, breakfast?' and I said, 'There's a good reason we're having eggs for supper. Mom had to throw the roast at the mad dog that was chasing Cathy and me.'"

"I thought fast, didn't I?"

"You did. And you promised to let me tell Dad the story. I had it all planned, and I rattled it off, something like, 'There was a Lassie dog and it came running into the backyard foaming at the mouth and followed us to the door so we couldn't get in, and Mom took the roast and threw it out the window into the yard so the dog would go after it and leave us alone and that's why we're having eggs for supper.' He looked like he didn't believe me."

"Oh, he believed you," Glorie said. "He called the dog officer the next morning. I guess I should have thought of that right away. They had no reports of a mad dog or a lost collie, so there was nothing to do."

"It must have been about a hundred degrees that day. Maybe it wasn't mad. Maybe it was thirsty. I always thought I could use that line someday if I forgot to go to the market and had to serve eggs for dinner," Louisa said. "Sorry, Patrick, I threw the meat to distract a mad dog."

Glorie could see that Louisa was going out of her way not to treat her like a crazy old lady. It was sweet of her, but it seemed like proof that she thought Glorie *was* crazy, or else why bend over backwards to deny it? Glorie would have to sort this out later, with Jack, because now Louisa was saying, "I can go over to your house and get anything you need from there. Is there anything special you want? Clothes or sewing or something?"

"I can't think of anything," Glorie said. Not anything I can mention, she thought.

She wanted her scrapbook. It would have been a comfort to look through it, to read about the swans and wonder about neck injuries at the hairdresser's, to run her fingers over Jack's name in print. But talk about loony. How could she explain Lucy Ball's death notice and the love letters the Duke wrote to the Duchess?

"Thanks, but I'll be home soon enough," Glorie said.

"After you see the doctor," said Louisa.

"She's fine for a woman her age," the doctor told Louisa after New Year's, as if Glorie weren't sitting right there.

"You're fine for a doctor your age, you baby-faced bastard," Glorie felt like telling him. She had spent six days pacing around her room, looking at her empty house, waiting for this juvenile delinquent to say she could cross the street!

Louisa walked over with her the first day. "I'll help you dust, clean out the refrigerator, get you settled in," she'd said the night before.

"I'll be fine," Glorie told her.

"Ma, don't give me a hard time. I want you to take things slow." And Louisa was up, dressed and waiting before Glorie opened her bedroom door in the morning. Louisa took her arm walking across like Ada had at the mall.

The house smelled stuffy as they walked in.

Hello, Jack, Glorie thought. We're home.

Louisa stayed all morning, throwing out sour milk, gossiping about the neighbors, vacuuming, spoiling Glorie as if she were her personal maid.

"Let me make you lunch," Glorie offered at noon.

"I'd like that, Ma, but I'm having lunch with Elaine, I haven't seen her in a while. I have to meet her at one. Sit down for a minute before I go, I want to talk to you."

"We've been talking all morning."

"This is serious. Sit down." They sat at the empty kitchen table and Louisa gave her speech as if she had spent hours rehearsing it, rattling it off as if she were still remembering her speech about the mad dog. "I was talking to Aunt Stella and Aunt Gemma the other day and they invited you to visit their apartments and stay overnight next week and see how you like it. You can sleep at Auntie Stella's and I think it's a good idea. Get a feel for it, see what the place is like, Ma. They really love it there and you know how independent they are."

"Independent? They're like three Siamese twins."

"They're on their own, in their own apartments."

"Why do I have to go overnight? I'll go to lunch, I can see it in daylight."

"Ma, give it a chance, please." Louisa's voice grew gentler, even pleading as she went on, but her eyes meant business. "What's one night? You'll go, you'll get a feeling for what it's like to live there, you'll come home the next day. No one's trying to force you out, but an apartment might be the best thing."

"I'm not going to an old folks' home," Glorie said, standing up from the table.

"Ma, it's not an old folks' home, it's an apartment building."

"I'm not going to an old folks' apartment building," she said, turning to look at her daughter. "What would your father say if he was here?"

"Ma, please, do it for me, OK? Do I ever ask you for anything?

Don't embarrass me with the Aunts, I already told them you'd come."

"Do I have a choice?"

"No."

We'll see about that, thought Glorie. "All right," she said, "I'll visit. Let's get this over with."

"Good. Thank you. How about next Tuesday? Will you call Auntie Stella and set it up?"

"*You* call Auntie Stella! You do what you want. You will anyway," Glorie yelled, walking into the next room and turning on TV.

Louisa put on her coat and said over her shoulder as she left, "Tuesday, Ma. No kidding."

Chapter 7

GLORIE COULD SEE HERSELF walking down the dim, narrow corridor, handcuffs cutting into her wrists behind her. She was wearing a faded, pale blue prison dress that did nothing for her complexion. The matron walked in front of her, carrying Louisa's flowered overnight case.

"Cheer up, Ma, you're not going to jail," Louisa said, but she was wrong. They took a sharp left down an even darker corridor. All the floors were carpeted in violent bright orange.

"This is what I get. I never even made you go to camp when you were a kid," she told Louisa.

"Camp never came up, what are you talking about?"

"Well, if it had come up I wouldn't have made you go."

"Don't let Aunt Stella hear you," Louisa said. "We're here." And she rang the bell.

Louisa had agreed to let Glorie wait until late afternoon to begin her visit, so she had almost a full day at home. After lunch on Tuesday she started packing the overnight bag Louisa loaned her. "Maybe I should have pajamas with feet in them and a sleeping bag. We'll probably roast marshmallows, this is supposed to be such a happy camping trip," she told Jack.

"Just go, get it over with, Glorie," was all he would say. "We agreed on this. It will be over soon and you'll shut Patrick up for a good long time."

I've never slept in a strange bed in my whole life. Never, she thought as she put a good, pink chiffon nightgown and her thick white terry robe in the bag. She had visited Frank in Pennsylvania a couple of times before he got too weak. In the year before Josie died, when she was so sick, Glorie had spent nights at a time at her bedside, holding her hand, giving her water, telling her about silly things to occupy her mind, praying whenever Josie wanted to, until Jack had put his foot down. "I'm taking you home for a while. You have to get some sleep." He had practically carried her home from Al Jr.'s. But she had never slept at a stranger's.

When she packed her toothpaste and face soap she felt nauseous. She checked the window locks, checked the doors, wondered if she should take the pans out of the big cupboards and leave those doors open so no one could possibly be hiding in them when she got back. As she walked down the front steps toward Louisa, waiting across the street in her driveway, she had a sudden flash of herself dragging the little girl kicking and screaming to first grade. "Don't leave me alone," Louisa had cried. "Promise me you'll stay all day." And Glorie had stood in the corridor for ninety minutes, until she was sure Louisa wouldn't rush out of the classroom looking for her. This was her thanks, sent to the electric chair. And for what? She hadn't killed anybody; she hadn't harmed anybody; she wasn't stealing the money to keep up this house — though bank robbery might come next if Patrick didn't leave her alone.

"I can carry this. It's light," she said, annoyed at Jack as she crossed the street.

What am I saying? she thought. Maybe I belong with those

crazy Aunts. I have to concentrate on this visit. I can't embarrass Louisa. Jack is right, it will be over soon enough. I don't have to like it.

"Ma, try to have a good time, will you?" Louisa told her on the way. "They're not strangers, you know, they're family, and they're being very nice to you, so please get rid of that long face."

"I'll smile when I get there," said Glorie, and looked out the side window of the car.

Glorie knew the building, a high-rise shoe box beyond the downtown shopping area, but she had never been inside. As she and Louisa walked through the wide lobby, they didn't pass anyone who looked especially feeble. There were no wheelchairs and only one man with a walker, who got on the elevator with them.

"But let's face it," she told Jack, "no one is jogging out the door here."

As they went up to the sixteenth floor, she asked Louisa, "What if there's a fire or the electricity goes out? Are we supposed to walk down sixteen flights? What kind of place is this for old people?"

"There are generators, Ma, don't worry," Louisa said. "Or maybe you should have packed a parachute for emergencies. That's what you and the Aunts can do, make parachutes for yourselves. I can see the three of you sitting around sewing. Yours would be pretty, with flowers, right?"

"You can't make me laugh, don't bother. What time will you pick me up tomorrow?"

"Ma, I'll call in the morning." They were at the end of the dim prison corridor with the orange carpets, and Louisa was ringing the doorbell of doom.

"Here you are!" Stella said as she opened the door and kissed

Louisa and Glorie. "I'm so glad you made it. Toni and Gemma are out shopping for dinner."

Thank God.

"We're going all out, making a real celebration for you, Gloria. Louisa, sweetheart, before you go can you help me open up the couch? It has a very good mattress, Gloria, Sealy Posturepedic, but I know you have a bad back, so you take my bed and I'll be fine here."

Glorie thought she was supposed to politely refuse this offer, but Sealy Posturepedic or not, she couldn't survive on that low sofa bed. Maybe she could pretend to sleep there and sit up in a straight chair.

"No, I can't take your bed," she told Stella. She sounded perfectly sincere; there was no need for Louisa to roll her eyes that way.

"I insist. It's my house, no arguments. You're the guest. Do you want to unpack your clothes, hang some things up in the closet?"

"I'm going to go now before I get a ticket," said Louisa. "I'll call you tomorrow, Ma. You have a good time," and she pecked her mother on the cheek as if she were going to the corner for bread. Behind Stella's back she opened her eyes wider and raised her eyebrows as if to say "Behave!" and walked away.

"Here's the bedroom," said Stella, opening the closet. "There are fresh sheets on the bed and an extra quilt and plenty of hangers, so make yourself at home. Would you like a nice hot cup of tea?"

"Yes, that would be good," said Glorie. "I only have this one dress to hang up." She put it in the neat, small closet, then went to join Stella. Her kitchen seemed efficient and snug.

As Stella made tea Glorie looked across the half-wall partition to the living room and said, "It looks very homey here, you have a very pretty place." She tried not to sound surprised.

Stella's living room was filled with embroidered pillows she had made over the years. On the mahogany end tables were white lace doilies, and on top of the doilies ornate lamps that looked old enough to be wedding presents. They were much too big for this apartment. There was a new beige couch and armchairs in nubby cotton, and big, blooming red geraniums on the windowsills. One table near the sofa was cluttered with framed photographs: a large gilt-framed wedding portrait of Stella and Gus; one of Louisa and Patrick with all the kids and grandkids; one of the Aunts on the Atlantic City boardwalk wearing sun visors that said MERV GRIFFIN'S RESORTS CASINO.

Stella seemed comfortable here, with her modern furniture and her little treasures. But how many mementos and pieces of oversized furniture had she been forced to toss out or give to reckless nieces and nephews who would never know what they meant?

Stella carried a tea tray into the living room, stepping around the pillows and sofa cushions Louisa had piled on the floor. "Look at this pillow," she said, holding up a white one with red and yellow roses embroidered on it. "Louisa made that for my birthday right after I moved in here. Gus didn't like so many flowery things, but now I do as I please."

"You've really made it lovely," Glorie said. There was a lot she needed to ask Stella. Toni and Gemma were probably closing in on them right now, already in the lobby, getting into the elevator. "How long have you been here?" she asked.

"Oh, it must be . . . eight years now. I didn't move here right away after Gus died. That was ten years ago. I remember you and Jack came to the funeral and then back to the house after. It meant so much to me to have everybody there."

"And you were at Jack's funeral," said Glorie. "I don't remember everything from that day, but I know you and Gemma were right there, and you sent beautiful flowers."

"Funny how that is. I remember every detail from Gus's funeral, and the wake too. I remember who showed up and who didn't, who sent cards and who didn't. And you know, I can't forgive the people who didn't. I never thought I'd be like that, but when it happens to you . . ."

A key sounded in the lock.

"Oh, that's the girls. We all have keys to each other's apartments. I better see if they need help carrying the groceries," Stella said, getting up and running to the door.

"Twelve dollars a pound for fish, could you believe it?" yelled Toni from the door. "We hadda get the chicken. Is she here yet?"

Glorie stood up. "Gloria," Gemma said slowly and formally, "welcome, welcome to our home. Really Stella's home, but welcome anyway."

"We gotta put the food away and then give Gloria the grand tour of the building," said Toni. "I didn't think you'd really come. I thought you'd pretend to have a sore throat or something." She said this as if it were a polite observation.

"Ooo-*maa,* look at that pretty suit you're wearing, Gloria. And look at us, we all look like we're going skiing in these big sweaters we knitted."

"We're gonna ski to the basement," said Toni.

As soon as they put the food away, the pack traveled. Glorie couldn't believe she was one of them.

Gemma's apartment was right next door to Stella's and looked so similar it was as if the apartments were sisters, with a family resemblance around the nubby couches and the old-fashioned lamps. Glorie couldn't pay complete attention because Gemma's cat kept trying to scratch her ankles. The Aunts treated that cat like a baby. "Did you miss us, Bambi?" Leave it to Gemma to name a cat after a deer. "Give me a smooch, Bambi." Glorie hoped Bambi didn't have fleas.

"I keep saying we ought to knock down the wall between Stella's apartment and mine, or at least cut a passageway through," Gemma said.

"Like those swinging dog and cat doors people have on their houses," Stella laughed. "We're always joking about that. Can't you see us walking through on our hands and knees to get across?"

"Come look at the view, Gloria," Gemma said, at the same time as a yappy dog in the apartment on the other side barked. "Excuse me, Gloria," Gemma said softly. Then she screamed in a voice ten times louder than Glorie had ever heard her use before, "Pipe down, Spike!" The dog stopped yapping.

"Was he barking at you, Bambi?" Stella cooed.

"As I was saying, there's a gorgeous view from here," said Gemma.

"That guy next door's a weirdo," said Toni. "His name is Spike, so what does he names his dog? Spike. They don't even look alike."

"Well, it makes sense to me," said Gemma. "If he yells 'Spike,' only the dog will answer. He's not going to answer himself."

"If he had a wife and she yelled 'Spike,' then it would be confusing," said Stella.

"What happens if the dog yells 'Spike'?" Glorie asked with a very straight face.

Gemma looked worried for a minute. "Oh yeah." She laughed. "Gloria has that same sense of humor as Louisa. That's something she would say."

"That guy's a weirdo, I don't care what anybody says," said Toni. "Let's leave him be and show Gloria my apartment now."

Glorie wished she had a camera for this one.

They took the elevator five floors down to Toni's place, which had orange-flowered drapes, a green paisley slipcover on the couch, a brown armchair, but at least no pets. The apartment was exactly the same as Stella's and Gemma's: a living room, a kitchen–dining area and a bedroom, all medium-sized, square, invented to make Glorie stir-crazy. In each one the pictures, vases, lamps — all the mementos salvaged from the Aunts' real homes — seemed less cheering, more pathetic than they had in Stella's.

"What do you think?" Toni asked. "You like it?"

"It's unbelievable what you can do with these places," Glorie told her.

"Wait'll you see the basement. We saved the best for last," Toni said with all the pep of a salesman showing a client the unique, irresistible feature that would clinch the deal.

"Get ready," Glorie told Jack, "for the thrill of a lifetime."

They stepped off the elevator into a dungeon of dark green cinder blocks. They peeked into a laundry room where some men and women sat at long tables folding clothes and talking, and others sat on benches staring at the dryers spinning around. The Aunts waved to people and said hi and Stella kept them moving.

They went into the game room, a big open space with dark wood paneling. This was the famous bingo basement of the shoe box building. A few people sat in chairs reading or watching some old Rock Hudson movie on television. A group of men in baseball caps sat at a round table playing cards. And a woman with long, frizzled gray hair and a dirty Red Sox sweatshirt wandered around the room mumbling to herself. "Poor soul," said Stella. "She talks to herself. Her neighbor says he can hear her through the wall sometimes walking in circles and saying,

'They killed my best girlfriend, I don't want them to kill me, I didn't know they were mob.' Her family doesn't want to take her back but something has to be done, poor thing. She's harmless, Gloria, don't be afraid."

"Too bad you're not here on luau night," Toni said. "We all come down and eat Hawaiian food and wear those leis, you know, those plastic flower things around your neck, and flowers in our hair. It's very exotic, you'd like it."

"What's Hawaiian food?" Glorie asked.

"Oh, you know, ham and pineapples, stuff like that."

"Here he comes," Gemma whispered to Toni. A man who had been watching television excused himself and headed toward the Aunts. "Good afternoon, ladies," he said. He was tall and bald and wore a suit jacket, and actually bowed in front of them. "You have a new neighbor with you today?"

"No, she's visiting," said Stella. "Gloria, this is Martin. This is our friend Gloria. She came to look the place over." Glorie could hear Gemma and Toni whispering and giggling behind her.

"You would be a beautiful addition to our building," Martin told her, and Glorie smiled and flushed and said, "Thank you," just before Toni broke in.

"Is it true you took Florence to the movies yesterday, Martin? We was wondering."

"We should go start dinner now," said Stella, and she took Glorie by the arm and led her away. "Toni, Gemma, we have to go now," she said firmly, and the other Aunts trailed behind, whispering to each other.

"Martin is a flirt and he talks like he came out of a book but he's harmless," said Stella. "He'd never try to corner you in the laundry room or anything, he's a real gentleman. I don't know why those two give him such a hard time."

In the elevator, Glorie told Jack, "They didn't cancel *Peyton*

Place from TV. They moved it to this old folks' apartment building." Did Stella like Martin? Did Martin like Glorie? Was the mob after the gray-haired woman's best girlfriend? They had reached the sixteenth floor again, and Glorie had lost track of what Toni was babbling about.

"So, what do you think, Gloria?" Gemma asked as they got back to Stella's door.

"I can see why all of you like it here."

"I told you she'd like it," Toni yelled. "Who wouldn't like this? We shoulda bet. I wanted to bet, Gloria, cause Gemma and Stella said this wasn't your kinda place, I wanted to bet but they wouldn't go for it. I knew you'd like it. Who wouldn't?"

They started, all three of them, to make dinner. "Gloria, you're the guest, you sit down and relax," Gemma said.

"Let me do something. I feel bad you're going to all this trouble."

All this trouble for nothing, she thought.

"Ooo-*maa,* it's no trouble," they all squealed.

"At least let me set the table," she said. She took her time, lining up the spoons and forks and knives just so. Gemma drawled, "Make sure the chicken isn't pink. You can get sick from eating pink chicken, I heard that on the news."

Toni yelled, "I wish I could make myself drink the broth from those boiled carrots. It keeps all the vitamins in, but pee-*uuu,* what a taste. I thought I'd throw up when I tried it once. Never again, only the carrots for me. Plenty of nutrition left in carrots."

"We usually watch the news while we're eating dinner, but tonight we're going to talk to you instead," Gemma said sweetly.

"Oh no, no, let's watch the news," Glorie said. "I want a picture of what it's like to live here. I want to know what your day is like. Don't do anything unusual for me." So she got out of hearing more details about window washing in the building ("You have to pay extra to have them clean inside but it's worth it, they do a bee-yoo-tee-ful job.") and got to watch Tom Brokaw ("He's the cutest one," said Gemma) while eating their chicken and carrots and salad.

"You sit there, Gloria, while we get dessert," Gemma said. Together, Gemma and Stella carried out a chocolate cake from the bakery and put it in front of her. WELCOME GLORIA was written in pink frosting.

"We were going to have you blow out candles, but Stella said that would be too much," said Gemma. "But you cut the cake and make a wish."

Glorie stood up at her chair and put the knife on the cake. "Thank you," she said. "What a sweet thing to do. This means a lot to me." It did. Why would they go to all this trouble for her? Would she have done it for them? She felt her eyes getting moist and stared hard at the cake for a few seconds until it passed. "I'll make a wish for all of us. To health and friendship," she said, pushing the knife into the cake.

"You're not supposed to tell," Toni yelled. "It won't come true."

"Too late now," said Gemma.

"Cut nice big pieces, Gloria," Stella told her.

"We're glad you didn't freeze to death in that storm," Toni said as she dug in. "What a shock that would have been to read about you in the paper the next day. What?" she said suddenly, looking at Gemma next to her.

"I don't think Gloria wants to talk about that," said Gemma. "Let's talk about happy things."

"What'd I say? I'm glad she didn't die. That's happy."

"I was very stupid," Glorie said. "I'm lucky Pat Jr. and Emily rescued me. They're such wonderful kids, both of them."

"But you musta been scared," Toni said to Glorie, then turned to glare bug-eyed at Gemma.

"I was at the time, but, you know, it left me feeling kind of brave. I figure if I can get through that, I can get through anything."

"You could survive living here," said Gemma. "Guys like Martin would be nothing to put up with after freezing to death in a blizzard."

"Martin's not so bad," said Stella. "Why do you two always pick on him?"

"That stuffed-shirt snob," said Toni. "Where does he think he comes from, England?"

"Maybe he does come from England," Stella told her. "How do you know where he comes from?"

"Let's behave in front of Gloria," Gemma said calmly.

"All I'm saying is, Toni could talk to him before she judges him," Stella said, still heated up.

"I don't need to talk to a stuffed shirt like that. I had a good man of my own. He was never a snob and he was never a dirty old man even when he was old."

"Speaking of dirty old men, where was Phil today?" Glorie asked. She thought she could help break the tension, but she did better than that. All the Aunts started giggling uncontrollably.

"You're not gonna believe this," Toni yelled. "He's got a part-time job . . ." They were all laughing so much they could hardly talk. "In a dry cleaner's."

Glorie didn't get it. "What's wrong with that?"

"Cause he's the one that never takes a bath," Gemma explained slowly. "Don't you remember, we told you at Christmas?"

"Gloria doesn't know him the way we do, but believe me, Gloria, it's funny," Stella said, wiping her eyes with her napkin.

Glorie smiled. "I'm in a loony bin," she told Jack calmly. "We'll probably have to play games next."

"We gonna play rummy?" Toni asked.

"Let's load the dishwasher first," Gemma said, starting to clear the table. "We have all the modern conveniences here," she told Glorie. "You'd like living here, I think."

Before she could catch herself, Glorie said, "Do you all work on commission?" She wanted to kick herself. After they'd been so nice about the cake, too. But no one seemed upset.

"I wish I worked on commission, I could rent this whole building," said Toni. "So we gonna play rummy or what?"

"I don't know," said Stella. "Gloria's the guest. Do you want to play cards? Or watch the TV?"

"Let's watch TV," said Glorie.

"Oh, come on, we'll teach you how to play," said Toni.

"You two play, and Gloria and I will watch TV," said Stella. "I think there's a good detective picture on."

Gemma headed toward the living room, then stopped and looked blank.

"We have to sit at the kitchen table and play tonight, Gemma, because there's no place left to sit unless we want to lay down on the sofa bed," Toni said. "Sit down. My deal."

Glorie relaxed in the armchair, pretending to be absorbed in the silly detective show. There was a man with a toupee and a fake mustache; you weren't supposed to know if he was a murderer or a hero in disguise. She could overhear the card game.

"I knock," Gemma said, tapping her knuckles on the table.

"You can't knock, Gem, this is rummy," Toni yelled. Glorie heard her say that several times.

Every now and then Stella would make some comment on the

show. "Ooo-*maa*, I bet he's gonna kill her to shut her up. What do you think, Gloria?"

"I think you're right," Glorie would say, whatever it was. If Jack were here watching this with her, the way they used to, he would have made up a story about these sisters: they could have their own TV program, three undercover detectives with gray bubble hair. They could go anywhere invisibly because no man would look at them twice. They could wear trench coats and men's hats and fake mustaches and not even look suspicious. Gemma would jump up from behind the checkout at the market, wag her finger and drawl to a well-dressed woman with a large leather purse, "Ooo-*maa*, I saw you put that steak in your bag." Then Toni would pop up and say, "Twelve dollars a pound, who could blame her for stealing?" Stella would stand up and say, "Twelve dollars, that's no excuse, Toni, what are you saying? Call the manager." They'd be so successful they'd have their own pinup, the three ooo-maas in trench coats and brown orthopedic shoes lining the walls of old folks' apartment buildings everywhere.

"Oh, look, she's finally smiling," Toni said from the table on the other side of the partition. "Gloria, you must like this picture. Gemma, come on, discard."

"Ooo, yeah, I forgot to discard. Let me count my cards."

At 11:00 Gemma said, "Wouldn't it be funny if we all stayed here tonight? Like a pajama party. We can make hot chocolate and sit up to watch Johnny Carson."

"Johnny Carson retired, Gemma," Stella said.

"Johnny retired? When?"

"A long time ago."

"So we don't have to watch him."

"You do what you want, I'm sleeping in my own soft, comfortable bed," said Toni, "and I'm going there now. How could you not know about Johnny Carson? You need a lot of sleep, Gemma. He's a multimillionaire, he doesn't have to work anymore."

"I thought we were watching Ralph Kramden cause we liked him better."

"They're not even on at the same time, never was."

"Oh, all right, I'll go, too," said Gemma. "We'll be back for breakfast." She kissed her sister and Glorie good night.

"Gloria, you can have the bathroom first," said Stella. Glorie hurried to wash her face and brush and floss her teeth, so she wouldn't keep Stella up.

"Let me know if there's anything you need," Stella said when Glorie headed toward the bedroom.

"No, I'm all set," Glorie said. "Are you really all right on that couch? It's not too late to trade."

"Oh, no, it's fine, believe me. I don't sleep that much anyway, I wake up early, I'll try not to make too much noise in the morning."

"Don't worry. Good night." But Glorie stopped as she was heading into the bedroom. She turned and asked Stella, "You are happy here, aren't you? You don't miss your old house."

"I can't say I don't miss it," Stella said, sitting on the edge of the made-up sofa bed. "But it wasn't good for me to stay." For a second Glorie shuddered the way she had in the blizzard; Stella spoke as if she had forced herself to say all this long ago and repeated it so often she was convinced it was true. "It wasn't good for me," she said again, like a brainwashed woman, and Glorie felt herself blowing down Hopkins Street. "I was so lonely there, you wouldn't believe it. I'd walk around and see Gus's chair or make supper for myself. Sometimes I would eat crackers and peanut butter for supper because I didn't feel like cooking just for me. Gemma visited, but she doesn't drive, so it was hard.

I was getting to feel so sorry for myself. I don't feel sorry for myself here, not very much."

"I don't feel sorry for myself alone," Glorie said matter-of-factly.

"No, I didn't say you did. We're all different. Moving here was the best thing I could have done. It would be different if I didn't have my sister and Toni, naturally. But it's healthier for me here."

Glorie stood still in the doorway. "Wasn't it hard to give up your house? I don't think I could leave mine. It's the last thing I have of my own. It's mine and it keeps me close to Jack, you know what I mean?"

"Oh, don't I know that feeling," said Stella. "I think that never goes away. But it's better for me here. Plus, the house was too much to handle by myself — repairs, the lawn, the snow, the boiler, I got so sick of it. I was always calling Patrick for help, so to say the truth I wasn't that independent."

"Did Patrick make you sell it?" Glorie asked.

"Oh, no, he didn't make me. He thought it was a good idea. And you know what? He was right. He means well, Gloria. He's not always wrong. Louisa and Patrick love you very much, they want the best for you."

Coming from a brainwashed person, that didn't reassure her.

"I know they do," said Glorie. "I'll see you in the morning, Stella. Thanks for everything. Good night."

Alone in the bedroom, Glorie changed slowly. "To say the truth," she told Jack, "I'm too jumpy to sleep."

She climbed in bed and noticed that Stella kept her most precious photographs in this room, as if to inspire her dreams — snapshots in gold or silver frames on the night table and dresser, all of Gus not long before he died. He was sitting under a tree in their backyard, dozing in his favorite chair in the living room, sitting at the kitchen table with company. He was an old man frozen in time, in the most ordinary poses, as if Stella could preserve him as he was in those last moments.

In Jack's last year Glorie wanted desperately to buy a camera, to photograph him endlessly, but it would have been too alarming, too obvious that she was hoarding these shots against the day when she would need them. It would have been too much like saying, "You're leaving me." So she stared and stared, memorizing every crease around his eyes, the way they looked when he was sad, how they deepened when he laughed. At birthdays she whispered to Blanche and Pat Jr., "Try to get your grandfather in that shot, but don't let on, you know he hates having his picture taken." When she had begged for these pictures after the funeral, it turned out Jack was usually hidden behind a child or a balloon or someone passing by.

She settled under the blankets in Stella's bed and turned off the light, feeling the strangeness of this dark, silent room. She put her right hand on her left shoulder. She wanted to feel Jack with her, protecting her from all these people who were tugging at her, trying to make her someone else, trying to make her leave him behind. In the dark they could be alone together; he could make her feel safe in enemy land.

Then she heard Gemma from her bedroom on the other side of the wall. "Dear Lord," Gemma said, and Glorie tried not to hear her pray. But she listened hard when she realized Gemma was chanting, "I can't sleep, I can't sleep, I can't sleep. Why can't I sleep? When will I sleep?"

Please take me home, Jack, Glorie thought, careful not to move her lips or breathe a word out loud in this room with Kleenex walls.

"Why can't I sleep?" was all she heard.

Do you hear her, Jack?

Of course he didn't. Why would Jack follow her to this place?

When he was alive he wouldn't even come into the supermarket with her. He sat in the parking lot and unloaded the bags from the cart when she wheeled it out. Why would he come to a pajama party at an old ladies' loony bin? He would never move with her to a brick shoe box like this, with luau nights and bingo sharks. The Spikes were pretty funny, though. A man and a dog named Spike; at least this trip was good for a laugh. She could tell him about it tomorrow.

Her body was jangly and achy, though she'd had decaf with the cake. It seemed like hours before she fell asleep to the sound of Stella and Gemma snoring, one on either side of the wall.

They even snore alike, she thought as she drifted off.

If Josie were alive she could come live with me in my house. Maybe we'd snore alike, who knows?

I could put rainbows on the walls.

Josie can have the sewing room, we'll get a pull-out couch.

We'll get a dog, a mad dog like Lassie.

She jumped awake, shivering and sweating, heartsick from a dream too terrifying to remember. All she knew was that in the split second before she woke, a moment she could almost reach back and recall, she was as frightened and as sad as she had ever been. It felt as if, inside the dream, the dream itself was a shapeless monster that chased her as she ran along a black corridor until she got to the edge of a well, a dark hole that held all sorts of horrors she had never imagined. This terror was new, different from those moments when her sleeping mind replayed Jack's death or funeral. This dream was out to get her. She was afraid to go back to sleep. She knew there was no use trying to remember what was inside the black shapeless dream that chased her. But if she slept it would be waiting for her.

She was awake for good, in the middle of the night, in a

dark, unfamiliar room. As her eyes adjusted she could make out Stella's dresser and the picture frames on the nightstand as they caught eerie glints of light poking in from a crack between the drapes. She trembled under two blankets and a quilt. Maybe this visit was some smart trick of Louisa's after all: send her to the Aunts for a night and her little bedroom across the street would begin to feel like home.

She imagined her bedroom transformed into a shrine like this one, with pictures of Jack everywhere. What a joke. To turn that room into a true shrine she would have to move in the double bed, the television, her gopher coat, a whole life. She didn't need pictures to remember Jack, not as long as her world stayed ready for him to step back into it.

Stella is more realistic than I am, Glorie thought. She's healthier. Jack belongs with those pictures on the table. Maybe I can be brainwashed too.

Or maybe it was Stella who should face facts. She dreamed that Gus could step out of those pictures, that's why they were all so new, as if she could reach out, pick up a photograph and have him appear, full-size, looking the way he had when he left.

I want those last years back, Glorie thought. If I could have any years back, I'd want those last ones.

It was just like Jack to make things easy on her. He managed things so smoothly that he never had to retire, he simply slowed down until he was running the business from the basement, with part-time help to do small jobs and renovations for old customers. Sometimes they needed a marble threshold like the ones he had put in years before and no one else had anymore. Sometimes bigger companies sent him repair jobs — a cracked tile, a patio table — too small for them to care about. It was enough to keep him busy.

He had kept an eye on Pat Jr. "He could be a businessman," he used to tell Glorie, and on the day their grandson graduated from college Jack took him aside at the family celebration and offered him the business. "It's all decided, I'm going to law school," Pat Jr. said. "I thought we settled this." Jack hadn't thought so; he thought he'd been hinting around and waiting for the right moment to bring it up.

"There are lawyers who are businessmen," Jack said.

"It's not practical, Grandpa," Pat Jr. said, and Glorie saw him throw a desperate look at his mother.

Jack was too proud to argue; he kept the business alive himself. "It's a little income," he said. "It's good to have something coming in."

He still went to the basement office early every morning, but in the last few years he started coming upstairs earlier and earlier — at first because he was bored. Then, Glorie realized, because he was tired. He would come upstairs for lunch, then come back for good at 4:00, then 3:00 or 2:00. Then he was coming for lunch and staying with her the rest of the day. Sometimes they went for a drive and ice cream after lunch. After the first year, he always took an afternoon nap. Those times reminded Glorie of the early days around the chicken coop when they were first married and his work let him stay close, drifting in and out of their house all day long.

Jack and his cousin were still scrimping to start the grocery when he started reading about the stock market crash and bad times ahead. At first he thought it had nothing to do with them; they didn't even know anyone who owned stock. Then he started worrying that bad times were ahead for everyone. "I read it in the paper, we better be careful. This is going to hit everybody," he said, but no one listened, until half the people they knew started losing their jobs at the mill. Glorie's father depended on Frank now. Manny's wife took in sewing at home. And Jack started to make money on the grain business.

"This isn't what I planned," he would say at night, doing the books and shaking his head. But almost every house in the neighborhood kept chickens for eggs and meat. They all needed grain and Jack was doing fine. Sometimes he was paid in credit at the hardware store or the cheese store or the bakery. He was paid in chickens more often than they liked, and Glorie found herself in the backyard again, less squeamish than before, shooing the chickens away as she walked toward the trough, training them with the stern tone of her voice to leave her alone. She tried barking, "Get out of my way!" but they scattered so quickly that feathers flew everywhere, on her hair, on her clothes, in her mouth. So she lowered her voice and spit out, "*Move!*" and tried to get it all over with in a few minutes.

She learned to pluck chickens, though she always made Jack wring their necks. "I mean it," he promised. "When we get out of this I'm going to wring their necks for fun."

He was around the house a lot, going out to make deliveries, coming home for lunch. When Louisa was an infant he could play with her during the day, hold her anytime. He could come home early and have a glass of wine with Glorie in the afternoon. And when he moved the marble business back to the basement all those years later, when he started coming upstairs for lunch and spending half the day with Glorie, it was like those early days only easier.

Glorie felt so safe and calm, until Jack finished his soup one afternoon and asked her to make a doctor's appointment for him. No one ever hated doctors more than he did. How awful he must have felt to be ready for that, how much worry he must have been keeping from her.

She called Louisa right away, and their daughter took care of everything. She insisted on driving them to the doctor's and to all the tests, and went back with them to hear that Jack had angina, not so unusual in a man his age. This doctor was calm, as if to say, "We all die," as he gave Jack pills and instructions and said he should be fine if he took care of himself.

Glorie wanted to see another doctor, someone with a magic cure and the fountain of youth bubbling out of his office water cooler. She needed someone to tell her how to save him. Jack refused. "You heard him, I'll be fine if I take care of myself," he said. "And if I'm not going to be fine there's nothing I can do about it, is there? I'm not going to let a lot of doctors waste my time and money for nothing. They all say the same thing, they're all in this together."

Glorie made healthier food, but Jack still wanted macaroni and meatballs twice a week, though he ate bird-sized portions. She made him fruit drinks, putting bananas and apples and oranges in the blender; they looked like gloop but tasted delicious and she told herself this would help him.

One day she looked at Jack as he walked into the bedroom for his nap and realized: He's an old man. She thought: He's going to die. And for a second it felt as if her own heart had stopped for good. Nothing was ever as terrifying as that moment when she knew she would have to lose him, not even the moment nearly a year later when it finally happened. She went on making health drinks with a smile on her face and a viper curled in her stomach waiting to attack.

She began to notice all the signs of his aging that she had somehow never seen. He didn't shave quite as well as he used to. His feet were freezing all the time. He walked more cautiously, and drove so slowly she worried that he shouldn't be on the road at all, but she didn't try to stop him. They always went out together now and she would rather die in an accident with him than suggest he was too old to drive. She treasured all these small signs that he was still alive.

They were pretending he could go on forever, so they never talked about what was happening. But whenever a thought of death crossed Glorie's mind — a mention on TV, news that a former neighbor had cancer — Glorie would say three Hail Marys very fast to protect Jack. She didn't believe it would help but was too afraid to stop. Sometimes dozens of times a day she would race through the prayers, skimming over the words so fast they were dropped and crunched together and made no sense. The prayer didn't matter; what mattered was that she made the gesture, these offerings of her time and her thoughts. What mattered was that she loved him enough to stop everything — blocking out the TV or the conversation, regardless how interesting or important — to protect him any desperate way she could.

One Sunday he sat at Louisa's dinner table and said, out of nowhere, "I don't feel just right." They all jumped and offered to get a doctor.

"I don't mean this minute. I mean all the time. I can't put my finger on it, but I don't feel just right."

Pat Jr. got the name of a good heart specialist, but Jack wouldn't go. His old doctor kept saying there was no reason he shouldn't be fine if he took care of himself. He said it again two days before Jack died.

Jack went away but Glorie's terror of losing him stayed. It had followed her here to this stranger's bed, to the edge of the black hole of her dream. She wasn't shaking anymore; she wasn't even scared. What else could anyone do to her?

The next morning Glorie waited until she heard Stella walking around before she got up. Too little sleep always made her nauseous, but she was so happy to be going home that she felt she could get through anything.

She dressed quickly for breakfast. Toni and Gemma turned up at 7:30 in their bathrobes. Toni had taken the elevator ride in a green velour robe and slipper socks. Glorie thought that was pretty comic. Now that she was about to be sprung, she was cheerful enough to joke with the Aunts.

"So you have to let me know about that Florence," Glorie said over coffee. "I want to know if Martin really took her to the movies. What did they go to see? And *what* was the rating?" They all laughed. Glorie was so tired she was goofy, but who cared? "Now you're gettin' into the swing of things," said Toni. "I like you this way. See, I told you she'd come around."

They like me this way, she thought, the way I like Ada when she's sad and acting like somebody else.

It was only 8:00 when the phone rang. Louisa wasn't letting Glorie hang in suspense after all. "I have some errands but I can be there around eleven, OK?" she asked.

"That's good, no problem. Come whenever you like," Glorie said cheerfully. She meant it. She could wait until eleven to be taken home. Her home would still be there and her plan could wait till then.

Chapter 8

"SO HOW WAS THE SLEEPOVER, Ma? Did they chain you to the bedpost and refuse to give you dinner?"

"Yes, as a matter of fact they did," Glorie said. "This is very good lasagna, honey."

Louisa had pulled up in her driveway without a glance across the street and said, "Come on in and have lunch with me," as if it were an order.

"OK," said Glorie.

It's only lunch, she thought. Might as well be agreeable and keep Louisa off guard.

"No, really, how was it?" Louisa was asking from across the kitchen table.

"They were fine, but it's not a place for me, you knew that. There's no privacy at all. Everyone's in and out of everyone else's apartment. Everyone knows everyone's business. If you try to do your laundry it's like going to the Fourth of July parade. Definitely not."

"You could have privacy if you want. You wouldn't live right next door to the Aunts."

"They'd find me. They have radar."

"There are other buildings like that, not as nice though."

"They'd still find me."

"What did they ever do to you, Ma? What was so bad about being there?" Now Louisa was getting annoyed, and Glorie had no choice. She was dazed and nauseous from lack of sleep, but it was time to put her plan into action.

"Well, for one thing they all talk to themselves." Her voice was full of concern.

"They talk to each other," Louisa said.

"No, they talk to themselves. Gemma talks herself to sleep, like a crazy lady. I heard her talking to herself and singing through the wall next door."

"You were eavesdropping again?"

"I couldn't help it," Glorie said. "And what do you mean 'again'? I don't pry into anybody's business, you know me."

"I know you hear every word we say around here, come on now."

"Don't make those eyes at me, Louisa. I never eavesdrop, I happened to overhear Gemma talking crazy to herself. She thinks the mob has a contract on her life, and she's afraid if she says anything they'll find out and kill her faster. She wanders around her apartment singing, 'If they could see me now, in my cement overshoes,' but she didn't sound too cheerful. Personally, I think she's been watching too much TV and now she's living in a dream world, poor soul. You and Patrick should have her examined. Living in a dream world is a terrible thing," Glorie said, shaking her head and looking down into her lasagna.

"All right, so she talks to herself. Aunt Gemma always had a vivid imagination." Louisa sounded sure of herself but looked worried. "She's old and she talks to herself. So what?"

"The chicken was blood red, the color of this tomato sauce.

You should see how they eat. They're going to poison themselves."

"You don't have to eat with them, Ma." Louisa's voice became playful, as if this were some new guessing game. "Besides, I know Aunt Stella is a wonderful cook. You're exaggerating."

"Louisa, this is serious." Glorie looked into Louisa's eyes so sincerely and sounded so concerned that Oprah herself would have been jealous. "Forget the chicken. Forget that they're crazy. I have something very serious to tell you. They're terrified of robbers. I'm telling you because they're afraid to tell you, and they'll deny it if you ask them, but they're afraid to go out of their own apartments after dark. They're afraid to go into the hall. Four people have been mugged in their hallway in the last month."

"In their building?"

"In their *hall*way, right outside Stella and Gemma's *door*. There's a big cover-up going on in that building. The superintendent threatens them. He says to stay inside and if they tell anyone he'll have them evicted. Why do you think they always make such a big deal about how much they like their apartments. 'Ooo-*maa*, how we love our apartments!' That guy is running some racket there." Glorie shook her head sadly. "Don't tell them I squealed, I promised not to. They trusted me because they didn't want to see me get in the same mess they're in."

Louisa looked suspicious. "They're not really good at keeping secrets, Ma. That would be a pretty big one for them to keep."

"They do it for you, dear," said Glorie. "Because they don't want you and Patrick to be upset, and they don't want to be a burden to you if they're kicked out on the street."

"Maybe I should call the police anonymously."

Glorie could see this was a trap. "Go ahead," she said, cool as could be. "And while you're at it tell them about the rats."

"Which ones are the rats? If someone ratted the police would check it out, that would solve everything."

"Not human rats, pay attention. Rats. Overgrown mice, rats. I saw one in the laundry room but I didn't say anything to the Aunts because I didn't want to embarrass them."

"A big rat?" asked Louisa.

"Not so very big," Glorie said primly, wiping her mouth with a napkin. "I'd say medium-sized."

"Well, I'm glad you didn't embarrass them."

"And there's gambling going on in that building too."

"Yeah, bingo."

"No, illegal, private games. One day they're all going to get raided and you'll have to bail them out. I don't want to be there when that happens."

Glorie had thought of telling Louisa that all the Aunts were having affairs, that low-class men were cheating them out of their life savings and exposing them to deadly diseases, but that would probably be going too far.

Louisa cleared the table, then sat back down and took her mother's hand. "Why don't you move in with us, Ma? We really want you here. *I* want you here. Patrick is always saying how he wishes you'd move in. You'd see the kids more, and you wouldn't have to worry about money. Please, please think about it."

"Don't make me give away more secrets, Louisa. The Aunts will never trust me again."

"Listen to me," Louisa said, still holding her hand. "I don't want to make you do anything you don't want to do. I'm glad you're healthy enough to go to your house every day, but we can't afford it and you have to make up your mind about that."

"One of those apartments would be expensive, wouldn't it?"

"But you'd have the money from the sale of the house. Now

you have nothing coming in except this little bit from Social Security, and the house needs repairs. We've had this conversation."

Louisa waited for a while, but Glorie had nothing to say.

"You have two choices, Ma. Move in with us, or go to a building like the Aunts'. It's entirely up to you, but it's got to be one or the other."

Glorie stared at the clock on the wall. "I'm too tired to decide right now. I didn't sleep well in a strange bed."

"You don't have to decide today. But you have to decide."

Louisa had just used up her last chance.

"I think I need a nap," Glorie said, and went to her room. She took off her shoes and panty hose, closed the drapes against the daylight and climbed under the covers fully dressed. Her stomach felt better, and she let her eyes shut. She would need to be rested to go ahead with the next part of her scheme. There were still a few details to work out, but she was ready.

From time to time she woke and lay there wondering if there might be another way out. Maybe I can sell the furniture, use the money to repair the roof and replace the heating system. I don't need all that furniture.

"You'll never get enough," Patrick would say.

"You're living in a dysfunctional dream world, you might as well live in my condo," said Blanche.

"I'm coming, Jack," she heard herself mumble out loud as she drifted off again. "You'll see."

When she woke again it was dark outside. She heard the sound of dishes in the kitchen. As the doorknob turned, she shut her eyes tight. A crack of light crept in and she heard Louisa whisper, "She's still asleep. Do you think I should wake her for a while so she doesn't wake up in the middle of the night?"

"She probably needs her rest," Patrick whispered.

Louisa crept out. Like a baby, they were talking about her like a baby. She wasn't hungry and she wasn't tired anymore. She was refreshed and thinking more clearly than she had in years. By the time Louisa checked in for the night, then turned off the lights and went to bed, Glorie had to pull the blankets up to her nose so Louisa wouldn't notice her grin.

I know what I have to do, she kept telling herself. I can do it. Other people do it, so can I.

She gave Louisa and Patrick a whole hour to fall asleep, then got to work. She turned on one small bedside lamp.

"See, this was meant to be," she told Jack as she took out the flowered overnight bag, still packed from her visit to the Aunts, and stuffed it with a few clean nightgowns. From the top of the white dresser she took the jewelry box with the diamond bracelet he had given her on their fiftieth wedding anniversary, and a bottle of Chanel No. 5. From the drawer, she took a few pairs of good earrings and a plastic bag that held the paper angels from Pat Jr. and Lily. She put all these things in her bag, then turned off the light, opened the drapes and sat in her chair to wait. She wouldn't set the alarm, she would wait. She looked across the street at her house, with the timer light peeking through from behind the living room drapes.

"That's a dead giveaway that no one's home," she told Jack. "Who has a light on in the middle of the night, every night? Why hasn't anyone ever thought of that before?"

"You're getting smarter already," he said.

She stood now and then to relieve her back. When it started to get light, she crept to the hall closet, put on her gopher, picked up her bag and crossed the street.

"I'm here, Jack," she said out loud as she walked in. "I'm not crazy and I'm here." She spoke so loud her voice echoed around the room.

At 10:00 she phoned the grocery store for a large delivery and made sure to tell them to come around to the back door. "The front doorbell isn't working," she said three times. The clerk might think that was weird, but better to have him suspicious than Louisa.

She wandered into the living room, sat on the couch and let her head fall forward, her hands covering her face. She was too tired to putter around, too exhausted to sleep, so she sat there, not realizing how hard she was pressing her fingers against her eyes. When she took her hands away the room was blurry and spinning.

Everyone was right, she thought. I never enjoyed this room, I haven't enjoyed my life. This room was beautiful, my life was beautiful and I've been mean and miserable, I'm a fake and a snob and now I'm paying for it.

"Can't we start over?" she asked Jack. "We can start again and make this room anything you like."

How could that happen?

I'll begin by enjoying it now, she thought. I'll bring a snack table in and have lunch right here on the green brocade couch, the hell with stains, what am I saving it for?

She put her head down on the arm of the couch.

Why was she being so hard on herself? Jack wouldn't have wanted her to be different, she knew.

Or would he? Maybe she had ignored all the signs of unhappiness the way she had ignored his cold feet and careless shaving until it was too late.

"Did I really make you happy?"

He said nothing to reassure her.

"Where are you?" she whispered. "I'm scared. I don't want to do this alone." He seemed far away.

The back of her neck was aching.

Just as well, she thought, getting up. I can't mope around,

there's no point. I have hours to kill and I have to do something to make them pass. Jack wouldn't want me to mope.

If she wrote a thank-you note to the Aunts, she could give it to the mailman when he came around noon. It would give her something to do.

Just because they're crazy, that's no excuse to be rude, she thought.

She got out the box of ivory stationery with her monogram embossed on it, a big set that had letter paper and notecards. She had ordered it from an ad that came with her Shepherd's charge bill and it had lasted for years, but now she was out of the notecards; they were exactly the right size for sympathy letters.

Well, she'd write the Aunts on real letter paper. In fact, she'd write three letters. Why not, she had time.

She sat at the kitchen table with the stationery and a pad of plain paper to practice on, to figure out what to say. *Dear Stella,* she started.

> *Thank you for your hospitality.*

That was too formal.

> *Dear Stella,*
> *Thank you for the pajama party. All that was missing was the roasted marshmallows.*

> *Dear Stella,*
> *Thank you for surrounding your bed with pictures of your dead husband and giving me one of the worst nightmares of my life. Thanks a lot!*

She switched over to the ivory notepaper.

Dear Stella,

Your apartment is lovely. Thank you for inviting me and for all the trouble you took.

She wanted to add something warmer, so she wrote:

And thank you for your kind words.

Gloria

She went back to the pad, wrote:

Dear Gemma,

and started laughing as she went on:

I can't sleep, I can't sleep, I can't sleep!

Dear Gemma,

Ooo-maa, what a nice apartment you got!

Dear Gemma,

Thank you for going to so much trouble to make me feel at home during my visit.

I'm not saying I did feel at home, I'm saying she tried. That's the truth. She wrote this on the ivory stationery, then added:

It was greatly appreciated. I enjoyed seeing your lovely apartment and meeting Bambi. Please give her my best and the same to you.

Gloria

Dear Toni,

Didn't anyone ever tell you not to ride an elevator in your bathrobe? Didn't anyone ever tell you not to scream? Didn't anyone ever tell you to get teeth that fit? I'm telling you this for your own good.

Sincerely,

A Friend

P.S. And you're not a real Aunt.

Glorie wrote this on the ivory stationery too. She folded the paper and sighed. It was worth wasting paper to feel this cheerful. Then she tore it up and started for real.

Dear Toni,

Thank you very much for your hospitality yesterday. It was very much appreciated.

Sincerely,
Gloria Carcieri

She got her address book and wrote out the envelopes. There was paper scattered all over the kitchen table. She had missed lunch, missed the mailman, and it was getting close to the time.

At 5:30 the phone rang, and as soon as she heard Louisa say, "Ma, dinn ——" she jumped in. "I'm not coming. I'm going to live in my own house from now on. I can take care of myself, don't worry," and hung up. She was thrilled for a few seconds, until she realized she had forgotten an important part of the plan. So she had to call Louisa back. "I'm unplugging the phone now," she said, and did. If Louisa worried, she would come right over; but if she thought Glorie was being stubborn, she might think it was smart to give in to her whims, at least for a while.

And I'm stubborn enough to outlast her, Glorie knew.

She closed all the drapes, zapped soup and ate on a snack table in the TV room.

This isn't so bad, it's like lunch here every day, she thought. All I have to do is stay calm. It's all right to be nervous, but I have to stay calm.

After she had cleared away the dishes she watched some more TV. She stayed with QVC as long as they were showing marcasite jewelry; she would never buy TV junk but it was pretty to look at. She drew the line at watching collectible dolls, and started flipping through channels restlessly. It felt as if Jack had gone to bed, tired from working all day. He would be snoring when she joined him later.

As she zoomed past commercials, she was wondering what to do about the lights. Would it be an invitation to burglars if there were no lights on at all?

Why is this so complicated? she thought.

She would let the timer lamp stay on in the living room. It would be like a night-light shining from the distance to their bed. Maybe she should close and lock the bedroom door. If a burglar broke in he could take what he wanted and leave her in peace.

Of course, why didn't I think of that years ago? I could leave a plate of cookies and milk, and a note: "Take what you want, just leave me in peace."

She chuckled. She could leave a hero sandwich and a thermos of coffee. "The good silver is on the top shelf, upper left cabinet. Sorry it's tarnished. Have a good night." She could leave notes on her ivory embossed stationery. She'd be OK.

She changed into her nightgown, went back into the TV room and tried to pay attention to Ted Koppel and Jay Leno and David Letterman, guys who were usually on long past her bedtime, but her mind was in the other room, where Jack would be waiting. Finally she walked through the house to the bedroom, closed and locked the door, pulled down the bedcovers and turned off the light. When her eyes had adjusted to the dark she was still standing there staring at the bed.

This is where I belong, she thought.

She couldn't move.

This is my first night back in my own home, what I've always wanted.

She stood there.

I'm coming, Jack, she tried to tell him.

"I'm sorry I deserted you," she whispered. "I should have stayed here." She grabbed the side of the mattress to steady herself, and felt her way along the edge of the bed in the darkness until she reached Jack's brown armchair near the foot. She took the extra blanket folded at the end of the bed, the one she used for naps. She settled into the chair, put her feet up on the footstool, spread the blanket over herself and settled down for the night. She put her head back and tried not to think about the empty bed.

"You can't stay there all night, Glorie, you won't be able to walk in the morning. Get into bed." That's what Jack would have said. It was an easy thing to guess.

Maybe Jack only tells me things I want to hear.

The idea hit her like a blow to the stomach, a knife through the heart, strong hands squeezing her neck. It passed in a glance of time, leaving her breathless, horrified, bleeding to death.

"Jack," she whispered. "Where are you?" Her soft whisper sounded as if she were afraid to wake him, as if he were there and she were lying next to him asking, "Are you awake?"

Maybe Jack only told her things she wanted to hear. Maybe it had been that way their whole lives and now he had nothing left to say.

What did you think of me, really? What did you feel? She wanted to make him say, "I love you, Glorie," but he had rarely said it in life. She always understood that wasn't his way.

She could imagine him saying, "Go to bed, Glorie."

"No, not without you," she whimpered, as if she had a choice.

She thought about sleeping on top of the bedspread, the way she did when she napped every day of her life. But that seemed so foolish.

She had never napped here with Jack, even in those last years. Why hadn't she simply crawled in beside him?

What's the difference? she thought. Under the covers or on top? Why should it bother me now?

She groped her way back to the bed, too tired and weak to argue with herself. She climbed into her side and lay on her back, arms tight beside her. She started to tremble, as if she had a high fever. She wanted the earth to open up and swallow this heavy bed, she wanted to sink to the center of the earth, to have the dirt close in on top of her and bury her alive. It wouldn't make her feel any worse, no more alone or hopeless than she did right now. In the morning there would be an empty space where the bed had been. It would be so simple; she would be erased, just like that.

She was still trembling and suddenly felt too frightened to move, as if someone — a burglar or a rat or the devil — were quietly watching her and would pounce at the slightest sign she was alive. She could never move fast enough to turn on a light and run to the phone for help. There was nothing to do except stay, alert and stiff, until morning.

There is no need to be scared, she told herself. I haven't heard anything. Nothing is wrong.

I live here now. I always said that I live here, and now I do. I better get used to it.

She made sure she didn't move.

She opened her eyes and it was daylight.

I slept, she thought. I did it.

Her shoulders and back ached, she felt exhausted, but it was 8:00 A.M. and she had slept here.

I had a bad night, she thought, still lying there.

She remembered doubting Jack.

She remembered the devil, holding his breath in the dark.

It was fear, that's all, I was being silly and scared. Now I have to get up. I have things to do. There must be things to do.

Of course. There was one thing she had to do right away.

She got up, went to the kitchen and opened the drapes so Louisa would know she wasn't dead.

She plugged in the phone. If Ada called and got no answer she might contact the police. Glorie would keep it plugged in during the day, to avoid any embarrassing police incidents or family misunderstandings.

Everything was back to normal until noon.

Ada called, furious. "Are you crazy?" she yelled. "Louisa is worried sick."

"You already talked to her?"

"She's worried, Gloria, now don't make things worse than they are. What are you up to?"

"I'm living here now," she said. "Louisa doesn't believe me, but I am."

"I don't believe you, either. Why do you want to do that? You had it easy. Besides, you're really hurting her feelings."

"They want me to give up my house," Glorie said. "Didn't she tell you that? They want to take it away." She sounded as if she were pleading. "Please, please, just be on my side, will you do that? Please just be on my side."

"Of course, honey, sure I'm on your side," said Ada. "But Louisa is awful worried, that's what I called to tell you. Are you sure you're OK? Do you need anything?"

"I'm fine. I'll call you in a couple of days."

"You want company maybe? I could come by. Why don't I come by?"

"No. I have a lot of things to do. I'll call you in a couple of days. Thanks for calling, now. Bye."

"Don't hang up, I have an idea," Ada yelled into the phone.

"You do?"

"I know I warned you to stay away from gigolos before, but you're desperate now."

"Huh?"

"You'll have to get married again. I know you don't want to, but find someone. So what if he's not rich, so what if he wants you for your money? Louisa can't expect *both* of you to live in her guest room."

"Good-bye, Ada."

"Think about it. Gigolos are people, too."

"Good-bye. I have to hang up. I have things to do."

"Bye, honey, talk to you soon. Think about it."

She did have a lot to do. She pulled out the yellow pages and looked up locksmiths. She couldn't go anywhere, couldn't leave this house for a minute, until the locks were changed. Patrick was waiting for the chance. When she was at the hairdresser's or the market he would come and change the locks himself, lock her out of her own house. Never! She'd beat him to it.

She looked at the listings, a strange promise in every ad:

Auto Lock Specialists
Panic Locks
Low Prices
Lowest Prices

Who knew how much it should cost to change every lock in the house? She'd have to make a lot of calls to get a feel for the right price. She'd probably have to make an appointment. Maybe she should wait until Louisa's hairdresser day. There was no rush, as long as she didn't leave the house, no rush at all. She put the yellow pages away.

She drew the drapes when it got dark, and every now and then peeked out the kitchen window. Sometimes Louisa was peeking back from the behind the curtains of Glorie's abandoned bedroom across the street.

Maybe I should put an ad in the paper, she thought: "Room to Rent," with Louisa's phone number. "Excellent listening post. Ask for Patrick."

They could go on this way forever, playing peekaboo across the street. Louisa always loved that game when she was a baby.

"Peekaboo," Glorie sang, pulling back the drapes, but Louisa was gone.

Each day passed faster than the one before. She worked on her scrapbook, adding a few new clippings she had brought over from Louisa's: the Christmas-card photo of Michael and Jeremy that nasty Blanche had mailed to her at Louisa's; a card signed by Lily; a newspaper photo of downtown in the blizzard, as a warning to herself.

She watched for the mailman, and made sure not to step on the porch to get the mail from the box until he was far down the block. Patrick could have gotten to him. Patrick might bribe the mailman to kick his way in and kidnap her if she so much as opened the door a crack. How did she even know he was the real mailman, not a private detective in disguise?

Every day one or two people would try to trick her.

Pat Jr. called and Glorie told him she was fine.

Blanche came to the door and stood on the porch for fifteen minutes watching Glorie wave from the TV room window, inches away. Then Glorie held up her forefinger to signal, "Wait a minute." She left the room and came back to the window with a piece of paper. She held up the sign: GO HOME, BLANCHE, I'M FINE.

Louisa left her alone, which meant she was probably planning something extra sneaky.

Ada called and almost acted as if everything were normal.

"I'm keeping my eyes open for someone in case you change your mind," she said.

"You never know," Glorie told her.

She had human contact. She had food. She got exercise by walking from one end of the house to the other. Once she counted how many small steps it took and then how many big steps. If she lost count she started over. She canceled the hairdresser and phoned a locksmith or two every day.

On the fourth day the family started playing dirty and had precious Lily call. "Grandma G, I miss you. When are you coming back to Grandma's?"

Of all the crooked tricks.

"Maybe your daddy can take you to visit me at my house sometime," Glorie said.

"When?"

"In a while."

At night she locked the bedroom door and lay on her back, as stiff and frightened and alone as on the first night. She caught up on her sleep in the afternoon, napping on top of the spread like always.

On the sixth day — it must be the sixth by now — she woke in the morning and looked at the clock. It was 1:00 in the afternoon.

I hate myself, she thought. I'm stupid and pathetic. I can't do anything.

She was so furious with herself, she rolled over and shut her eyes again.

I'll lay here until I figure out what to do next.

She was running out of milk and bread. She could call the

store and ask them to charge another delivery, but eventually she would need to transfer money to her checking account and she hadn't figured out how to do that yet. Besides, what if Patrick were hiding in the bushes and raced at the door when she opened it for the groceries?

Her best idea was to get up at dawn tomorrow and go to the twenty-four-hour diner downtown for breakfast, to get her strength back. She could call a cab. She would be out and back before anyone noticed. Then she could come home and she'd be up to dealing with the locksmith. When the locks were changed, she wouldn't be a prisoner anymore.

It will be fun, it will be like hiring servants, she told herself. I always wanted servants. I would have been good at it.

"Don't you think I would have been good with servants?" she asked Jack. "I'd be strict but kind, like Lady Marjorie on *Upstairs, Downstairs.*"

She looked at the clock again and it said 2:00. She sat up so fast she got dizzy — or was that from hunger? She got dressed quickly and thought about food but felt too nauseous to eat. She looked out the window, hoping to spot some neighborhood kid who might want to make a few dollars by going to the market for her. She ate a few crackers and watched the evening news. And while she tried to concentrate on the news and how to pay the bills, now and then she heard her own voice in the back of her head, maybe even in the air, saying, "Jack, come back to me. Where have you gone?"

She was wandering from room to room, dressed but barefoot, saying, "Jack, come back to me," over and over.

She would have to scheme to get him back. After all these years.

She needed a charm, the opposite of the Evil Eye, a good eye, a love eye.

Snap out of it, Gloria, she told herself. Be sensible. Think.

She would call him back if it was the last thing she ever did. She knew how.

She opened the kitchen junk drawer and found the flashlight Jack always kept there for emergencies. She picked it up and gray powder fell out of a hole on one side. On the other side bubbly batteries were eating through the metal.

Good, it's a sign, she thought, and gathered up what she had been looking for. Candles, pastel candles she had bought over the years simply because they were beautiful and elegant. At first she had told herself she was being practical, stockpiling candles for emergencies. Then she admitted she was treating herself, they were so irresistible, cheap but luxurious. Now she knew what they had been meant for all along.

"Jack, come back to me."

She piled them on the counter. There were thirty. She found every candleholder in the closets and every saucer from the best sets of china. Then she went to the bedroom to get ready. She took a box down from the shelf of the closet and lifted out the long white silk nightgown and robe she used to wear on Jack's birthday and her birthday and Christmas, and hadn't put on since he died. She changed into the lacy gown and robe and the delicate white satin slippers that went with them.

As she passed through the living room she lit the candles already standing on the mantel, then turned off the lights. She went into the kitchen, lit the candles in holders and dripped wax into the saucers to hold the others. She put four pink candles in holders on the counter and carried one in her hand to light the way as she went from room to room with the others. She left golden candles on the television and lilac ones in the bathroom. She put four pale blue candles on the kitchen table.

"You never wanted to dine by candlelight," she told Jack.

He had always grumbled, "I want to be able to see what I'm eating, Glorie."

"I should have insisted," she said. "You would have liked it, I know you would have. You're more romantic than you think. In your own way, you're very romantic, Jack."

She put two pale green candles close together on the living room floor right in front the couch, where his feet were when he died, and said, "Come back to me, Jack."

She walked from one end of the house to the other by candlelight, and in each room she said, "Come back to me, Jack," as if it were a spell. "Come back to the room where we watched TV. Come back to the room where you watched my bath. Come back to the room where you left me."

She had saved the most beautiful rose-colored candles for the bedroom, and she put one on each night table on either side of the bed. She took off the robe, slipped into her side of the bed, and waited for him to come. There were things he said in the dark that she treasured. Once he had kissed her neck and said, "Your skin is as soft as rose petals." He had a romantic soul, she knew. She was as quiet and nervous as she had been on their wedding night, and she knew that he would come out of the bathroom soon. He would be that wrinkled man with the fringe of white hair and the musty smell, but he would be as eager to hold her as he had been all those years ago. He would kiss her lips, and run his hands up her thighs, he would raise her nightgown and kiss her breasts.

"Your skin is as soft as rose petals."

She ran her hands up and down his back.

"Don't be afraid, Glorie."

"I've never been afraid of you."

She felt his hand stroke her breast and kiss it. He kissed her lips. She felt like she was floating, she knew he had come back to her.

She opened her eyes. Her empty arms were reaching up to the sky and her cold feet flailed as they reached to grasp the body that wasn't there.

She turned on her side and looked at the empty space next to her. She could imagine him there, rolled over onto his side, his back to her, calmly sleeping as if he would wake up in the morning. She imagined him there.

Then she got his pillow, put it on top of her own and arranged both of them in the middle of the bed. She slept dead center.

Why not? she thought. I'm alone, aren't I?

She lay there in the candlelight and thought, Let them burn.

I hope the house burns down. I'll be like one of those widows in India who burn themselves up after their husbands die.

We'll burn up together, Jack.

She was an old woman rolled up in blankets on the deck of a ship, sliding from side to side, but this time she knew she was dreaming. "Where did you get that red-haired woman?" a man's voice said. "Her skin is as soft as a rooster's." The ship rocked. She heard a noise, footsteps. Someone was on the deck, someone was in the house, this time for real. It was happening, she wasn't dreaming anymore, she wasn't just being afraid, this time it was true. She was wide awake hearing slow, light but definite footsteps creep down the hall toward her open bedroom door. There was no way to escape, no one to help her.

I don't want to die this way, she thought. She shivered and lay very still in the center of the bed as the footsteps crept nearer.

"Ma?" Louisa's voice called softly as she peeked into the bedroom. "Ma, are you OK?"

"How did you get in?"

"I used my spare key."

Stupid, I'm so stupid, Glorie told herself, sick at this proof of how her memory had failed.

"What time is it?" she asked in a slow, heavy voice.

"It's late. I saw there was something funny about your lights. As long as the lights kept going on and off and you answered the phone I knew you were OK, but I got worried when the lights looked strange, so I came over. Didn't you plug in the phone today?"

"I'm all right. I'm just tired."

"What are you doing with all these candles? Is the power out?"

"The power's fine."

"Do you want me to stay here with you for the rest of the night?"

"No. Go home."

"I can't do that, Ma, you know I can't." Louisa was suddenly frantic. "I gave you as much time as I could, but I can't leave you alone anymore. I can't worry like this."

"I said, go home."

Louisa sighed. "Maybe I'll rest on the sofa in the TV room," she said, patient once more.

"Do what you like. I'm tired. I'm going to sleep."

Louisa walked away.

Glorie sat up. She sat up in bed for hours watching the candles burn down. As the room grew lighter she memorized every piece of furniture, every fold of the drapes.

She heard the television go on. Louisa was watching some old movie.

Jack, she thought. Jack, help me. Don't let them take me away.

She rested her head against the pillows propped behind her.

She and Jack were lying side by side in each other's arms, and rose petals were raining down on them. They were covered with layers and layers of rose petals, the scent was so strong they could hardly breathe. As they clung to each other the rose petals kept falling, covering the bed, weighing it down until the bed started sinking to the center of the earth.

"Jack," she said. "Talk to me, Jack."

He held her close. His eyes were closed. His jaw fell open and he looked like a drowned man, rose petals falling into his mouth.

"Ma," Louisa whispered, gently shaking her awake. "It's morning, Ma. Get up. I made you breakfast."

Glorie got up and did as she was told. She sat at the kitchen table and Louisa put a scrambled egg and toast in front of her. Glorie stared at the plate. Louisa hadn't set a place for herself. Her daughter was sitting across from her.

"Come on home, Ma. You can take a hot bath, wash your hair, change into fresh clothes."

"No."

"I'm not leaving without you," Louisa said, as calmly and firmly as she had ever said anything.

This was it. Glorie heard a long, hideous shriek, but she knew the sound was only in her head, or Louisa wouldn't still look so calm.

From now on she'll never stop asking if I want a bath, if I need my hair washed, if I have to go to the bathroom, Glorie thought. I'm dead.

Louisa got Glorie's coat and put it on over the nightgown. She got Glorie's pocketbook from its hiding place under the counter, then took her mother by the arm.

"Come home with me, Ma. We'll come back and get some more things tomorrow," Louisa said, as if Glorie had never heard anything like that before.

As Louisa closed the door behind them, Glorie looked back. "Good-bye, Jack," she said out loud. She knew it was showy.

I've earned it, she thought. Fuck anyone who thinks I haven't.

Chapter 9

GLORIE WAS SIPPING her morning coffee from the thin china cup with the orchids on it, looking out the window across the street, noticing that weeds were cropping up where they never had before. It was 9:00, he should have left fifteen minutes ago and there was no sign of life in the house yet. Suddenly he raced out the front door looking flustered, jumped into his car and drove off. Even from the window of her little room Glorie could tell he had bags under his eyes. She laughed so hard she almost choked on her coffee.

"We did it," she told Jack. "Serves him right."

"I don't see how this is going to help, Glorie."

"We'll see. Besides, it can't hurt. And this is only the beginning."

He shook his head. "Fine, we'll try it your way. Just make sure Louisa and Patrick never find out because there'll be hell to pay."

"Don't worry," she told him. "I've been careful."

Glorie hadn't been sleeping too well. Some mornings she woke at 4:00 and couldn't get back to sleep at all. She had to find something to do. During one long sleepless dawn she'd had a brainstorm. She couldn't do anything about it right away because she didn't have the man's phone number and couldn't risk Louisa or Patrick hearing her call information in the middle of the night.

But the next time she was alone, she hit 411 in a flash. "Do you have a number for Edward Brown on Jasmine Street? It might be a new listing." They did. She could hardly wait for night. She woke and saw by the red numbers on her bedside alarm that it was 2:00 A.M.; she peeked out the window. His lights were out, but it was still too early.

I need patience, she thought. I've got all the time in the world.

She dozed until 4:00. By then she could make out the dial on the big gold clock in the center of the white dresser, the clock that used to be on the mantel in her living room. The phone reached from her bedside to the chair by the window. The angel picture in its golden frame was on the wall over the television now, guarding her, giving her inspiration. She dialed and saw a light go on in the bedroom across the street.

"Hello?" he asked, sounding worried. She kept her hand over the receiver. "Is anybody there? Hello?" She didn't hang up until he did.

She waited half an hour — gave him time to get back into a deep sleep — then dialed again. This time she hung up before he did because she was afraid he might hear her chuckling.

She went back to bed herself, smiling, and luckily woke up at 6:00 to dial again. He sounded suspicious when he said "Hello," but he had definitely been sleeping.

Now here he was, late for work, exhausted, racing his ugly black car out of her driveway. And she had plenty more tricks where that one came from. Or at least she'd come up with them. She had big plans ahead.

"I wish you'd help me think up some tricks," she told Jack.

"Maybe," he muttered.

She rolled her eyes at him. "OK, don't help me."

She sat and sipped her coffee and imagined more ways her house might help her get even. She could bribe the locksmith to let her in.

Why was I ever afraid of locksmiths? she thought.

Now that the house was sold, she had plenty of money to invest in her project: getting her home back from that intruder.

Too bad it's summer or I could go to the basement when he's at work, turn off the water and let the pipes freeze! It was something to look forward to — *if* he was still there in the winter.

The oil tank! There must be a valve that would let the oil drip out slowly onto the cellar floor. But then the oil might catch on fire and the whole house would blow up. Maybe that one wouldn't work, but she was excited about all her possibilities.

She knew where the fuse boxes were.

She remembered where there was a weak spot under the carpet on the cellar stairs.

If I sneak in every day and pull away a little bit more wood from the steps, one day he'll fall through the hole and crash down to the cement, she thought.

And of course, her dear towel bar, that shaky bar Jack had put in for her as a birthday present. She could imagine the scene when it would come out in Edward Brown's hand, making him slip and crack his tailbone when he fell in the tub. She didn't want to kill him. She just thought he deserved to be miserable. No stranger deserved to be happy in her house.

"Can't you help me, please?" she asked Jack. He was beginning to get on her nerves about this. "You're dead. Why can't you haunt him? Scare him away? What good is it to be a ghost if you can't put it to use? Do I have to do this all myself?"

"Let's save that for an emergency, Glorie," he said patiently. "Let's save that for a rainy day."

"You're just trying to shut me up," she said sweetly.

"This is your project," he told her. "You're on your own. I have confidence in you."

"Thanks a lot."

He smiled. "Oh, come on, you can do this yourself. And you're cute when you're annoyed."

She tilted her head and fluttered her eyelashes, joking. "If you say so."

For weeks after Louisa had taken her back to her small room, she had wanted to do nothing but sleep. The doctor said, "Let her, it's the best thing for now." She wasn't ill; she was worn out.

By the time she decided to wake up, it was as if she had been hibernating all winter. It was early spring and people off the street were traipsing through her house.

She sat at her window one day and saw Patrick's friend Tom drive up with a young couple, take out a key to her house and let them in. She knew what was going on, she knew the house was being shown, but the shock made her close the drapes as if she were blocking out some vision too nightmarish to bear, an ax murder or a car crash. And as she sat in the dim room, she found she could see straight through the heavy drapes. She thought they must have become magical, for she could look into every room of her house, could hear what was going on.

She could hear Tom's sales pitch. "Perfect condition. Only

used by a little old lady during the day." How dare he insult her that way? How dare he suggest her house wasn't lived in?

He was taking the young couple around and they were laughing at the old-fashioned knotty pine paneling in the TV room, planning how they could knock down the wall between the living room and the sewing room to make one large, L-shaped room. They were hysterical with laughter when they saw the purple bathroom. "This will have to go," said the wife. Tom laughed too. "Like I said, a little old lady." What did they know? Who did they think they were to laugh at her like that?

She was relieved when the house was sold, in no time at all, to a single man, an insurance executive who looked to be in his midthirties.

"Is he gay?" she asked Louisa.

"I don't know, Ma, who cares? He got the mortgage."

I care, Glorie thought. I don't want children destroying my property. I don't want another woman in my house. I don't want another couple in my bedroom. I hope he *is* gay or else such a hopeless loser he'll never get a girl.

His lonely life didn't stop her from wanting him gone, though.

Meanwhile she signed everything Patrick put in front of her, without reading any of it. Whenever Louisa began to explain something, she would say, "I don't want to hear about it, you take care of it."

A few days before signing the final papers, she said to Louisa, "I want to get the packing over with in one afternoon. Tomorrow." That would give her enough time to think about what she needed to move, and not enough time to torture herself. There were very few things she wanted with her now.

After Jack's funeral, before she had recovered the strength to leave Louisa's, Glorie had fantasized about walking into their bedroom closet. She was wondering how long that musty smell she loved would cling to his clothes, linger in the air. Maybe if she rarely opened the doors, the scent would stay trapped inside for months, years. More than anything, when she went back she wanted to slip in the closet and stand among his clothes.

When she got there and opened the door, the closet was half empty. Louisa had packed up all Jack's clothes, every shirt in the drawer, every pair of socks, tossed the small things away and stored the rest in the basement.

"How *could* you?" Glorie screamed at her.

"I thought it would make things easier," Louisa cried. "It wasn't easy for me to do, you know. I thought it would help."

"I don't need your help."

Now she was glad his clothes were already packed away. She told Louisa to move them to the storage room next to Patrick's office in the basement, where they had made space for Glorie's things.

Her own clothes had already been brought over, and she had given Louisa instructions about almost everything else. Sitting on a shelf in the cellar near Jack's clothes were four big boxes filled with Mother's Day cards, Louisa's report cards, pressed flowers from her wedding. Glorie didn't want to open the boxes or sort through them; she simply told Louisa to take them across the street. She had already given her daughter the best china and silver and linens. Louisa could use them, she thought, and Glorie would still have them around her. Louisa put them in boxes in the basement, too.

Glorie insisted that all the furniture go to the Salvation Army. Let any poor stranger have it; she didn't want it turning up in some relative's house.

This must be what a divorce feels like, she thought. She wouldn't want some ex-husband who had dumped her hanging around the same neighborhood, running into her at the market.

She was divorcing her furniture, making it move where she'd never see it again. She tried not to think about the green brocade couch. It would never fit in her room at Louisa's, so she decided not to think about it.

Still, she had to go back home at least once. There were private things only she could identify: her scrapbook, a few piles of Christmas and birthday cards scattered in drawers and cupboards, her china teacup for morning coffee, Jack's shaving brush, family photographs slipped under the mattress to thwart the midget thieves. There was the receipt for the secret safety deposit box where she had stored the deed to her house — the deed that turned out to be a copy and not valuable at all. "Tomorrow," she told Louisa, and meant it.

She ate breakfast with her daughter the next morning, intending to go across and be back in an hour or two. Then Blanche showed up. "There's more stuff there than you think, Ma, we can use the help," Louisa said.

They're ganging up on me, Glorie thought. They're not going to leave me alone in my own house, not for a minute.

They would spy and see what she had hidden all those years, then laugh about it later. There was no point in fighting. She wanted it to be over.

The three of them crossed the street and Blanche started going through the hall closet, the one with the vacuum cleaner and brooms. "Do you want anything from here, Grandma?"

"Why are you going through my junk closet?"

"I figured we should start at one end of the house and work our way to the other."

"Let's just get what's important. Do what you want with the rest, as long as I don't see it again."

"Do you not want to be here, Grandma?" Blanche asked, as if she thought little Glorie had a tummy ache.

"I do not want to talk about it," Glorie snapped. "I know exactly what I'm looking for. Why don't you pretend you're in some cherry orchard, Blanche, far away."

"Don't get excited, ladies," Louisa called from the sewing room. She was packing dress patterns in a box.

Glorie walked in and said, "I don't want them." She had no room for new clothes in the small closet across the street, even if she'd had someplace to wear them.

"You might change your mind. We'll keep this in the storage room for now."

"Please yourself," Glorie said.

Louisa was on a stepladder taking down boxes of old patterns from the top shelf. "Do you want to go through these boxes?"

Glorie opened one. The pattern must have been twenty years old, a dress that would make no sense now. She opened another package and the thin yellow tissue paper nearly crumbled in her hands. She threw it back in the box. "Throw them away, all of them. I'm through with them, they're old."

"Don't you want to look? There might be something you want, something with sentimental value. Didn't you keep the pattern for my First Communion dress?"

"You look for it. There's nothing else I want," Glorie said, leaving the room.

"I'll put these boxes in the basement, too," Louisa said. "Maybe another time you'll want them."

"No!" Glorie yelled. "I said throw them away, I mean throw them away!"

Now Blanche was in the room. "Is everything all right? Should I make some tea?"

"No, no, please, no," Glorie said, her voice weary.

Tea in my house for the last time?

"No, please," she said. "I want to get this done."

Glorie found the flowered overnight case where she had left it, in the bedroom closet. She carried it to the purple bathroom, closed the door, got Jack's shaving brush from the medicine cabinet and packed it. She went back to the bedroom, opened the drawer on the night table and packed her scrapbook. She pulled the photographs from under the edge of the mattress, and took others from the drawers. She opened the door. Louisa could pack the things on the dresser, the jewelry box and hand mirror and perfume bottles. She left in a hurry.

In the kitchen she got her address book by the phone and pointed to the orchid teacup. "That's very fragile. Would you wrap it up and carry it over by hand?" she asked Blanche.

Then she walked back to the living room. She wanted more than anything to sit on the couch one more time. Instead, she looked at the clock. It had run down and stopped ticking in the weeks she'd been gone. It should have stopped forever the minute Jack died, like clocks did in stories. She called Blanche and said, "Would you carry the clock across, too? It stopped when your grandfather died."

Blanche looked confused and began to say something. Beyond the doorway Louisa held her hand up and signaled her to stop, thinking Glorie couldn't see.

"I'll take it, Ma, don't worry," she said.

Honestly, that Blanche had no imagination. Her father's daughter through and through.

Glorie put on her coat and walked out the door without saying another word.

At the end of the day, Patrick and Bob carried the boxes across. She arranged her few precious objects the best she could: the china cup in Louisa's kitchen closet, the gold clock and the angel picture in her room. Far into that night, she woke and felt at last that Jack had returned and was sleeping beside her in their single bed.

"I had no choice about the house, I had no choice," she cried to him quietly. "I'm sorry, I'm so sorry."

"I know, Glorie, I know," he said, putting his arms around her. "It's not your fault, I don't blame you, I'm not upset. Come on now, don't cry. You know I hate to see you cry."

What else *could* he say? How would she ever know if she had let him down?

"I'm sorry," she cried into her pillow. "I'm so sorry I let you down."

"You've never let me down," he said.

She looked up into his eyes. "I love you, Jack," she said, and he kissed her. She didn't ask where he'd been all this time or why he'd abandoned her when she'd moved back home. While she had been looking right through her drapes at those house thieves with Tom, while she had been dealing with all the nasty details of the move, she'd been wondering if he'd ever speak to her again, and she had made a decision. If he did come back, she would ask no questions. She would be warm and loving and seductive, so perfect he would never want to leave her again. That, she was sure, was what Wallis would have done.

She kept the drapes in her little room closed for a full week after Edward Brown invaded her house, but she couldn't see through them anymore. She avoided looking across the street when she walked to the bus stop to go downtown to the hairdresser's and to shop like always. Louisa opened the drapes while she was gone one afternoon; Glorie walked into her room and before she knew what was happening saw her house straight ahead. From then on she couldn't take her eyes off it. She knew everything about that intruder, when he came, when he left. She knew he was usually out for dinner and that he never had company. He was wasting her house. Why should she give him any peace?

"I think I'll go for a little walk," she told Louisa one early summer morning.

"Do you want company?"

"No, I just want some fresh air."

"That's good, Ma. Don't tire yourself out, though."

Glorie took a walk around the block. The next day she walked up and down Jasmine Street, first up Louisa's side then back down her own. She varied her pattern a bit every day. She didn't need fresh air. She wanted Louisa to get used to the idea that she could go out anytime, innocently, by herself. This was a long-term campaign.

"Don't tell me. You've got nothing but time," Jack said.

"I've got nothing to lose," she told him. "I don't even care if they think I'm crazy anymore."

"Oh yes, you do."

"Well not as much as before."

She had short-term maneuvers, too.

One day when Louisa was out she called Edward Brown's office.

"Who's calling, please?" asked his secretary.

"Exotic Escort Service," she said, holding a Kleenex over the phone. "The collection department. He's seriously in arrears on his bill. It's a very big bill."

While she was on hold, she hung up.

"Now what good did that do, Glorie?"

"If he loses his job he can't pay the mortgage. Do I have to explain everything? Do you think I should call his boss?"

Edward Brown's hair was thinning, so she called some 800 numbers on TV and had them send him information about Rogaine and the Hair Club for Men.

"Some people might say I'm doing him a favor," she giggled to Jack.

But she could imagine how upset Edward Brown might be, wondering who was sending him anonymous hints that he should cover his bald skull.

After a couple of weeks, she put the big plan into action. She rode the bus for two stops and got off a block from the post office. She was wearing an old coat that no one ever saw her in anymore, and before she went in the building she put on a black knit hat that covered all her hair. She didn't look dressed for the weather, but at least no one would be able to identify her as the redhead. Then she got a change-of-address form, filled it out with Edward Brown's name and a forwarding address a street over from that rotten Margaret's. They belonged together.

She chuckled to herself as she waited for her turn at the window. She hoped he had been planning to get a lot of important mail at her house. Checks. Stock dividends. He'd miss his mortgage payments and the foreclosure notice would be lost with the rest of his mail, floating around the other side of town.

A bored-looking man behind the counter took the form. "Who is the person moving?" he asked her.

"My son," she said. "He asked me to drop this off for him."

"Well, he has to sign it himself," the man said, pointing to the signature line. "Then you can drop it off."

"But I'm his mother." She paused for a minute. This was bad news. She should have planned better, taken a bunch of forms home and practiced copying his signature, but it was too late now. "Isn't there any other way?" she asked feebly.

"The person moving has to sign the form," he said, pushing it back at her. "You want anything else? A stamp maybe?"

She shrugged and walked away. On the way out she picked up some of those helpful what-to-do-when-you're-moving pamphlets from the Post Office itself. Inside were change-of-address postcards to send to friends, loved ones, people who sent you bills. She took plenty, enough for the electric company, the phone company, the oil man and anyone else she came up with. It might not be official but it would do.

She printed in a different style on every one; let them try to trace her! She made up account numbers where she needed them, and copied his signature the best she could from papers she found in Patrick's files. A week later she mailed them all at once to cause the most confusion possible. When she learned to do his signature perfectly, she'd go for the big one, the official change-of-address form.

This was a challenge. She was having a great time.

She went on walks nearly every day, but Louisa kept pestering her. "See some people, Ma. Invite Aunt Ada over, do something!" she said.

"You always said Aunt Ada was dizzy."

"But if she's dizzy in my house I don't mind."

"Well, if you want me to," Glorie sighed. "I'll do it if you want me to, dear."

"Are you up to something? You've got that *I Love Lucy* voice. 'Oh, Ricky, I wouldn't think of going to the club,' and the next thing you know she's wearing a banana hat and dancing in the chorus line."

"What would I be up to?" said Glorie.

Louisa looked like she wasn't convinced.

"I'll call Ada now." She picked up the kitchen phone right in front of Louisa.

"Hi, honey. It's me. I was wondering if you'd like to come over and have lunch with me here tomorrow."

"What?" Ada said. "Tomorrow? I'll have to check my busy calendar — oh, what a surprise, completely empty. Of course, I would, I'd love it. But don't go to any trouble. Just throw together a sandwich, it'll be good enough for me. Let me bring dessert."

"No, just bring yourself. I'll see you around noon, OK?"

After Glorie hung up she told Louisa, "You're making me have this party so I might as well do all the cooking."

"What do you need? I'll go to the store."

"Oh, never mind. You can set the table. You don't have to stay around for lunch, either. Maybe you can drop in on Blanche."

"I could do that," Louisa said very slowly. "I could do that as long as I take Aunt Ada's car keys with me."

"Don't you dare try it."

"Well then, I'll stay downstairs. It's your party."

Now Louisa was really thrown off guard. Glorie didn't need to go to any cemetery, but she needed to have a private talk with Ada.

In the morning she made tiny finger sandwiches of tuna with celery and onion powder. She tossed a big salad and put some Pepperidge Farm cookies on a plate for dessert.

Louisa was true to her word. She didn't even complain when Ada parked partway in a flower bed. After she had chatted with her aunt for a while Louisa excused herself. "I have some things to do downstairs. Yell if you need anything," she said, and disappeared. Glorie gave it a good five minutes before she crept to the cellar door and closed it almost completely, just to the point where it wouldn't click shut and make noise.

Then she sat down across from Ada, who was working on a plate piled high with sandwiches. "This is yummy," Ada said. "What do you put in here?"

Laughing gas, Glorie wanted to say, but what came out was "Onion powder."

"Aren't you eating, honey? It's delicious."

"Oh, I've lost my appetite," Glorie said, and sighed as heavily as she could. "I'm too worried about what's going on across the street."

"What? The new people?"

"It's only one man, but I think he's bad news. I think he's running a drug house or something like that. All sorts of people go in and out at all hours, and you know how Louisa is, if I mention it she thinks I'm crazy."

Ada frowned but she kept on eating. She thought for a minute then said slowly, "You *might* be crazy. This is still a good neighborhood. You can't be too careful, though. What does a single man want with that big house, anyway?"

"Right! That's what I always said."

"And Louisa doesn't believe you?"

"She won't believe me," Glorie said, shaking her head sadly, with the straightest face she could manage. "I can't call the police without proof. If I could only get him out of there somehow."

"You mean drive him away. Let him know he's not wanted around here. Get someone like that Charles Bronson from New York after him."

"Ada, I don't think Charles Bronson makes house calls and he must be our age by now, anyway. You're watching too many reruns."

"So what would get rid of him? Wait. What if you made an anonymous phone call? Tell him you know what he's up to?"

"Yeah, and what if I ordered twelve pizzas delivered to his house?" Glorie said sarcastically. Ada laughed and almost choked on her tuna.

"That's it, that's it," she said, and Glorie knew she meant it. "With the works, pepperoni, mushrooms, extra cheese," and Ada went on laughing till she had to take off her glasses to wipe her eyes.

"That's kid stuff," Glorie said, the way she used to scold Louisa when she was little. "I asked you here to help me, I'm really worried."

"Sorry, honey, I can see how worried you are," said Ada, straightening up and wiping her mouth on her napkin to prove she meant business.

Glorie thought she might as well give it another try, since Ada was already here. She didn't have time to hint around, though. "We have to do something that will really mess up his life, make him so miserable he'll want to leave. Listen, don't tell anyone this." She lowered her voice and glanced at the door. "I'm going to go to the Post Office and change his mailing address to a fake one, so his mail will be delivered to outer space." Glorie giggled. "I just haven't learned to copy his signature good enough yet."

Now Ada turned deadly serious. "You don't mean that."

"I did it halfway already. I sent change-of-address cards to all the places I could think of, phone company, every place. I just can't get the big one."

"You didn't! That's tampering with the U.S. Postal Service. That's a federal crime. You could wind up in jail."

"You have a better idea?"

"First of all, you better not call the police now that they've got a federal crime on you," Ada said, beginning to panic. "I don't believe it. I say you better lay low and hope they never find you. My lips are sealed."

"OK, Ada," Glorie said. "If that's what you think, then it's going to have to be the Evil Eye."

"I've never done the *mal occhio,* Gloria, never, I don't care what anybody says." Ada was getting agitated. "I told you that millions of times, I told everyone millions of times. I only ward *off* the Evil Eye."

"But you must know how to do it."

"You're playing with fire," Ada said, crumpling her napkin and getting more nervous. "I got to tell you, you're playing with fire from hell. Whatever curse you put on someone will come right back at you and kill you or worse. You'll burn in hell forever."

"Just teach me how to do it."

"It might not work, you know, you're not Italian."

"So what's the harm in trying?"

"Because I don't want it on my head if you burn in hell forever."

"Will you help me or not?" Glorie was getting annoyed and her voice was getting louder.

"I'm thinking," Ada yelled.

They jumped when Louisa appeared at the top of the stairs.

"You two having a nice visit?" she asked.

"Oh, we were reminiscing about the good old days," Ada said, smiling. "Remember when your aunt Margaret spread that rumor that Aunt Delia had VD? Gloria made a delicious tuna salad, by the way."

"Why don't I make you some coffee?" said Louisa.

"Yes, why don't you join us, honey?" Ada said.

As Louisa went to the sink, Ada mouthed behind her back, "I'll think about it."

Three days later, minutes after Louisa had driven off to the hairdresser's, Ada rang the bell. She was wearing dark glasses and a scarf around her head.

"I waited around the corner till I saw her leave. I wore the dark glasses so no one would notice it was me coming in."

"But your car is parked in the driveway."

"I still don't feel right about this. I'm only doing it to help you."

"I appreciate it. I'd do the same for you."

"Let's get this show going. You got the plate and the oil?"

"Right here on the counter."

"Oh, good, extra virgin olive oil, that's good. Where is he now?"

"At work."

"Where's that?"

"East County Insurance."

"I mean *where,* what direction?"

"Direction?"

"You have to point in the direction of the person you're putting the *mal occhio* on, don't you know that?"

"I guess. I thought we'd just aim at the house."

"He's not *in* the house, Gloria," Ada said impatiently. She seemed to enjoy being in charge here. "We have to point it at him. We'll have to look up the address in the phone book."

"It's in a big building downtown, I remember now."

"You're sure?"

"I'm sure."

"OK. You're going to do this yourself, I'm not involved."

Ada poured the oil in a plate and put it on the kitchen table. "You face downtown," she said. "You put your fingers like this over the plate and point in his direction." She held out her index and pinkie fingers and held back the middle fingers with her thumb. The devil's horns were hovering over the plate. Ada pulled her hand back quickly. "Then while you're pointing — I'm not saying this now, I'm not saying it while my hands are over the plate, so it doesn't count. You say — "Ada whispered something in Glorie's ear. "You got it?" Ada made the sign of the cross so fast her fingers were still in horns.

"Got it. Let me at him."

Glorie stood at the table, made the horns over the plate.

"You sure you want to do this?" said Ada. "It could come back at you bad."

"I'm sure."

Glorie held her hand over the plate and took a deep breath.

"You remember the words?" Ada said, making Glorie jump.

"I *remember.*"

Glorie held her hand over the plate again, took another deep breath. "I just thought of something. What if he's out at a meeting? What if he's not at his office?"

"Put your hands *down,*" Ada said. "We got a problem. It's no good if you don't aim it at him."

"So what do we do?"

"You'll have to wait till he gets home. Now that you know what to do."

"I could. But I kind of like the idea of not having the Evil Eye enter my house, you know what I mean?"

"You've got to aim it at him, that's all I know. I wouldn't send it out into a crowd if I were you anyway. You never know what'll come back."

"What if I catch him in the driveway, before he gets into the house?"

"Does he walk fast?"

"Sort of."

"Then you better talk fast. It's worth a try. I got to get out of here, I'm giving myself the creeps."

"Don't you want to stay for lunch?"

"Not today, honey, I want to stop by church, then go straight home."

"You want a cup of coffee?"

"You want to come to church?"

"No. We'll have lunch another day."

"Absolutely," Ada said. Then she whispered, "Call me tonight and let me know how it worked out." She put her scarf and glasses back on and left, shaking her head.

Glorie took the plate of olive oil into her room, cleared a space on the floor of the closet and put it down. The olive oil wouldn't be so fresh later, but at least she wouldn't get caught if Louisa needed the bottle of oil for supper. Then she ate a big lunch; she'd have to skip dinner and sit by the window, in case he came home earlier than usual. She was determined to do this today.

"Do you feel OK, Ma?" Louisa asked when Glorie excused herself from dinner.

"Yes, I had a big lunch. And I feel tired," she said, trying to slow down her words. "I think I'll rest for a while. Don't worry."

She went into her room, and stood by the door until she heard some pans clatter, then clicked the lock fast so Louisa wouldn't hear. She got her plate of oil and sat at the window to wait, the oil ready on her lap as she glanced back and forth between television and the street.

"The only reason I'm not trying to stop you is that I don't believe in all this bullshit," Jack said.

"So what's the harm?"

"You could slop that oil over everything and have a hard time explaining it to Louisa."

"I'll say I was having a salad."

"An oil salad?"

"Is that him?"

"No, it's another car going by. It would serve you right if he got home at midnight."

"You had a choice. You could have haunted him. But, no, you left it up to me."

"You and Ada. You're taking advice from Ada now? That doesn't strike you as strange?"

"Well, she can't be wrong about everything. Is that him?"

"It's another car."

At 9:00 Jack said, "That's him."

Glorie stared. She made the horns. She moved the plate to keep up with him as he walked from the car and said the secret curse. She imagined bright red electrical currents, like maniac bolts of lightning, racing across the street and zapping him. The red lightning was inside him, like evil Mexican jumping beans. It would only be a matter of time before he exploded, or self-destructed like the tape at the start of *Mission Impossible.*

He walked through her front door and she was left holding a plate of extra virgin olive oil. Now what?

What have I done? she thought.

Maybe the evil red currents would crawl out of Edward Brown and into her house. The house would be cursed, the rays would get into the walls and under the carpets, into the faucets in the purple bathtub. One day she would walk back into her house feeling happy and secure, and when she least expected it the red currents would leap out from the walls and zap her in the heart so she would suffer a painful death. Is that what happened to Jack? Was he zapped in the heart? Was it painful?

She sat there frozen for a while, holding her plate of oil, before she heard a knock on the door. She put the plate on the floor under the chair and covered it with a magazine.

"Come in."

Louisa turned the knob. "It's locked. Why is it locked?"

Glorie got up and opened the door. "Sorry, I didn't realize."

"Are you feeling better? Your eyes are all bloodshot. Have you been crying again?"

"I've been watching TV," Glorie said, sitting in her chair. "I'm watching a sad program."

Louisa looked at the screen. "Seems to me like they're giving away prizes."

"So I rooted for the wrong person. I hate to lose."

"OK, Ma. Good night."

Glorie went to bed and said a whole rosary lying in the dark. No need to take any chances. She would have to get Ada's trick for warding off the Evil Eye first thing in the morning.

"I'm not sorry I did it," she told Jack. "It might do some good. He could lose his job tomorrow."

"He could. He could wake up changed into a dog, too, but I wouldn't count on it."

"Do you think I cursed our house?"

"No, I don't think you cursed our house. I don't think you cursed him, either. I think you wasted good olive oil doing something foolish."

"We were so happy there," she said, still clutching her rosary. As if Jack needed to be told. She saw the two of them in the purple bathroom. She was in the tub; he was sitting in the chair reading the paper. Then he helped her dry off, put his arm around her and started to lead her to their big bed.

"Maybe I should take a bath too before I get in. I've been working all day," he said.

"No, no," she whispered into his ear, kissing his neck. "I love the way you smell. Did I ever tell you that I love the way you smell?"

"You know you're not going back to that house, Glorie," Jack told her, his arm around her in their twin bed.

"I know. It's the principle of the thing."

She thought for a minute. "Maybe you could just push him down the cellar stairs so he'd crack his head on the concrete floor."

"Don't be cruel, Glorie. We can get rid of him without hurting him."

"Whatever you say."

She kept waiting for the Evil Eye to kick in, hoping for it and preparing for the worst. Every day she did Ada's charm for warding off the curse if it boomeranged back at her. She poured water into a dish, took some oil on her fingers and sprinkled it into the water, saying the secret prayer. She watched to see if the oil drops came together to tell her she was doomed, or spread out to say she was safe. She was always safe.

"You put those drops together on purpose," Jack said.

"I do not."

She took a knife and cut through the water and oil in the dish. Then came the hard part. She had to throw it outdoors, the way Ada taught her, without Louisa knowing. This was not an easy activity to hide every single day, and Glorie got to be expert at doing it fast. She kept a bottle of mineral water and one of oil in her bedroom closet, hidden among the shoes, so she'd be ready at any opportunity. Sometimes the used water and oil went out the front window, sometimes out the back door. No one had caught her yet.

Near the end of summer she had to admit that the Evil Eye had probably failed. She could see that Edward Brown was getting his mail. She knew he had gotten an unlisted phone number. The weather was still unbearably hot, and Glorie usually stayed indoors. Sometimes she walked around Louisa's backyard, but when she came into the air-conditioning again she felt so chilled at the change she was dizzy. She wasn't eating much.

"No one is hungry in this heat, I guess," Louisa said as she cleared away her mother's almost full plate.

"That's true," Glorie said.

She felt sick from the heat. Or from not eating in the heat. Or from not sleeping because she was worried about not eating.

It's nothing. I always get nauseous when I'm too tired, she told herself.

After a few weeks Louisa got worried too. "Ma, you're not eating enough. Do you feel OK?"

"Yes, it's like you said, it's the heat."

"You've been in the air-conditioning for days."

"Don't tell me what to do. And don't snap at me. I'm not stupid, you know, I'm a grown woman and I can decide when to eat. Did it ever occur to you that maybe it's your cooking?"

"All of a sudden? All right, then you cook. You don't want to eat my cooking, you cook."

"And have Patrick complain? Not on your life!"

"What do you want, Ma? I'll make anything you want to eat, any way you want it. Just tell me what."

"No."

"Ma, stop being stubborn."

"I'm not being stubborn. You're being stubborn."

"How?"

Glorie walked into her room and slammed the door. Then she opened it again, a crack, and said, "Your cooking's fine."

She closed it while Louisa was saying, "Then why won't you eat for me?"

She opened the door a crack again and peeked out. "I'm sorry I yelled. You know I love you, don't you?"

Louisa looked concerned. "I love you too. Are you OK?"

"I'm fine, stop asking me that," she said, and shut the door.

She sat and looked across the street. She liked to pretend she could still keep a secret from Jack if she wanted to. But she never was very good at keeping things from him even when he was alive.

"Are you worried?" he asked.

"I'm being silly. It's like that time I thought I was pregnant again, remember? When I felt so sick to my stomach but it turned out I was late because I had the flu? My body fools me sometimes."

"We know you're not pregnant."

She smiled.

"And you're not sick to your stomach," he said. "I can tell. You have your arm over your stomach. That's a pain, Glorie, don't try to put it past me. You have to see a doctor."

"I know."

"Come on. Remember what you always said, what you used to tell me. You're not some ignorant greenhorn about doctors."

"I'm not. But I was hoping it would go away."

"Me too. I wish I could make it go away for you."

"You know what you *can* do for me?"

"What?"

"You can wrestle with the intruder," she said, smiling. "He's younger, but you're still tough. Plus, you're invisible." She didn't want him to feel sorry for her, no point in having him worry more than he already was.

"He'll never know what hit him," Jack said.

"There isn't enough insurance in the world to save him," she laughed.

"It will be all right, Glorie," he told her. "Don't worry, one way or another, it will be all right."

"Ma, you're mumbling to yourself. Were you falling asleep?" Was Louisa always at the door, or did it just seem that way? "Why don't you go to bed? It's eight o'clock, get comfortable and go to bed. You're not sleeping much anymore, it's not good for you."

"I don't feel just right," Glorie said.

"What's the matter?" Louisa said gently, putting one arm around her and feeling her forehead with the other hand. "Are you sick?"

"My stomach's upset all the time. My head aches and I feel tired. I think I need to see the doctor."

"Get some sleep, we'll call the doctor in the morning. Don't worry. Everything will be all right."

Chapter 10

IN HER DREAM Glorie's hair was long and white, flowing past her shoulders, wild as a troll's. She was alone in a forest and with every minute she looked more like a troll: her hair kept growing, a flowered cotton nightgown fell away from her body and she saw that she had a huge, puffed up belly. Jack came out of the woods and rubbed her stomach, as if for good luck. "I'm bad luck," she warned him. "Stay away."

This couldn't be happening.

Then she wasn't a troll anymore, she was a giant black dragon towering over the trees. Jack looked up at her; he looked through her; he didn't know her. "Jack," she tried to call, but sparks flew out of her dragon's mouth.

And when she woke, she had no greater wish than to escape again to that horrid forest of her dreams. The woman in the bed next to hers was moaning, calling, "Nurse, nurse," so loud it had awakened Glorie from a drugged sleep. Whenever she awoke these days she felt worn out, as though her body had been punched and beaten until she was sore everywhere. Her arms and legs felt like they were filled with lead. She could hardly move her head from the pillow.

Her dreams were disturbed and twisted, hard to remember. Jack was always there, but Glorie was someone else or something else, some creature he couldn't see. She woke from those dreams with her mouth hanging open, her muscles too slack and her tongue too parched to say the words "Water" or "No more pills." Her mind was clearing enough now to realize that Louisa was sitting in a chair by her bed, reading a thick book.

Louisa looked up and saw that Glorie's eyes were open. She jumped forward in her chair. "Ma?" she said quietly. "Do you know who I am?"

"Yes," Glorie managed to mumble. "Thirsty," she whispered.

Louisa gave her water from a cup with a straw, and called the nurse to check her. They raised her to a half-sitting position in the hospital bed and she began to wake up more.

"I have bad dreams," she told Louisa. "How long have I been here now?"

"Three weeks," her daughter said. "You've had trouble recovering from the operation, that's all."

Glorie wanted to ask, "Am I all right?" but how could the answer possibly be yes. "What next?" she asked.

"You'll get a little stronger, we'll take you home to get more strength there. Then we'll talk to the doctor about the next step. You just concentrate on getting some strength back for now."

"I don't want any more bad dreams. The pills make me dream," Glorie said, but already she was feeling the dull pain in her abdomen that she knew would get much worse. She heard the woman in the next bed moaning, "Sarah, bring me my medicine, I need it now!" to no one at all. Could her nightmares be worse than this?

"Maybe they can cut down the medication, I'll talk to the doctor later," Louisa said.

Glorie closed her eyes and tried to imagine herself in her own room: in the tiny white bed, with the gold clock on the dresser and the angel picture over the TV. She tried to imagine she was sitting up in that bed looking out the window at her old house.

She opened her eyes and turned to Louisa. "I dreamed I had long white hair," she said, and Louisa looked alarmed.

"Don't worry, we'll have the roots touched up when you get better," she said.

What must I look like? Glorie thought, but she didn't want to know. If she asked for a mirror, the sight might send her into dreams uglier than any she had ever had. She tried to picture herself fresh from Gilda's, her hair done, her dress crisp, her feet in pumps, instead of this sweaty mess she was now.

"What do I look like?" she asked Louisa.

"You look tired, like someone who's been sick, but you'll get over it. If you're worried about your looks, I'd say that's a good sign, Ma."

"I feel wilted," Glorie said. "I must look like a lettuce leaf."

From then on, every night that she was in the hospital she fell asleep pretending she was back in her twin bed at Louisa's, as if her mind could carry her through space. Sometimes she imagined that Jack lifted her into his arms and flew through the air like Superman, laying her softly on the bed and joining her there. "We'll have to get back to the hospital by morning so they won't know we're gone," he said.

But she could never imagine him peacefully with her for long; they had cut down her medication and she rarely slept through the night without waking to footsteps, or strange lights flashing on, or her own stomach sending a fierce electrical charge through her body.

"I don't want you to have to share this," she told Jack.

"I don't mind," he said, whenever he could, but he seemed to drift in and out of the room, caught in a wave that carried him closer and farther out at its whim.

When she did get home, she found she could only lie in bed, her head aching too much to talk or watch TV. She spent hours wondering why she was going through this. Over the years her body had turned on her in hundreds of small ways, but no matter how badly her back ached or her bones stiffened, she had never believed that a slow painful death was possible. She was convinced that the small betrayals of her body would mount up until one day she turned to stone and ceased to breathe. This pain was too shocking to be real; it belonged in someone else's life.

She woke in the middle of one night to a pain so brutal she couldn't move. She was curled up on her side like a baby, clutching her stomach. Her pills and a bottle of water were on the table by her bed, but she couldn't uncurl herself long enough to turn on the light and pour the water. She could hear herself breathing loudly, struggling to catch the air.

She didn't want to call Louisa. She remembered the ugly moans of the woman in the next hospital bed. She remembered all the terrible old women she swore she would never become. She remembered Josie's mother-in-law, a fat old lady who used to sit in a big armchair all day long. When Josie would visit she would call in a shrill voice, "Josie, where's my lunch?" as if her family were her servants.

I still don't want to be like that, Glorie thought, and she was almost relieved that she couldn't have yelled loud enough for her voice to reach Louisa anyway.

After twenty minutes she forced herself to move. Slowly she sat up, turned on the lamp, took her pill. She settled back into bed.

It will be better soon, she thought. It's only a matter of time. Did I feel pain like this when Louisa was born?

Yes, she decided, but it was different.

Some people said that women forgot their labor pains as soon as they ended, but she remembered. Between each contraction she had remembered, and steeled herself for the next. Who could forget such a thing?

She had heard that some women screamed and cursed their husbands during labor, angry at what they had caused.

"I never regretted a minute," she told Jack, as she felt the pills working and her pain getting weaker. "I was never angry at you. I remember everything."

But it was so long ago. How could she be sure she remembered?

Jack was lying next to her, stroking her stomach to ease the pain as if she were a child. "It will be all right," he told her. "You'll either get better or you'll be with me."

Where is that? she wanted to ask, but she knew he couldn't say.

If her memory was all that kept Jack alive, what would happen to him when she was gone? What would happen to her?

"Louisa loves you, don't worry," he said, but it wasn't the same. She and Jack would both vanish, they would be nothing. All the mementos they left behind—their house, their wedding rings, their beds—would be hollow. What comfort could there be in vanishing together?

I have to stay alive to keep Jack alive, she thought.

"Don't worry," she told him fiercely. "I'll fight, I'll keep you with me."

And he stayed. He followed her back to the hospital, though neither one of them wanted her to go this time.

Louisa insisted. "I don't want you to go either, Ma, but we can't make you comfortable here anymore. You have to go back for a while."

Her days got busier in the hospital, she had to admit. She felt a little better at first and could stay awake longer, sitting up almost all afternoon. She had company every day.

Ada came with her daughter-in-law, who had driven her over. Ada rolled her eyes at Glorie and whispered loudly, "They won't let me drive anymore, honey, but don't you worry. When you get out of here, we'll find a way to escape to you-know-where."

Glorie wasn't so far gone that she didn't see how Barbara talked to Ada like a five-year-old. "Of course, you'll have lots of fun together," she said, patting Ada's arm and smiling like an idiot.

"Leave me alone, I have something to say to Gloria," Ada snarled, shaking off Barbara's arm. Barbara backed off and Ada bent closer to whisper.

"I'm so afraid this is the *mal occhio* backing up on you, honey," she said, her eyes teary. "I feel so bad I let this happen."

Glorie would have laughed if Ada hadn't looked so sad. "That's not it, it's not your fault," she said. "I don't have the Evil Eye."

"But you have all the symptoms. Your head ached for a long time before you came in here, I know, and that's the biggest sign."

"My stomach hurt," said Glorie. "It's my insides. That's not the Evil Eye, is it?"

"Sometimes it is, it could be. It travels," Ada said.

"It's not the Evil Eye. And if it is, it's my own fault. And I don't regret it," Glorie said. "Cheer up or I'll put the Evil Eye on you."

Ada laughed. "You could do it."

Glorie looked forward to visits from everyone, even Patrick. Any excuse to turn off television. Why had she ever cared about these stupid programs? She knew they had mattered once, but no one on TV seemed worth her time anymore.

"Tell me about work, Patrick," she said, and he seemed tongue-tied and shocked.

"Work's fine," he said slowly, as if it might be a trick question. "It's good."

The Aunts came bringing flowers and fruit. "Ooo-*maa,* what a pretty nightgown," said Stella. "You look a little pale, but you'll get your color back," which made Glorie more self-conscious than ever about the inches of white at her roots. She wanted to say, "My skin is so dry I itch all over. My hair is dirty and ugly. I'm too weak to put on lipstick. I can't leave this bed." But she just smiled.

Gemma stood near the door and seemed frightened to be in the room. Then she walked over to Glorie bravely and kissed her cheek. "Ooo-*maa,* how good to see you," she said, and Glorie could see that, scared as Gemma was, she meant it. Gemma had never been much of an actress. Even Toni was quieter than she had ever been, like a regular human being.

When they were leaving, Toni took Glorie's hand. "We'll be seeing you very soon, we'll come back again. I'm not going to say good-bye because we'll be right back here. And we'll bring you all the gossip from the building."

"She doesn't want to hear that stupid stuff, Toni," said Stella.

"Why? What's she got better to do?" Toni answered. "Am I right?" she said, turning back to Glorie, still holding her hand.

"You're right. When you come next time I want to hear everything."

"Atta girl," said Toni, bugging out her eyes at Stella.

As they headed for the door, Glorie crooked her finger at Stella, gesturing her to come closer, and whispered, "How is that nice Martin? Why don't you think about marrying him?"

Stella laughed, "Ooo-*maa*, you still have that sense of humor," but she blushed bright red.

"They're kind, aren't they?" Glorie asked Jack after they'd gone.

Maybe she could live with these people after all. Why had they gotten on her nerves so much? "I must be delirious to be saying this," she giggled.

"You must be."

"Do you think Stella will take my advice?"

"We'll see."

Jack could tease her about getting softhearted, but she wasn't soft in the head yet. She lost her patience when Father Mignucci came around to hear her confession and told her that Our Heavenly Father Has His Reasons for Everything and We Must Accept His Will.

"You accept it," she snapped, "and don't come back here again."

"I understand—"

"Get out!" she screamed with more strength than she thought she had.

Louisa had been standing in the hall and raced in when she heard her mother yell. "What's wrong?" she asked.

"Did you tell him to come?" Glorie asked. "Did you tell him I was here?"

"I thought it would help," Louisa said. She looked in pain herself. "What did he say to upset you? I'll talk to him."

"Keep him away," Glorie said firmly. "I'll decide what to accept, not that moneygrubbing priest. Why should I tell my sins to him, that goddamn fool. What does he know? Damn him to hell."

"I'm sorry, Ma, I thought he could help. I should have asked you first, but I thought it would make you afraid if you knew he was coming. I didn't want you to think it was a bad sign or anything." She was so flustered, but Glorie was calm again.

"A bad sign? This is all a bad sign, Louisa, it's one big bad sign, dear. Don't you think I know that? I'm past bad signs. Just keep the priest away. I'm sorry I yelled."

"I'll tell him that."

"No!" Glorie yelled again. "I'm apologizing to *you*, not him."

"You sure sound lively today, Ma. You sound better."

Jack was proud of her for sending the priest away, of course. "Goddamn fool, as if he can fix anything," he said. "You're not afraid, are you, Glorie?"

"Of course I'm afraid," she told him softly. "I'm afraid of everything."

Were you afraid? she wanted to ask, but it was much too late. He had gotten sicker and weaker. He drove too slow and he stopped shaving right, and she had never been able to bring herself to say, "Are you afraid?"

"Should I have asked you?" she wondered now. "Maybe I could have helped you the way you're helping me."

"It was faster for me," he said, but she guessed he was just trying to make things easy for her, as usual. She was furious at herself. "I'm so sorry I let you down, but I didn't know what to say."

"I've told you before," Jack said, "you've never let me down. Never."

She started to chuckle. "Do you think Ada's right?" she asked. "Do you think this is the Evil Eye coming back at me?"

"Could be. Let's get some olive oil and water and send it away," he laughed.

"Let's. I still have a few tricks up my sleeve. But not many."

She felt her energy slipping away, so slowly and steadily only she could notice it, as if she were bleeding to death from a pinprick in her finger and was too weak to call for help. She slept for days at a time it seemed. She could hardly keep track of who was in the room.

One day Pat Jr. brought Lily and Jeremy, the littlest kids. "They shouldn't be here," she tried to say. "They're too young." But she was so glad to see them. They stood by her bed and gave her cards they had made. She was too tired to read, so Pat opened them and read, "Get well, Great-Grandma. Love, Michael and Jeremy," and "Hello, Grandma G. Love, Lily."

She reached her hand out across the covers toward the children. Jeremy was standing closer so she took his hand and held it between hers. "Honeys," she said, looking from one to the other. "I don't want you to be afraid."

She knew what she was saying now. She was helping them.

"Afraid of what?" said Lily.

"Of me. Of anything. Don't be afraid of anything, dear. You'll rise above everyone."

The next morning, as soon as Louisa showed up, Glorie started talking and couldn't stop. She could hear herself talking in a fog, the words all cloudy and muffled, but now and then the fog cleared and she realized she must have been babbling. She tried to grasp what she was saying, to slow down and hang on to the words, but her voice came racing out like a flood too strong to stop. It seemed like all her life became a story she had to tell Louisa, even if it made no sense.

Louisa held her hand and listened, drank coffee and ate part of a sandwich Patrick brought her. Glorie knew that. Nurses came in and closed the blinds. It was night and Glorie was still talking, though she couldn't remember what she was saying. She was losing her voice but she wasn't through telling everything yet.

"Josie never liked dresses made from newspaper," she heard herself say. "Aunt Margaret should have been born a chicken." Where did that come from? And why wasn't Louisa laughing?

She drifted into the fog again and saw the ship. "Where did you get that little red-haired girl?" He would get her in the end, she always knew he would, he was nearby and no one could save her now.

"Jack," she called. "Jack." But he was out fighting a mad dog.

"Mad dog," she heard her voice say. It wasn't what she meant to say, it wasn't what she wanted.

"Give the angel picture to Lily when she gets old enough," she said next, relieved to get out something that made sense. "Tell her to go to the Sistine Chapel and kiss the Pope." Jack was cooking Christmas Eve dinner in the Sistine Chapel and the whole family would be there, sitting at a long table in the aisle, eating baccalà.

"I never wanted another man," she said.

"I never wanted anyone but you, Glorie," Jack told her.

She knew Louisa was holding her hand tight and trembling. "Honey, don't be afraid," Glorie tried to say, but her voice gave out. She was flying away. She rose up in the air, standing straight while a shower of red fireworks fell all around her; the sparks looked as glittering and sharp as rubies but felt soft and smooth like rose petals. She kept flying higher, up through the red fireworks, and in their light she saw all the treasures of her life tumbling past her as they headed down the other way—her gopher, her scrapbook, the big bed and the little bed all tumbled past. She was laughing now because she knew where Jack had been. He was hiding up in the sky, like Jack on top of the beanstalk. He had met her mother there and they liked each other. Now they were hiding and laughing and waiting for Glorie to get there. "I'm coming, Jack," she said. She chuckled as she rose higher, flying up through the ruby rain.

A PENGUIN READERS GUIDE TO

GLORIE

Caryn James

An Introduction to *Glorie*

Glorie is a sparkling debut, a heartbreaking and funny first novel with a brilliantly drawn and compelling character at its center—Gloria Carcieri. Gloria—she only lets her husband call her Glorie—had that rare and enviable thing, a truly happy marriage. Now a widow for seven years, Glorie is not quite able to let Jack go. In her heart, he is still alive, and in her head, she keeps up a running dialogue with him. She saves her slyest comments and deepest longings for his ears only. In some ways she has never had to let go. She spends her days in the house where they lived, and simply crosses the street at night to sleep at her daughter's house. But as the novel begins, a crisis looms. Glorie's accountant son-in-law, Patrick, wants to sell the house and even Glorie's highly patient daughter, Louisa, agrees that it is time.

Glorie's action and much of its comedy is fueled by Glorie's pretense of openmindedness. She agrees to spend a trial night with the colorful trio of Patrick's aunts in their retirement community while she secretly plans to foil the sale of the house, plotting late-night pizza deliveries and dabbling in the Evil Eye. The novel is also highly interior. Facing the world alone while trying to keep Jack's memory alive proves to be a complicated ordeal. At times fiercely determined, at others gripped by doubt, Glorie wars even within herself to find an acceptable way to live the rest of her life.

At the heart of this novel is a fifty-year love story. What is Glorie without Jack? If she moves on with her life, does it mean letting Jack go? Does loving someone so completely allow you to truly love anyone else? Caryn James has interwoven Glorie's widowhood with flashbacks that illuminate her immigrant childhood, her youthful dreams, and her passionate marriage. The skillfully entwined past and present evoke a unique character, headstrong and imperfect, whose story is completely her own yet speaks to every reader who has ever known or lost love.

A Conversation with Caryn James

How did you come to choose an octogenarian widow as a heroine? Was it difficult getting into her head?

Years ago, I began noticing how my grandmother and other women of her generation were getting along in their old age, when they were suddenly alone for the first time in their lives. After their children were grown, after their husbands had died, what happened to these women whose whole lives had been invested in other people? They were intelligent, but hadn't had many opportunities for education; they had strong emotions that were completely poured into marriage and family. I became fascinated by how different all that was from my generation. Eventually, that idea became the story of one unique woman from that era.

Glorie isn't meant to represent a generation, though; she's entirely herself, an individual who's wildly in love with her husband, happy in her marriage, and sheltered from practical, financial worries. And that comforting life is suddenly pulled away from her when her husband dies. What does she have to fall back on? It turns out her emotions and imagination are more powerful than she knew.

I didn't really worry about getting inside her mind. Obviously, I don't know what it's like to be eighty, but I know Glorie's character inside out. It was a matter of extrapolating from there, of saying, "I know this person; how would she react in this or that situation?" Her personality is the touchstone for everything that happens. It didn't matter to me whether gerontologists would be able to say, "James got it right," or "She got it wrong" in every clinical detail. I wanted the character to be believable.

You've dedicated the book to the memory of your grandmother, and in your acknowledgments you thank your family for allowing you to "take the seed of a family story and turn it into make-a-believe." How autobiographical is the novel? Is the city of the novel the Providence you grew up in? Are you Blanche, the overeducated wise-ass granddaughter?

Glorie is loosely based on one central element from my grandmother's life: after my grandfather died, she really did use her house only during the day. Every night, she slept at her daughter's across the street. I found that amusing and touching and ultimately very strong of her; it's certainly a better story than anything I could have made up. There are other bits and pieces of family history; she really did come from Portugal as a little girl. But I've made up almost everything else. I don't think of the book as veiled family memoir or autobiography in any way, and never meant it to be. I simply used some convenient details and invented the rest, including her inner life, which was what really intrigued me. It was a storytelling impulse that set me off, not any historical impulse. If I had been writing a memoir, I never would have been able to get inside the character's thoughts.

I did have Providence in mind while I was writing, but only as a loose visual map of streets and neighborhoods. I wanted the setting to be more general, any one of a number of unnamed New England cities. And by not tying the story to the real Providence, I felt freer to invent what I needed. Of course, I was being practical, too; by not calling the city Providence, I didn't have to worry about having one-way streets going in the right direction; I just made up the street names.

As for Blanche, I think she's by far the least likable character in the book, so imagine my surprise when people, especially relatives, started asking, "Are you Blanche?" As a character, one of Blanche's functions in the novel is to give us an unflattering, outsider's perspective on Glorie. It's Blanche, for example, who says Glorie lives in a dream world, which comes as a shock to Glorie. But I have to admit, I also created Blanche so I could say some things in a voice — I guess it's my voice, that smart-ass voice — no one else in the book would use. I didn't *mean* to be Blanche, but I can live with it.

The Washington Post *gave* Glorie *a rave review and said, "It is an unflinching portrait, merciless as certain Rembrandts, of a shrewd, sly, vain, tough old lady . . . . Only the bravest would relish her as a close relative." Did you intend her to be more sympathetic than that?*

I was thrilled with that review, which really grasped what I was trying to do: to make Glorie both sympathetic and imperfect. She's a deeply loving woman who sometimes acts like a pill. I wanted to avoid the clichés of the lovable, feisty old lady, and I wanted to avoid any excess of sentimentality, so she's difficult, a flawed human being. That was the only way to make her real rather than a caricature. Glorie is self-absorbed, but not malicious. She can be terribly annoying; and, remember, we're seeing things from her point of view, so she's probably sugar-coating her own annoying tendencies. And she finds it so hard to express her emotions, which means she is misunderstood by many people around her. Yet because we know her thoughts, we see her true emotions, her good intentions, her genuine hurts and loneliness, and her undeniable snobbery. I wanted the book, and the character, to be as ambiguous as life. *I* like her.

Though the novel has a third-person narrator, we only know what Glorie knows as it's told from her perspective. Did you ever consider telling the story from another point of view?

At one point very late in the writing, I did ask myself why it was a third-person narrator if we're restricted to Glorie's point of view (which we are). Why isn't she telling her own story? The answer came pretty quickly: I have a bigger vocabulary than she does. If she had been telling the story, I would have been more restricted, in the tone and style even more than in the words. The trick for me was to try to stay extremely close to the way she would have talked and thought, without limiting myself to her exact language; it's really a kind of illusion, a narrative sleight of hand. So, for instance, there are colloquialisms the narrator uses because Glorie would have: "sister-in-laws" instead of "sisters-in-law." But I thought I could create a more fluid, graceful prose in the third person.

One striking aspect of this story is Glorie's fierce devotion to Jack. Yet there are suggestions throughout the novel that this has limited her life in many ways; despite the novel's great comic energy, Glorie seems terribly isolated. Is Glorie *a love story? A tragedy? Something else?*

It's absolutely a love story; Jack is the grand, defining passion of Glorie's life. She isn't sorry she devoted her life to Jack; she's just sorry he's gone. (Whether he, and their relationship, are as ideal as she recalls is another matter). Her story is also a domestic comedy. The tiny details of life can give her a hard time. But it's not a tragedy: she's had a rich, happy life, and as it winds down she faces normal, inevitable problems. There is sadness, though. I think it's overstating things to call her story a tragedy, but if there is a tragic element, it's in the way Glorie is unable to connect with anyone other than Jack. She can't express her emotions easily even to people she dearly loves, like Louisa, or might have as a friend, like Stella. And you're right, that tragic element of her character and her isolation are completely intertwined.

You're the chief television critic at The New York Times *and have also been a* Times *film critic and an editor at* The New York Times Book Review. *How does your sophistication about these other art forms—film and television—inform your fiction? Do you feel differently about writing fiction and writing criticism?*

I think I've absorbed a sense of dialogue and setting from having watched all those movies and television shows. I didn't consciously think of the novel as cinematic; in fact, it's very interior. But I think there's a sort of breathing room in the prose that comes from the way scenes play out on screen.

I like having the freedom to invent in fiction, where "facts" can be inventions and the only logic has to do with coherence of character and setting. That's completely different from reviewing, where you're handed the material you have to deal with: the book, the movie, the miniseries.

But I love reviewing, too. People often ask if, as a critic, I get tired of having to have an opinion all the time; that question gets something fundamentally backwards. I don't always have an opinion because I'm a critic; I'm a critic because I always have an opinion anyway. I see fiction and reviewing as very different kinds of writing. I think some readers were surprised that *Glorie* is so different from my journalism, in its subject and its voice. But what would have been the point of writing the same thing I write for the paper? It was the difference that intrigued me and kept me going.

As a book reviewer, what was it like to read reviews of your work? Do you think the reviewers "got" your book? Was there any criticism you felt was way off the mark?

As a reviewer, I knew going in that I wouldn't have the luxury of pretending reviews don't matter. I knew that most critics really grapple with the books they review and are honest in their opinions, so I'd have to take them seriously even if I disagreed. I was relieved that the reviews were not only good, but that they understood Glorie's character, with all her imperfections. If there was anything off-kilter about some responses, it was the tendency (understandable as a convenient shorthand) to describe *Glorie* as a book hermetically about old people. I think of it as more encompassing than that. To me, it's a book about one woman's entire life, from childhood on, as she looks back on it from her old age.

Are there any writers whose accomplishments inspired or challenged you while writing Glorie*? Are there any books in particular that you would recommend to people who love* Glorie*?*

The book I love the most, my deepest literary inspiration, is Virginia Woolf's *To the Lighthouse.* It wasn't a model or direct influence on *Glorie*; it was more of a talisman. And because it is an elegy for Woolf's parents, and in a sense *Glorie* is an elegy for my grandmother, looking back I can see a link. My own shorthand description of *Glorie* has always been *To the Lighthouse* meets *I Love Lucy*, which probably says all anyone needs to know about my influences. I also adore Chekhov's *Three Sisters* (my favorite play) and *The Cherry Orchard.* Again, they were not direct influences, but I kept their tone—sometimes sad and elegiac, yet insistently hopeful rather than depressing, and always lyrically beautiful—in the back of my mind as inspiration. There is even a brief reference in *Glorie* to *The Cherry Orchard,* which is a play about a woman who loses an orchard instead of a house. That line, of course, could only come from Blanche, my evil twin.

Are you working on another novel? Is it in similar territory, or are you drawn to something completely different?

I am working on another novel. I didn't talk much about *Glorie* until it was nearly done because you never know what direction a book will take, so I'm reluctant to say too much too soon. I will say this about the next one: it's not about a critic for a major newspaper (that's the first question everyone asks when I say I'm writing a novel). And it's not about a self-absorbed octogenarian widow. I think the scope will be wider and the tone very different.

Questions for Discussion

1. The book begins with a story Glorie heard throughout her childhood and often told Jack. The man on the boat coming to America asks her mother, "Where did you get that little red-haired girl?" The story ends with her mother saying, "You'll rise over everybody, Gloria.

You'll better us all." Why is that dream so important to Glorie? Does she fulfill her mother's prophecy? How important is her family's immigrant background in shaping Glorie's life, her character, her aspirations?

2. What does Glorie gain and lose by devoting her life so completely to Jack? Does that choice have any relevance to women today who struggle to balance families and careers? Was she better or worse off than women are now? Throughout the novel Glorie struggles to preserve her independence. How independent was she when she was married to Jack? How independent is she as a widow?

3. Glorie says of her daughter, "Wonderful Louisa had turned out just like her father. She was smart, she was funny, she could blow up at someone who treated her wrong and be their best friend the next day" (p. 26). Do you see ways in which she is like her father? Are there ways in which she is like Glorie?

4. How would you describe Glorie and Louisa's mother-daughter relationship? Why do they argue? When Blanche tells Louisa, "You always say she was awful when you were growing up, she gave all her attention to Grandpa and none to you" (p. 114), Louisa denies this. Do you think there is some truth in what Blanche says, or is she distorting things, as Louisa says? Was Glorie a good mother to Louisa?

5. What do you think of Jack? How accurate are Glorie's memories of him? Do her imaginary conversations with Jack help her cope or distance her from reality? How firm is Glorie's grip on reality? Does that change as the novel goes along?

6. Glorie thinks her son-in-law, Patrick, is so boring she calls him "Ivory Soap" and so stupid she makes fun of him as "the Italian

Patrick." Do you agree? What do other characters—Louisa, his children and his aunts—think of Patrick? Is he the book's villain?

7. Who are the people Glorie truly loves? Why does she find it difficult to express her affection for them? Who are the people she detests? Does she have the same problem expressing her feelings for them?

8. Throughout the novel Glorie recalls dreams and stories. Among them are the story Jack used to tell the grandchildren about the rooster who went to fight with the king, and a dream Glorie has in the hospital in which she has flowing white hair "wild as a troll's" (p. 219). What other stories and dreams does she recall? What role do these fairy-tale elements have in the novel? What do they reveal about Glorie's thoughts?

9. Glorie has rich memories of her sexual life with Jack and misses their physical relationship. Does that seem surprising in the depiction of a woman in her eighties? What stereotypes do we have about old people, and how does Glorie fit into or defy those images?

10. Why does Glorie finally sell her house? How much of that decision was really about money? Did it have anything to do with Glorie getting caught in the blizzard? Or was it just a matter of time?

11. Glorie compares the Aunts to circus performers. ("Elephants, trapeze artists and performing old people," she tells Jack on page 116) and sees them as "three organ grinder's monkeys lined up across the table" (pp. 123–4) on Christmas Eve. Why is she so hard on them? Do they have distinct personalities? Do you think Glorie should have moved into their apartment building? Why does she almost see Stella as a confidante? When she tells Jack at the end of the book, "They're kind, aren't they?" has she come to her senses or is she being, as she suspects, "delirious" (p. 226)?

12. When Ada teaches Glorie to do the Evil Eye, does she really believe that curse will force the new owner out of her house? How clever are the practical jokes she plays on him? What might these tricks be signs of: her desperation? her boredom? her state of mind?

13. At the end of the book, when Glorie is in the hospital, she tells her great-grandchildren, Jeremy and Lily, "Honeys, I don't want you to be afraid" (p. 228). What does she mean? At the very end, when she sees Jack "hiding up in the sky, like Jack on top of the beanstalk," and says, "I'm coming, Jack," what does that suggest? Do you think they're together in the afterlife, or is this another of Glorie's fantasies? Is it a happy ending for her? For you?